"Is he going to win?" Christy asked Michelle.

"They've only run ten laps," Michelle said, checking, like a veteran, the scoring pylon behind her. "There are still over a hundred laps to go. Lots of stuff can happen in a hundred laps!"

"It seems like he's been leading forever."

Rob showed no sign of being willing to surrender the point. Jodell Lee had suggested it already.

"You may want to let one of them lead for a while, kid," he had said. "Give you a chance to see how your car feels in the middle of the draft. Maybe feel out if you got what it takes to pass him back."

But Rob had only bumped the microphone switch to signal he had heard. He didn't want to ever let go of the lead. Never!

Follow all the action . . .
from the qualifying lap
to the checkered flag!

Rolling Thunder!

Rolling Thunder

STOCK CAR RACING

FIRST TO THE FLAG

Kent Wright
& Don Keith

TOR®

A TOM DOHERTY ASSOCIATES BOOK
NEW YORK

This is a work of fiction. All the characters and events portrayed in this book are either products of the author's imagination or are used fictitiously.

FIRST TO THE FLAG

A Tor Book
Published by Tom Doherty Associates, LLC
175 Fifth Avenue
New York, NY 10010

www.tor.com

Tor® is a registered trademark of Tom Doherty Associates, LLC.

ISBN: 0-812-54507-9

First edition: July 2000

Printed in the United States of America

0 9 8 7 6 5 4 3 2 1

THE TEST

The tall, sandy-haired young man sat slouched in a heap in the private plane's stuffed-leather rear passenger seat. He appeared to be fast asleep, even though he was arranged in what might have been considered to be an awkward position for a catnap. But with his mouth open and his eyes tightly closed, he snored softly anyway. The kid was clearly oblivious to the awkward tilting of the King Air as it circled for its approach to the airport, to the bumpy air it chopped through as it descended, to the casual conversation between the plane's pilot and the other occupant who sat in the copilot's seat.

Rob Wilder had become a master at grabbing sleep wherever, whenever, he could manage it. The cabin of the King Air was downright luxurious compared to some of his more recent accommodations.

The other passenger, the older man who occupied the right seat up front, dropped his chat with the pilot when he got busy on the radio talking and responding to his landing instructions. He turned then to see how the kid was doing and was not at all surprised to see him still dozing peacefully.

Billy Winton smiled. It had been only a short time ago when the young man had been petrified at the very thought of flying, terrified most of takeoffs and landings. Now he was usually fast asleep on the taxi out to the runway and had to eventually be shaken awake when the plane had already been parked.

Then, as he watched the handsome youngster sleep, Winton noticed something else telling. The kid's right foot twitched slightly. So did his right hand, as if he was performing some sort of coordinated maneuver in his sleep.

Billy smiled even more broadly. He's dreaming of driving that race car, he thought. And likely of being first to the checkered flag.

That was a safe guess. That was about all Rob Wilder dreamed about, all he talked about, all he seemingly lived for. Driving Billy Winton's race cars as fast as he could until he could finally win his first big-time stock car race on the Grand National circuit.

Now they were on an approach to a legendary place where he might just do that very thing. It was a shrine to speed where, Billy suspected, young Rob Wilder would feel very much at home, though he had never been there before in his slightly less than twenty years on this planet. At least not while awake. And within an hour, they would not only be there but they would be testing one of the new cars they would soon use to start their first full season of serious racing together.

He hated to wake the kid from his dreams.

The last several days had no doubt been far more tiring for Wilder than driving a five-hundred-mile race in a day at Charlotte would have been. The young man had been pushed and shoved through a three-day series of promotional stops and special appearances on behalf of their team's major new sponsor. Billy had been his constant companion on the trip and he was admittedly sapped, bone-tired as well. But he had merely been along for the ride and had not had to shake hundreds of hands or sign all those autographs or answer all those silly questions with a good-humored smile and pretend it was the first time he had ever heard them.

Even now, this far down the road, Billy sometimes wondered why he had stepped back into the middle of the swirling tornado of serious stock car competition and dragged all these other lives along with him on his obsessive quest. As the chief mechanic of one of the most successful teams in the sport's history, he had gotten more than his fair share of the glamour and glory during the seventies and eighties. And the money, too. Enough of the spoils of victory that, well invested as it was, he could have lived comfortably for the rest of his days without ever having to do any more grueling personal appearances or gritty all-night work sessions, or brutal early morning track tests.

But the money and glory were not what had drawn him to the game in the first place. It was the winning. And Billy Winton had missed that one addictive element so badly he had willingly stepped back into the maelstrom. It had been on a limited basis at first, but he had soon realized that halfway didn't quite feed his habit. Then he took the plunge again big time when Rob Wilder had dropped into his world.

No, normally he would have let Rob sleep all the way to the terminal so he would be a few minutes better rested for the job ahead of him this day. But something was coming up he wanted the kid to see. The turboprop engines changed pitch again as the plane made another turn, a course that brought them perpendicular to the shimmering white-sand beaches and put the orange ball that was the morning sun directly behind them.

He touched the boy's sneaker with his own boot.

"Robbie! Wake up, son. You'll want to see this."

The youngster's eyes popped open and it was clear he was disoriented for a moment, maybe still chasing checkered flags in his sleep. Then he blinked in the bright sunlight that filled the cabin, rubbed his eyes with the backs of his hands much as a child might, and then leaned forward as much as the seat belt would allow to see what Billy was pointing at below.

A green carpet of pine and scrub oak and pasture stretched off into the far distance, while houses and streets and store parking lots claimed the foreground. The towering beachfront resorts and condos seemed to reach up toward them from directly below where they flew. The ocean was a cold slate gray behind them except for the fiery streak painted by the rising sun.

"Hey, kid," Billy shouted over the drone of the engines, and indicated he should be looking down and to the left. "There she is."

It took Rob a moment to see what Billy was pointing at. Then it emerged from beneath the plane's wing. Even then he had to look twice to make sure it was what he thought it was: a perfect replica of a big framed photo that hung on the wall in Billy Winton's office back in Chandler Cove, Tennessee.

And it was one of the most beautiful sights he had ever seen. The gigantic speedway at Daytona Beach! He glanced over at Billy and there was a look on the young man's face that hinted he might think he was still dreaming.

"That's her, all right. Daytona. What you think?"

"Whoa! That *is* Daytona!"

"The grand old lady herself. The place where legends are born. Built for speed and nothing but speed. Beautiful, don't you think?"

Rob didn't answer as he stared out the plane's window, his nose against the glass, again almost kidlike. The stands were empty, the pits and garage almost deserted, but for an instant he thought he saw movement out there on the track. Petty and Pearson dueling for the checkered flag. Earnhardt nudging someone aside to take the lead. Bobby and Davey Allison, father and son, finishing one-two. Rob could almost see the highlight reels spinning in his mind as he stared at the hook of the tri-oval track down below, its famous tower overlooking the start/finish line.

"It's hard to believe we're looking down on the same place where all those great races were run," he said.

"I've been lucky enough to see a bunch of them from down there close at hand. I watched Richard Petty and Jodell Lee and the others come to the checkers at two hundred miles an hour. And even after five hundred miles of racing, they'd get to the finish and be so close that you still couldn't tell who crossed the line first. Lots of guys who can win races can't win on that track down there, Robbie. It's where they separate the car jockeys from the racers."

Billy left his next thought unsaid. That strip of track that was sliding beneath their airplane would be the next place this young driver would have a chance to prove his own mettle, too. So far, so good, in this young driver's career, but Rob Wilder had not yet faced Daytona.

"It is hard to imagine all that speed from up here," Rob was saying. "It almost looks like an interstate highway with sharper curves."

"Oh, she's plenty fast. Too fast sometimes."

Billy let the words hang as he allowed a whirlpool of memories to claim him. He had spent times both wonderful and tough down there when he had worked with Jodell Lee and his team. Lee had been one of the best the sport had seen, but Daytona had taken a bite out of him more than a time or two as well. Billy Winton and Jodell Lee, along with Jodell's engine builder and first cousin, Joe Banker, and their crew chief, Bubba Baxter, always came to this place fully expecting to win whatever race it was that had brought them here. They had cut their teeth on this track before Billy had joined them. Besides, most of the other teams readily acknowledged that Jodell knew the banks of Daytona even better than he did the mountain roads where he had once run illegal moonshine whiskey for his grandfather. Yessir, this place held special memories for Billy Winton, and now he had high hopes of adding some new ones with his fresh, young crew.

The King Air glided in low over turn three, making its final descent down along the track's long backstretch. For an instant Rob thought the pilot was going to set the plane right down in the racing groove itself, but then he remembered another detail from the picture on Billy's wall. The Daytona Beach airport was right next to the track.

The kid could not take his eyes off the place. That is, until it disappeared out of view as the plane's wheels finally touched down on the runway with a screech and a puff of blue smoke. And even as they taxied over to the flight service hangar, Rob replayed in his head the majestic view he had just commanded.

So this was it! He had finally seen the speedway he had every intention of conquering when they came back here to race in just a bit over a month. Today was to be only a test.

This was Daytona!

From the ground, as he hopped down from the plane's steps, he got a much better perspective of the actual size of the place. It was massive! There was no other way to describe it.

Will Hughes, their crew chief, was waiting for them at the door of the flight service building. He showed them his usual dour expression as he watched them walk his way across the tarmac.

"Billy Winton, you look like you just pitched a five-day drunk," he observed matter-of-factly when they were within earshot.

Winton tried to smooth his rumpled clothes and ran a hand through his long, thinning, red-mixed-with-gray hair.

"Well, Mr. Hughes, we've been on one airplane or another most of the night while y'all were down here taking it easy," Billy said with a grin. He knew the crew had driven all day the day before and had probably been working on the car most of the night. And he knew, too, that they were already at work again early this morning.

"And you . . ." Hughes gave Rob's tousled hair, swollen eyes, and pale white countenance the once-over. "You look like you might have just seen a ghost."

But Rob was paying him no attention. He was already striding toward the car, looking in the direction of the track, ready to go take her on. He was quiet on the short ride over, too, letting Billy and Will compare notes on the car. They were quickly at the tunnel that ran beneath the "short chute," a brief stretch of linear track coming out of turn four on the front stretch. He watched as the monumental piles of sand and dirt that made up the outline of the track slid past, towering over nearby Highway 92.

Once through the tunnel and inside the speedway, he found it difficult to actually see from one end of the facility to the other. If the banks had not been so tall, it would be impossible to see where the turns made their graceful arc toward the front and back straightaways. And though he knew to expect it from all the races from here he had watched on television, he was still shocked to see an actual lake in the middle of the speedway. Lake Lloyd was formed when the construction crews had dug up all the sand and dirt for the banking. He knew some of the drivers and crew actually fished its waters when they took breaks from practicing or preparing their cars.

Once again the realization of what he was about to do struck him, and the anticipation continued to build as they bounced across the flat of the infield over to where their tractor-trailer transporter sat waiting for them in the garage area. It had brought down from Tennessee two brand-new race cars, the products of many shop hours and hard work over the last few months. Will and his crew had carefully crafted the engines and the actual shapes of the cars so they could have the necessary power and the aerodynamics required to be able to cut through the wind while still staying earthbound at almost two hundred miles per hour. That would be faster than the takeoff speed of the King Air they had just flown into the airport.

As he walked around one of the cars, the one he was about to climb into and take for a spin on this storied track, he stopped, cocked his head, and listened. For a moment there he thought he had heard his name being called from a distance, but there was only the whistle of the cold January wind. He smiled. Maybe it was the track, beckoning him, challenging him to tame her. Or the voices of those who had driven here before but had gone on, men like Fireball Roberts and Neil Bonnet and Davey Allison. Maybe they were urging him out there, encouraging him to make that car go fast, real fast, the way she was supposed to.

"I'm ready," he murmured to no one in particular.

"What you saying?"

It was Donnie Kline, the tire man and one of the key crew members. But if Rob had confessed to the big man with the shaved head that he was answering ghost voices, he would never hear the end of it.

"I said I was ready to take her out," he said.

"Danged good thing. Hate to think we drove all the way down here to watch the seagulls."

Then Donnie was back at work, helping the crew get the primary car rolled out and ready for a spin. Around them several other teams were busy, working on their own race cars. Despite the chill in the air and the early hour, they all seemed as excited to be back at it as Rob and his crew were. It was finally about time to go racing. All would soon be right with the world.

Just as the Billy Winton Racing team had done, the rest of them had passed the last few months building or modifying cars, getting them ready for this day, their first crack at the speedway where the season would truly begin as it always did, with Speed Weeks in February. It was their first true opportunity to see what kind of fruit would be borne from the frantic couple of months of work they had done back in the shops. A successful test here would go a long way toward building confidence and it would generate valuable knowledge that could be put to use when the teams came back for Speed Weeks. A sour day today, though, and it was back to work with a vengeance to try to fix whatever seemed to be the matter. And it would be another long, cold, bitter month before they would know for certain if they had done so.

The Winton Racing team was especially apprehensive about the approaching Speed Weeks. This would be their first trip to Daytona with their young driver. It had been the legendary Jodell Lee himself who had discovered Rob Wilder at a small, out-of-the-way track the year before. Knowing exactly where Wilder's talents were most needed, Lee made a quick telephone call to his old "chief wrench," Billy Winton, and a test had been set up for the kid at the Nashville Fairgrounds track in Tennessee. He had easily passed the coming-out exam, then he had gone on to drive the balance of the Grand National season for the Wilder team. He had been spectacular in the contests he had run the last third of the year, showing an almost uncanny ability to put the car exactly where it needed to be. Though he still had not won a race, it was clearly only a matter of time. And though no one had said it out loud, everyone on the team, from Billy and Will on down, was pointing to the Grand National season-opening Daytona 300-lapper as the race. Today's run would go a long way in either boosting or deflating that feeling, and everyone knew that, too.

So far, the pressure didn't seem to be bothering Rob Wilder at all. And that was another reason Billy and Will felt they had the right driver. The kid was supremely confident without being cocky.

That had been one of the traits their new sponsor liked about the young driver, too. Liked so well that they had chosen to back the team this year with very large checks and a massive public relations commitment. Ensoft, a huge computer software company, had come aboard for the last couple of races the year before and they were now full bore into their relationship with Rob, Billy, and the bright red Fords they would run in 2000.

They, too, had high expectations. And they, too, planned to stay with Winton Racing as they made the next transition, likely at the end of the season, depending on how they did, to the sport's big league, Winston Cup.

Rob seemed unfazed by that pressure, too. Though the promotional schedule he had been keeping for Ensoft the last few months had been brutal, he seemed to have quickly grown into the role of spokesperson. He had even bought himself a laptop computer and learned as much as he could about the company's products between airports and hotels and the shop.

Will Hughes took one more sip from the paper cup of coffee he had set within reach on the car's frame. Cold already. He was especially anxious to get rolling. He had been in the game long enough to know when his cars were close to right, that a little work after some hot laps would likely get them totally race-ready. But today he wanted to see how the kid would take to the high banks and the blistering speed this place could generate. Would the youngster be up to it? Will had seen other drivers who weren't, good ones with wins under their belts who couldn't master the old lady by the beach. They had taken to the track and, for some reason, had not been able to get the speeds out of their cars that they had been perfectly capable of running. Something always seemed to keep them slower than they could have been. And many of them had not even come back to try. Or they had settled for a finish somewhere back in the pack but still in the money and had gone on to somewhere less challenging to try for the all-out wins. A special breed of driver was required to be able to run a race car right out there on the ragged edge around Daytona's high banks.

Today they could find out if they had such a special driver behind the wheel of their car. Totally distracted by the effort, Will took another sip of the coffee, and this time he didn't even notice how bitter and icy it had become. It could have been raw gasoline and he likely would not have taken note.

Inside the hauler, Rob was shucking his Ensoft Racing windbreaker and golf shirt and khaki slacks and pulling on his racing suit. His mind was already on the high banks that awaited him out there. He had spent many hours over the last couple of months walking the woods of East Tennessee with Jodell Lee, or sitting around Lee's fireplace in the home he had inherited from his moonshining granddaddy. Most of the talk had been about this track. And the old driver had been perfectly willing to share what he knew with his protégé.

"Son, that old hunk of asphalt is really deceptively easy to drive if you pay attention," he had told Rob. "The banking is so high and the corners so wide it makes the car seem to sail right on through them. You got to stay alert, though. You make the slightest bobble anywhere and you end up like I did a couple of times. Lose the air off the spoiler and around and around she'll go. Get just the wrong gust of that tricky old wind out there at the wrong time. Or try to force a line the car don't want to run, then look out. And when you lose it, you'll either hit the wall real hard or somebody's gonna tag you and send you into the middle of next week. That's the voice of experience talking, son. I know. There's not much room for error out there on that thing."

The race car itself even looked chilled this morning. Instead of its racing paint, it was a dull gray color, wearing only a coat of primer. The Winton crew had rolled her off the hauler and now stood, hunched over and shivering in the cold, and waited for Rob to climb in and take to the track for the first time. As he stepped from the hauler, Wilder smiled. Paint job or not, the car looked absolutely beautiful to him in the dull sunlight. As beautiful as if she were all decked out in her brilliant red war plumage, her shimmering gold numbers and trim, and her blue Ensoft logo.

He quickly swung his long, lanky legs in the open window of the race car, then bent his frame to slide into the cockpit. As he settled in and began strapping himself to the car, he allowed the words of Jodell Lee to flow through his head.

"Patience . . . let the car find its own groove . . . stay alert . . . don't panic if she wiggles . . . patience."

The seat in this race car felt wonderfully comfortable, almost as if he were climbing into the big recliner in Billy Winton's living room, ready to watch a football game or the replay of any of the races Billy kept in his own exhaustive tape library. The comfort of the car's seat was, of course, by design. The driver's compartment of a race car is his "office." His and nobody else's. It should be contoured to his body, his frame, so he can concentrate on the car, the competition, winning the race, not how badly his back or his butt hurts.

It was a far cry from the car Rob had been piloting less than a year before when Jodell found him. The old Pontiac the kid drove to victory the fortuitous night Lee dropped by the out-of-the-way track was merely an old bucket seat tightly bolted to the frame rail. That old seat tended to numb his backside, requiring constant mid-contest shuffling. With the belts holding him in tightly, that was tough to do in a long race with few caution periods.

Rob buckled himself in while Will and the crew busied themselves with several last-minute checks. Rob methodically hooked up the belts and went through the rest of his usual checklist as he prepared to take the car out onto the track. By now he had completely replaced any apprehension about his first tour of Daytona with the thoughts of how he would attack the track. How he would handle any situations that might arise. What he would be looking and feeling and listening for from the car itself so he could report them back to Will and the crew.

He idly listened to the chatter on the radio as Will finished the last bit of preparation for this very first run of the brand-new season. The season that was being birthed with so much optimism, so many grand plans.

"Okay, cowboy, talk to me."

Rob pushed the radio button on the steering wheel with his thumb.

"Got you loud and clear, Will. Ready when you are."

"Well, let's fire her up and see if she'll crank. Time to see what this baby can do," the crew chief said,

"Roger!"

Rob flipped the starter switch and immediately felt and heard the mighty engine grumble to life without even a cough or hiccup. With a deep, throaty rumble, the engine idled happily beneath Rob's feet, seemingly as excited to get this season under way as its helmsman was. Soon the heat off the headers coming up through the floorboard had begun to warm the interior of the car. The men who huddled around outside the vehicle still shivered, but Rob was comfortably warm.

He didn't even wait for Will's order. Rob shifted up into gear as the crew backed away from the car.

"Let's see what kind of jalopy we got here, Rob."

"I'm ready. The motor sure feels good, though."

"Sure ought to. Nobody builds a better restrictor-plate motor than Joe Banker. He was building them while you were still teething."

Joe Banker had made a name for himself building fine racing engines for the Lee Racing team, and these days for anyone else willing to pay the price. Of course, the price might vary depending on who the customer happened to be. He was especially adept at the unique racing engines required for the superspeedways at Daytona and Talladega. The sport's governing body required a special part be installed between the carburetors and the intake manifold to restrict the amount of the fuel-and-air mixture that could be sucked in. This robbed the cars of speed and power, but according to the rule-makers, the plates helped keep the cars on the tracks, not letting them be as fast and dangerous as the tracks would otherwise allow.

Many begged to differ, but rules were rules. And that meant that someone needed to be able to build engines that could do the most possible with the built-in hobble. That someone was Joe Banker. When the Ensoft sponsorship had been signed, the money at last a certainty, that had been one of Billy Winton's first telephone calls, and the new, powerful motors were being crafted within the week.

"Well, I'm tired of waiting." Rob spoke into the microphone. "I want to see what this bad girl can do."

"What are you waiting for?"

Rob didn't answer him. Instead he punched the gas and felt the car leap forward as if it had suddenly been cut loose from its moorings. He steered the racer out of the garage area and carefully pulled out toward pit road, the strip of asphalt leading out onto the track.

Still being admirably deliberate, Rob fed her more gas as he cleared the opening in the pit wall that allowed entrance to the track. As he rolled along pit road, Rob took a second to glance over at the famed tower overlooking the bend in the tri-oval. For a moment he allowed his mind to wander. He imagined himself flashing across the start/finish line there, leading a giant pack of cars beneath the flag stand, the grandstands filled with cheering fans as the rest of the field desperately chased him as he thundered first to the checkered flag.

He shook his head and tried to regain concentration on the job at hand. He would have to wait to win the race in a month, but his work this day would go a long way toward realizing that fantasy.

But it was good to dream. Lord, it was good to dream!

The car exited pit road and pulled out onto the wide, sweeping track. There were already several other cars out testing, making their first runs of the new racing season. The steady drone of the motors was carried on the stiff breeze across the speedway, and the noise firmly announced the impending season as surely as the blaring of trumpets. It was like the smell of freshly mown grass for a new baseball team or the squeak of sneakers on a gym floor at the initial basketball practice of the year. And the air inside the cold, empty speedway was still electric with the anticipation.

The pitch of his engine picked up as Rob jammed the accelerator to the floor. But the car seemed sluggish to him, only slowly picking up speed as they headed off toward the first turn no matter how urgently he spurred her on. For an instant, Rob was concerned. Then he remembered the restrictor plate, sitting between the carburetor and the intake manifold, cutting the fuel and air mixture that was flowing into the cylinders. The effect on the motor was immediately noticeable to Rob and he determined to talk more with Jodell Lee about how he had overcome the sudden loss of power back when the restrictor plates had first been mandated.

Now Rob took notice of the towering banks as the car rolled into turn one for the first time. The banking was so steep that it appeared it would be difficult for a man to even walk up it from the bottom to the top. The car, which was sitting down low on her back springs, bottomed out several times as she hit the small bumps that dotted the track's surface through the corner. He wondered what it would be like when he hit them at speed.

The ride was rougher than he had anticipated. Rob could feel it each time the car struck bottom, as the wheel seemed to want to jump out of his hands, and as the force of the big bump resonated up through the floorboard of the car, shaking car, driver, and everything inside them. But the engine continued to build RPMs as the car shot out of turn two and onto the long backstretch, and the ride seemed to smooth out some as he gained momentum.

Rob immediately noticed one more thing about driving with the restrictor plate. There would be no need to lift his foot off the throttle in the turns. He could keep the gas pedal pegged to the floor all the way through the corners. Running wide open around the big track would be no trouble at all. Rob had never run a car flat out through a corner before, and he had to fight the urge to lift off the gas as the car set its line into the turn.

The car was beginning to get up a good head of steam now as Rob sailed into turn three, his right foot still firmly shoved to the floor. He began to revel in the tremendous velocity as the car rocketed out of turn four and on to the tri-oval. Coming down to the start/finish line at a speed approaching 195 miles an hour, the grandstands were nothing but a blur out his right side window. It would have been hard for Rob Wilder to describe to anyone else the sheer exhilaration that coursed through his body as he crossed that start/finish line for the first time.

He'd made his first lap around the famed Daytona Speedway and he could already tell that he loved the place!

With the first lap completed, it was now time to see what both he and the car could do to find more speed. Would he be up to the task? Could he expect to step right in and conquer the track that made legends out of Petty, Pearson, Yarborough, and Baker? Those questions might not be answered this chilly January morning, but he was about to learn all he could as he zoomed down toward turn one again, the Ford now approaching maximum speed.

The crew stood tensely outside the garage, watching their car run those first few laps out on the track. While they had gained plenty of respect for their new, young driver already, they also knew that the first few laps in a new car on an unfamiliar track could be shaky. A loose bolt or fitting on the car at these speeds could send the thing into the wall in an instant. A miscalculation by their driver could do the same.

Will watched stone-faced as the car slowly came up to speed on that first lap. He squinted into the sun as Rob brought her around to the line for the first time. He could well imagine the thrill the kid must be feeling inside the cockpit of that machine out there, but he also hoped he would temper his excitement and go on about the business at hand.

He clicked the button on his stopwatch as Rob flashed by their position, then he paced back and forth as he watched the car push higher up on the banking of turns one and two. Rob was clearly trying to use every inch of the track to keep from losing any of the precious speed he had built up over that first lap. The driver had likely already sensed how hard it was to gain impetus with the restricted carburetor and he didn't want to lose a bit of it.

The car disappeared from Will's view then, rumbling on down the backstretch while he fiddled with the stopwatch, his ears keyed to the roar of the motor of his car as opposed to the others circling out there. He turned to pick Rob up high in turn three and then watched the car ride all the way through the corner. He sneaked one quick peek at the watch, trying to get a feel for the lap Rob was turning as he waited for him to roar back past their position.

The car flashed by in front of them and Will clicked the watch. When he took a look at the time, he couldn't hold back a broad grin no matter how hard he tried. Only then did he realize the entire crew was watching him for his reaction.

"A tick over one hundred and eighty-five miles an hour."

He had done the math in his head, converting the seconds on the watch into miles per hour. Everyone else seemed to breathe for the first time in the last couple of minutes. The primary concern they had, in addition to their green driver, was for the bodywork that they had done during the winter, getting the car's aerodynamics just right. The kid had just proved he could get the car around the place quickly. Now, over the next day and a half, they needed to tweak some to get the car itself more capable. The watch had confirmed that they were about as close as they expected to be. When they had worked a little magic on the machine, everyone else had best look out!

Everybody was still smiling the next day when the team loaded everything back up on the hauler. Will was relieved to see that all the work they had put into the car over the winter had taken her in exactly the right direction, that it had been effort well spent. Some of the other teams had tested cars and had discovered they had been on the wrong road all along and had a tough month ahead of them.

Billy Winton was smiling because he knew how difficult it would be for his young team to win a good starting spot in the field for the Grand National race, the one they would run the day before the Daytona 500. Or to even make the field at all, for that matter. These last two days showed the team had taken a huge step in the right direction to make that a possibility. If so, there would be a confident excitement in the Winton Racing shop the next few weeks.

Rob Wilder was floating a foot off the ground. He had immediately liked the big, fast speedways, the ones like Charlotte and Michigan that he had run on already, but they were nothing like what he had experienced over the last couple of days. He knew now that this was where he belonged. He had discovered what other drivers before him had learned, the appeal of this track which had drawn generations of racers before him to come to the beach and challenge its towering high banks and lofty speeds. Rob told everyone who would listen how he wished he could drive this track every day, that the middle of February could not come soon enough for him.

As the King Air lifted off the runway and turned out toward the ocean the next afternoon, Rob twisted around and watched the speedway until it slipped out of view in the dusky winter haze. Then he leaned back in the seat and closed his eyes, but not to sleep this time. He was imagining that the throb of the airplane's engines was that of his race car, and the wind whistling past and over the wings outside was the sea breeze buffeting the car as he steered it out of the second turn at Daytona at nearly two hundred miles per hour. The kid's throttle foot twitched, his shifting hand tugged at air, and his left-hand fingers clenched an invisible steering wheel.

With his eyes closed, he couldn't see Billy Winton

watching him from the copilot's seat up front. Or see the pleased smile on the man's face. The old mechanic knew exactly what the kid was thinking. And he, too, couldn't wait to get his driver and his car back out on the track they were quickly leaving behind.

It had been many years since Daytona had first grabbed hold of Billy Winton, captured him so completely, and she still had not loosened her grip on him. It was good to see the boy-faced young driver he had chosen to shepherd his own car could be so completely seduced by her curves, too.

"COASTIN'"

The oddity was not lost on Rob Wilder at all. He could be perfectly comfortable, almost relaxed, sitting back in his race car, zooming along in the middle of a pack of other circling machines, hurtling around a speedway at nearly two hundred miles per hour, the whole world passing by his window in a blur and a roar. But sitting there in a corner of the cavernous studio, closely surrounded by gangly light standards, madly rushing stagehands, odd-looking cameras and recording equipment, and a cast of brightly costumed extras, he was actually on edge, uneasy.

He didn't let it show, though. He had gradually accepted that this was as much his job as steering the car in a race. But he certainly had an opinion on which part of the job he preferred.

It was now a couple of weeks after the Daytona test and it was still hard to believe that he was back in California, "coastin'," as Donnie Kline put it. That he was actually sitting there in a studio in the San Fernando Valley, just over the hill from Hollywood. And that he was, at that moment, over two thousand miles from the rest of his crew, the guys working away on the cars in the shop back in Chandler Cove, Tennessee, getting ready for Speed Weeks in Daytona.

I oughta be back there helping, he kept muttering to himself. He couldn't remember when he had last held a wrench. When he had been beneath a car, performing some kind of operation on it.

But he and Billy had had that conversation already. Had it several times.

"You're helping the effort far more by doing the best commercial you can do for Ensoft," he had said. "And besides, they may be casting you in a movie or two before this thing is over. You even look a little bit like that DiCaprio kid."

Rob had scrunched up his face at such an outlandish suggestion. But he knew the boss was right about the importance of what he was doing.

This was his first trip out to California without Billy, and that felt strange, too. He had flown out on a commercial flight two days before and it had been his first flight alone, too. That had been no problem. Ensoft had booked him in first class, in the middle aisle of an L-1011, and one of the cabin attendants had recognized him and got his autograph, and the guy in the seat next to him was from North Carolina and they talked racing practically all the way to Los Angeles.

And so far, so good on the commercial shoot. In fact, it would be almost a pleasure if the director weren't constantly yelling at the crew and retaking the same scene a thousand times and muttering under his breath about how someone with his talent should be doing "features."

Finally, as he became more accustomed to all the

flurry of activity around him, Rob admitted to himself that it wasn't such a bad place to be. It was actually closely akin to being in the pits at a racetrack, where the work was hard, repetitious, sometimes even boring, but the end result was well worth it. And besides, having all the attention centered on him wasn't such a bad deal either. It was certainly easier work than he had been doing less than a year before. Sitting in the bright lights in front of a camera reciting the same few memorized lines over and over while dancers cavorted all around him was a far cry from the his old job at Brandon's Cabinet shop back home in Hazel Green, Alabama. He often caught himself wondering what his old buddies were doing back there.

When the exasperated director finally grabbed his head with both hands, screwed up his face in disgust, and called a break, Rob took the chance to seek out a pay phone and dialed the number for the cabinet shop. It would be fun to tell them where he was at that very moment. That he was right there in the same studio where they had shot some of the great movies they had watched at the twin theaters in Hazel Green. That he was right down the hall from where one of those soap operas was recorded.

But there was no answer back in Alabama. Then he remembered it was two hours later back there and that his friends had likely gone on home by now to their families. He suppressed a quick stab of loneliness. Billy's race crew and the boys in the cabinet shop were the only family he had.

He hung the phone back on its hook, then wandered outside and across the parking lot to a small grassy park with a stand of palm trees and some carefully planted flowers and a few playground implements. The commercial shoot had been going on for the better part of two days now. All that filming and reshooting the same bit over and over again would end up being only thirty seconds on the screen in the final version. Rob had kept his frustrations to himself so far, though. It was like driving another few laps to check the setup one more time when Will demanded it. He never complained about that either. Better to do it enough to get it right. But he still didn't understand why they had to keep doing it "one more time, people!" Not when it had seemed perfectly all right to him several hours and many feet of film before.

Rob stretched out on the thick grass in the shade of the palms, leaned back against a trunk, and stretched out his long legs. He knew from the experience of the last day and a half that it would take at least an hour, maybe longer, for them to make the changes to the set and get ready for the next scene. And that was more than enough time to work in a good nap if he got to it.

Back inside, Michelle Fagan was trying to keep her cool. She was head of marketing for Ensoft, and this day she was trying to keep up with everything going on back at the office in San Jose and still hold watch over the commercial shoot. The task was stretching her nerves taut. She had her usual army of assistants and all the people from the advertising agency running in every direction, taking care of details, while she oscillated from her cell phone to her computer hooked up to E-mail in the corner of the studio to the temperamental director who thought he was overseeing another *Star Wars* sequel.

And now she had temporarily lost her star.

"Anybody seen Rob?" she shouted to no one in particular.

"He probably slipped outside again. Over by the picnic tables and swings. That's where he's been going between takes," one of the assistants volunteered.

"Darn him!" Michelle said, half under her breath. "I wish he'd stay put."

But she had immediately felt bad about fussing. Rob had been great so far, willingly redoing the shots over and over, even though he had done them perfectly every time. And he had not complained to her once.

She started to ask someone to go out to look for him, but then she decided she could probably use a breath of fresh air herself. She made her way for the side door, stopping only long enough to grab a couple of soft drinks from the caterer's wagon.

The brightness of the late afternoon sunlight blinded her and she covered her eyes with her free hand while her vision adjusted to honest light as opposed to the fake stuff inside. Then she looked across the parking lot to the park for some sign of Rob. She didn't see him anywhere and was about to go back inside when she finally spied him, stretched out beneath one of the trees. He seemed to be deep in sleep, his chin on his chest and hands crossed over his belly. She smiled as she made her way over toward him, once again amazed at the young man's ability to catch forty winks practically anywhere.

"He drives fast, he recites his lines like a natural-born actor, and he even sleeps like a baby in the midst of utter chaos," she said in her best *Inside Hollywood*–host voice. "Is there no end to the young man's talents, ladies and gentlemen?"

He opened one eye and looked up at her sideways.

"Oh, hi, Michelle," he said, cheerily enough for someone just awakened from a deep sleep. "Is Mad Max ready for me again?"

Rob had quickly bestowed the nickname on the wild-haired director, whose first name really was Maximilian. Now most of the crew was calling him "Mad Max" behind his back, too.

"No, I just need to go over a couple of things with you before we finish up at the beach tomorrow. It ought to be a little less intense than things were yesterday and today."

She offered him one of the sodas and settled down on the grass beside him, her legs crossed, and then leaned back against her own palm tree. The kid thanked her politely for the drink and took a big swallow. Rob Wilder's easygoing nature had won Michelle Fagan over the very first time she met him, and her high opinion of him had only increased since. She sat there for a moment, closed her eyes, took a deep breath of the fresh air while she gathered her wits, and allowed herself to enjoy the cool breeze.

"Are we almost done for the day?" Rob asked her hopefully after another big draw on his soda.

"Sorry. Afraid not. We probably have another couple of hours before we'll be finished. We have to get all the soundstage stuff done today."

"The way that guy keeps making me redo things, we might be here all night. I don't know why he doesn't like what I'm doing. I'm trying to be as natural as I can be."

"You're doing fine. He just wants to get as much footage as he can so he can have the perfect shot for every second of the commercial."

"Michelle, I've done so many takes already today that I don't think there's a perfect shot left in me."

"Look, hang in there and I promise I'll make it up to you with a great dinner. How's that?" Michelle said with her usual direct look.

"Well, I was about to start gnawing on this tree trunk. I don't think I could stomach any more of that 'finger food' they got in there. We still going to try that place on the beach you've been telling me about?"

"Yeah. Anderton's. It's down at the end of Sunset Boulevard near Santa Monica. I hope you don't mind. I invited my sister to join us. She's a student at U.C.L.A. and could probably use a good meal, too. And besides, I'd like to introduce you to her. She's about your age and I think you'll like her."

"If she's half as pretty as you . . ."

He stopped short, clearly embarrassed by what he was about to say, and blushed as red as his Ford race car.

Michelle just laughed and let him off the hook by taking a swig of her drink, standing up, and then grabbing his hand and pulling him to his feet.

"I'm sure Mad Max is about ready for his star again," she said.

"I believe I'd rather rub fenders with Earnhardt Junior, but you're the boss."

Fortunately, the rest of the afternoon went easily, the temperamental director apparently running out of fire, actually admitting reluctant satisfaction with a shot or two. He even had a precious few words of praise for Rob. The kid grinned and winked at Michelle behind Max's back when he actually called him a "photogenic flower."

Soon after wrapping, they were in Michelle's rented convertible, heading over the Hollywood Hills and down toward Sunset Boulevard. Michelle insisted on driving. She told Rob it was so he could relax and have a chance to take in some of the local scenery. But he suspected she was afraid he would drive on the streets of Los Angeles the same way she had seen him do on the track at Charlotte. But for once, he didn't mind letting someone else behind the wheel. He enjoyed the warm weather, the view of the houses on stilts perched on the near-vertical hills around them, the stunning homes and coifed flowered lawns. After all, it was still winter back home in the foothills of the Smoky Mountains, a bit of hominy snow having sifted down the day he left, but there was no hint of cold or snow here.

Michelle noted that traffic was light by California standards and they were driving through Coldwater Canyon in no time, dropping down to the broad, king-palm-lined streets of Beverly Hills. Rob tried to look nonchalant, his arm draped over the door, but behind his sunglasses, he was busily looking for celebrities working in their yards or walking the sidewalks that ran in front of the swank shops. But all he spied was still more tourists, some of whom were staring right back at him, trying to figure out what famous person the good-looking, blonde-headed kid behind the sunglasses in the convertible might be.

Michelle smiled as she pointed out another house where a big star was supposed to live. She knew he was still somewhat in awe of all he was seeing, and could only imagine how different all this was from his small town home back in Alabama, or where he lived now in East Tennessee. And it also occurred to her that it was likely that Rob was already much more famous than most of the folks he was likely to spot walking the streets of Beverly Hills.

Anyway, she was glad he was enjoying seeing the sights. She had picked this particular route instead of winding around to the 405 for precisely that reason. It was also a direct route past the U.C.L.A. campus in Westwood where her sister was halfway through her junior year in prelaw.

"You sure know your way around this place," he said as they glided along Sunset out of Beverly Hills and into Bel Air.

"I went to school at U.C.L.A. right up the road here. Christy used to come down and spend weekends with

me, and that's why she decided to come to school here,
too."

He was quiet for a while as the wind whipped back
his longish blonde hair, the waning sun glinted off the
rims of his sunglasses, and the singer on the radio war-
bled about having some fun on Santa Monica Boulevard.

"I was just thinking . . ." he finally started.

"About what?"

"Aw, nothing really," Rob said, apparently wishing
now that he had kept his mouth shut.

"No, come on. Tell me what it is."

He grinned sheepishly. "Well, when I was a little kid,
I used to always watch the *Beverly Hillbillies* on television.
Never missed a show. I guess us riding through here
where they filmed it just kinda brings it all back. Sometimes I feel a little bit like Jethro. Just a hillbilly kid from
the sticks running round lost in the big city."

"Hey, you're not lost. You're here with me. And this
is a big city even for somebody who used to live here.
It's really just a bunch of little towns all lined up, actually. There are plenty of people from Glendale who have
never been to Torrance. Wouldn't know how to begin
to get there even." She stopped at a red light and took
advantage of the chance to look directly at her passenger. "Oh, and you can cut the 'hillbilly' stuff, too. You're
about as cool as anybody I know, Rob Wilder. You just
turn on that country-boy charm for effect, don't you?"
She said it with a smile and she saw the corner of his
lip move as if he was about to grin himself. "And by the
way, most of that show was shot in a studio like the one
you've been in all day."

"A production studio? I thought it was shot all over
Beverly Hills," Rob replied, clearly surprised.

"Of course not, dummy. Where did you think?"

"I don't know. I reckon I thought they just picked a spot and started filming."

Michelle simply laughed as she pulled away from the light. That was one of the things she liked about this young man. He might come across as naïve, but never a bumpkin. And he was so natural. So real one had to wonder sometimes if he was putting them all on, if he was actually too good to be true. But she had long since decided Rob Wilder was the real deal. Never mind the amazingly dangerous and breathtaking thing he did so well for a living. He also had just enough of a southern lilt in his voice to be oddly intriguing, had all the attractive vulnerability of a boy on the verge of becoming a man, and was definitely movie-star-handsome, all blonde hair and flashing white teeth. And his innocence only served to make him all the more attractive.

Those were the very qualities that had made him and his race team such an obvious choice for her company's huge investment as its sponsor. Sure, Billy Winton had put together a competitive team, one that could get their logo on television and in the newspapers on a regular basis no matter who drove the race car. But meeting the kid, letting the other key players at Ensoft meet him in person, had sealed the deal. Michelle had known immediately that he was the perfect match for the target demographic they wanted to reach with the campaign for their new Internet-related software systems. The others had agreed and had gladly written the checks. He had taken to the personal appearances and the commercial shoots as naturally as he had to guiding Billy's Ford racing machine around a superspeedway. Now, if he could actually win some races this upcoming season, make impressive showings in most of the others, then make the move next year to the Winston Cup, the whole plan would come together.

They finally turned off Sunset through the gated entrance to the U.C.L.A. campus. Michelle wound her way through the narrow roads as Rob watched the students hurrying in all directions, carrying their backpacks, all of them apparently off to somewhere in a mighty big rush. And he realized where all the California women the guys in the shop had kidded him about had gone. They were everywhere, in such abundance he had trouble deciding which direction to gawk.

As they headed toward one of the residential quads, Rob gazed across an open stretch of green lawn and spotted a particularly striking blonde standing on a small plaza in front of several tall buildings. He couldn't help himself. He craned his neck as he tried to get a better look at the tall, slender woman standing casually at the curb, likely waiting for her boyfriend to come by and pick her up.

"You wanna get your tongue back in your mouth, lover boy?" she kidded.

Rob blushed as he realized he had been caught staring at the blonde.

"Sorry, Michelle. I've just been spending too much time with hairy, greasy old mechanics and with my head buried in an engine, I guess. I'm kinda overwhelmed with all these beautiful women congregated in one place."

"Well, Casanova. I noticed you were staring at that blonde over there on the curb. Why don't we just drive on over and let you see if she might like to meet a real, live race car driver?"

"Uh, that's okay now, Michelle! Don't we have to go pick up your sister?"

"She'll wait. I think we need to stop and give you a chance to meet a new California friend. Maybe we can give her a lift somewhere. That is, if you can untangle your tongue long enough to maybe ask her where she's going."

"Aw, Michelle, stop it!" he half whined in a voice hardly associated with a rough-and-tumble stock car racer.

"Okay, big boy. You're up."

She had wheeled the car to a stop at the edge of the curb, not three feet from where the striking blonde young lady waited.

But Rob could only drop his head and try to slide low enough in the convertible's seat to actually disappear from sight. He had never been so humiliated in his life. Under Michelle's mocking gaze, he straightened up and tried to speak, but nothing would come out. One thing was for certain, though. He was looking at the fresh face of one of the most beautiful women he had ever laid eyes on. And she had turned her head expectantly, as if waiting for some glib pickup line. A line Rob Wilder couldn't seem to utter.

Michelle rescued him.

"Hi!" she said to the girl. "Looks like the cat's got my friend's tongue here, but he was just wondering if you needed a lift somewhere."

The girl's eyes sparkled mischievously as she flashed a blinding smile.

"Why, thank you. As a matter of fact, I sure do. I could use a ride down toward the beach if you wouldn't mind. If you're going that way."

Rob couldn't believe it. This stranger was going to climb right into the car with them without knowing who they were or what they were up to. He was hardly aware of Michelle digging him in the ribs, urging him to open the door, to lean forward so the beautiful woman could climb into the backseat.

"Climb in. Just happens we are heading to the beach ourselves," Michelle said cheerily.

Rob finally fell back on his good manners, offering the stranger the front seat while he crawled into the back, then held the door open while she slid in. It would be better to be behind her. That way she couldn't see the deep shade of crimson his face had turned or that he had absolutely no idea what to do next.

"So who is your friend back there with the tangled-up tongue?" the blonde asked, pointing over her shoulder with a thumb to where Rob sat in the middle of the backseat. Now he could only imagine her smile.

"That's Mr. Rob Wilder, a soon-to-be-very-famous race car driver," Michelle said with a hint of a giggle.

Something was going on here and he wasn't sure what it was. Then he caught the young woman's deep blue eyes in the rearview mirror. She was watching him. He managed a sickly grin. And he vowed when they dropped this woman off and before they picked up her kid sister, he would give Miss Michelle Fagan a piece of his mind for embarrassing him so. He didn't care whether she was the sponsor's rep. This wasn't fair!

Then, as Michelle pulled back out onto Sunset, the blonde student twisted around in the seat, showed him her perfect teeth again, and offered her hand.

"Well, Rob Wilder, it's nice to finally meet you."

Finally meet me? he thought.

Rob took the offered hand and didn't try to hide the puzzled frown on his face. Was she a race fan? What were the odds of that?

"My name is Christy Fagan. Michelle has told me all about you. But hey, Michelle!" Christy said, nodding over toward her sister but not taking her eyes off Rob. "You left out the part about him being so cute."

"I figured I would let you make up your own mind."

"It's nice to meet you, Christy," he finally managed to spit out, but the words still came out sideways. Her hand was warm. He felt as if he had just touched the hot terminal of a car battery.

"You didn't say 'y'all.' "

"Huh?"

" 'Nice to meet y'all.' Isn't that the southern way?" She didn't say it in a snide way at all.

"Not unless there's more than one of you. Yankees never get that right in the movies."

Something about her manner put him immediately at ease and he was actually able to manage what he hoped was a coherent sentence. Not that he wasn't still miffed at Michelle for playing the trick on him. He'd get even. Somehow he'd get even.

Christy turned back and watched the road ahead while she asked him questions about racing, about the commercial they were shooting, about what little she knew of Alabama. But Rob watched her the whole time, the brilliant, sunny scenery now no longer of interest to him. Her long hair blew gently in the wind as they drove on toward where the sun was already sinking. He could not keep his eyes off of her. And he would blush whenever she would turn to look at him to hear his answers to her questions, giving him that smile again each time.

Finally they dropped the car with the valet and walked into the restaurant. Rob couldn't believe the way the orange sunlight reflected off the ocean. He admitted to the women that it was his first time to actually see the Pacific. Michelle asked the hostess to seat them on the patio, overlooking the water. The sisters sat together, across from Rob, and seemed not to notice that the sea-gulls were flying in and out between the tables, helping the busboys do their jobs.

Rob watched the sunset as they chatted casually. He

couldn't help thinking about how beautiful it was here in this place. And how unlikely it was for him, of all people, to be here, in some swank restaurant on the West Coast overlooking the Pacific Ocean, sitting across the table from two beautiful women, about to order a slab of grilled mahimahi, acting for all the world as if he actually belonged here. It had all happened so fast it made his head swim worse than a hard lick in a crash on the track might.

Then, as the sun seemed to touch the water out there on the horizon and they paused in the conversation to eat, he glanced over at Christy and caught her looking at him. It was her turn to be embarrassed now. She quickly went for the straw in her drink and poked herself in the lip. That only embarrassed her more, but she smiled at him all the same. Basking in the glow of the gorgeous sunset, seeing that smile aimed his direction, only made Rob Wilder realize what a special day this had turned out to be. A day, he suspected, that he was meant to remember for a long time to come.

As the evening wore on, as the delicious fish was followed by a fancy piece of fudge pie and then cups of some kind of strong, foamy coffee, Rob realized that he now could talk with Christy as easily as he could her sister. He had gotten over his case of stumble-tongue and was actually enjoying talking with her, hearing what she had to say. He had often wondered if he wasn't developing a crush on Michelle. Now he knew for certain he had a serious one on her baby sister.

When Michelle pulled the car around to the front of Christy's residence hall, Rob had to fight a swell of disappointment. The evening had been special and he suddenly realized it was coming to a close much sooner than he would have liked. And try as he might, he couldn't come up with a way to extend it.

Christy said her good-byes to Michelle and Rob, then hopped out of the car, leaving the door open for Rob to climb back up into the front seat. He stepped out onto the curb beside her.

"It was so nice to finally meet you," Rob said, extending his hand to her. "Good luck on that exam tomorrow. I hope we haven't taken too much of your study time."

Christy took the hand, squeezing it tightly. "No problem. It's only sociology, and a Scantron multiple choice at that." Even in the dark, her eyes sparkled when she looked up at him. "After Michelle told me so much about you for the last several months, it's nice to finally meet you live and in person. I'm going to take you up on that offer to come to a race. You can count on that."

"Anytime you want to come, just let me know."

She still held his hand, and now leaned closer and whispered to him. "You know, she's been trying to set us up for the longest."

"Really?" was all he could whisper back.

"Yep. I don't mind. I hope you don't."

"No. Absolutely not. No!"

"You two gonna talk about me, at least do it where I can hear it!" Michelle said loudly.

Christy squeezed his hand again, then suddenly reached up and wrapped her arms around his neck and gave him a tight hug. The surprise as much as the force of it left Rob breathless. He loved the feel of her next to him. Then, just as suddenly, she gave him a quick kiss on the cheek, a grazing peck that was so quick he was not sure at first that her lips had even touched him.

Then she was gone with a quick bounce of her long hair as she hopped up the steps and through the doorway of the dorm.

He was set for what he was sure would be the inevitable teasing from Michelle. Surprisingly, she only turned up the radio and said nothing as they rode in silence back toward their hotel.

Was she mad at him? he wondered. Jealous maybe? Could there be some sibling rivalry going on here? Or had the whole evening been as obvious a setup as it seemed and Michelle was only allowing him to be alone to sort out his thoughts?

Whatever it was, Rob was running on all cylinders. If it had been possible to get out on a racetrack with the high he was on at that moment, then the rest of the field would have had to look out! Christy Fagan had lit a spark inside him like he had never felt before. There was a new level of confidence bubbling inside him.

With both of them exhausted from the long day and the prospects of an even longer one tomorrow, Rob and Michelle said quick good-nights in the hotel lobby and agreed to meet for breakfast the next morning. But once in his room, Rob couldn't find sleep.

He could still feel a warm spot on his cheek where her lips had touched his skin. He could feel her hand in his and still hear her voice, her soft laugh when he said something that had not actually been all that funny.

As he tossed and turned, wide-awake, he even wished a time or two that he had brought his old scrapbook with him on this trip. He usually did. The clippings taped and pasted inside the torn and tattered old book had gotten him through many sleepless nights before. But maybe it was best he had left it home this time. With him on the verge of a wonderful, hopeful new season, with the amazing new feelings this special evening had set off inside him, maybe it was best he didn't have those old memories, those lingering demons, to fall back on.

That was when he realized he had gone hours without

even thinking a single time about the race car, about the upcoming race at Daytona, about the crew or Billy or Will or the shop. He stifled a strong stab of guilt. Then he finally rolled over on his side, took in and released a deep breath, and slept a dreamless sleep.

BACK TO THE BEACH

The guys at the shop noticed a difference in the kid as soon as he got back from the West Coast trip. Now he actually beat them to the shop each morning. It was hard to get an earlier start than a race-team crew, but Rob managed it. He also seemed to work even harder around the shop than he had before, diving in with even more dedication and fervor. And he now seemed almost totally immune to the constant torrent of jokes and tricks that rained down from the other crew members. But sometimes they would catch Rob staring into space with a half smile on his face. Or lying flat on his back on the creeper beneath a car with a tool in his hand. But often it was not engaged at all, and the kid seemed to be contemplating something pleasant, something very distant and not at all related to the rear end of a Ford race car.

There was plenty of speculation about the change in their driver's demeanor. Everyone in the Winton Racing shop had an opinion. But only Will Hughes and Billy Winton knew the real answer. Billy had briefed Will after he got a full report on the trip from Michelle Fagan. She had told him about the commercial shoot, the photo sessions for the print ads, the quick visit to the Los Angeles Ensoft office where Rob signed autographs and gave out team T-shirts. Then they had talked about the upcoming plans for Speed Weeks in Daytona. And she had finally told him of the evening Rob had spent with her and her sister and that it had apparently gone well. Very well.

"Well, if he's going to fall in love, it's best it's not somebody around racing," Billy told Will.

"True. We don't need the constant distraction," Will agreed. "Do we let him know we know?"

"Not just yet. He may get over her in a hurry if he doesn't see her for a while. Let's don't make it a problem if it's not a problem. And for God sakes, don't let anybody on the crew know!"

Not that Rob had actually fallen in love anyway. He only knew that he couldn't stop thinking about Christy Fagan. He had politely refused her dorm telephone number when Michelle had offered it. He actually did want it in the worst way, but he doubted she would really care to talk to him again after he had been so thick tongued and awkward during their first and only evening together. Why in the world would someone as special as she was want to get a phone call from some redneck race car driver?

Now he was kicking himself and trying to figure out some nonchalant way to bring it up to Michelle, some excuse to get in touch with her so he could get her sister's number. Or maybe he would just wait until he saw her at the next appearance and ask for it then.

He mentally kicked himself. How could he be so sure,

so confident, when he was behind the wheel of a race car, yet so timid when it came to someone like Christy Fagan? And why was he still so preoccupied he could hardly work? Thinking about her and the evening at the beach restaurant, even as he lay there underneath the car they planned to use in the race in Rockingham, the one right after Daytona. He was supposed to be changing out the rear end, but as he lay there in a pool of tools, parts, and grease, examining the gear, he was thinking about her deep blue eyes, her laugh, the gentle way she had teased him. And he had completely forgotten how this thingamajig was supposed to fit.

It was a blessed relief when the truck finally pulled away from the shop on a frosty morning, the gleaming new race car carefully loaded aboard, heading for Daytona Beach. Now they were finally going to go do some racing! And he could think about something besides blue eyes and long blonde hair.

Rob left right behind the truck, but he was en route to the airport for a flight to a software convention in Atlanta. He would be in the Ensoft booth for a couple of hours, signing autographs and meeting vendors and distributors. He was to meet up with Will and the rest of the prerace crew at the hotel in Daytona the night before the racetrack opened. He was anxious to put all the sponsor appearances he'd been doing behind him, to get to some place where he could smell gas fumes and have his ears stunned by the roar of a collective cadre of engines. It would be wonderful to actually concentrate on driving and racing for a change.

The long winter off-season had been hard on him. Other than the Daytona test and the few times he had crawled into one of the Fords to remind himself how it felt, he had spent no time in a race car at all. The sponsor appearances had been fun, a real boost to his ego, but it was not racing. He needed to feel the powerful earthquake of a six-hundred-horsepower motor beneath him. The momentum had been building the previous season, the excitement heading for a peak, and then they had run out of events in which to run. The season had ended just when they were ready to challenge anybody who wanted to run against them. It felt like years since the last time he zoomed down with a pack of cars to take the start and try to be first to the flag at the end.

It was time to go racing. But first he had to do the show. And be with Michelle Fagan for a day and a half without mentioning Christy. Or thinking about her. But Michelle seemed very busy, always running or on the cell phone, and never talked about her sister at all.

The second time he saw the Daytona Speedway from the air was just as exciting as the first for Rob Wilder. He twisted around in the seat of the Ensoft corporate jet and pointed excitedly out the window as they banked to line up with the Daytona Beach airport.

"Look, Michelle! There she is. Ain't she beautiful?"

He immediately bit his tongue, ashamed he'd said "ain't," but Michelle seemed preoccupied and missed it. But then she, too, was clearly impressed with the gargantuan speedway slipping by beneath them. The largest track she had seen so far had been the mile-and-a-half at Charlotte.

"It's huge, Rob. It must take five minutes to make a lap around that thing."

"It's big, all right, but it's also lightning-quick. You can do the whole two and a half miles in under a minute."

She tried to do the math in her head but gave up. "Whoa! That is fast!" She could only imagine what a car moving that quickly would look like from ground level, down close. And she knew she would likely soon find out.

"I can't wait to get the car out there and set her loose. You can run wide open all the way around the place, you know. You never even have to crack the throttle anywhere, not even in the corners."

"I can't imagine forty cars running along like that. It has to be dangerous," she said with a worried look. But she had to smile when she caught the euphoric expression on the young driver's face. "Kid looking through a candy store window" came to mind.

She got her chance to see the wildness firsthand the next day. She was there when they rolled the shiny new red Ensoft-sponsored car out of the garage stall and headed it toward the inspection line. Will Hughes was already fretting about the once-over the car was about to get. With all the tweaking they had done on the bodywork over the winter, he was concerned that they may not have hit the templates close enough to pass the meticulous once-over. He knew for certain that they were pushing the limit in several spots, trying to get air to flow as smoothly as possible over the car's surface. But it had to meet the sanctioning body's rigorous standards or they would have plenty of work to do in the next little while. He doubted they would ever get the car as perfectly shaped again as it was now. And redoing the body would be time and manpower wasted that could be better spent with other testing and tweaking to make the car even faster.

The impact of the draft on the cars running Daytona, the ability to tuck in behind and follow other cars around the track, made it critical to have a racer as aerodynamically perfect as possible. The airflow rushing over the body of the vehicle had everything to do with how fast the car would go. Have the hood or front end or roofline only a tiny bit out of kilter and you might just as well run with an open parachute hanging off the back. That was why Will and the crew had spent so much time over the winter perfecting the body shape on the new race car.

Now Michelle watched as the team's engine man stood in the fender well of the car, making a couple of last-minute adjustments. With the power plant built by Joe Banker, Billy had explained, they knew the motor had plenty of horsepower at the disposal of young Rob Wilder, regardless of how hog-tied it might be by the restrictor plate. It certainly looked powerful, filling the entire engine compartment. And when they cranked it up, it sounded plenty potent. Then why was everyone suddenly so nervous?

That was one thing she had noticed about racing folk already. Everyone was supremely confident one minute, ready to take on the world. Then, a second later, everything was wrong, the engine sour, the track too hot or too cold, the sky too cloudy or the sun too hot, the body of the car about as aerodynamic as a cement block.

When they finally rolled the car off to inspection, Michelle stepped back into the lounge in the hauler, putting into the refrigerator the things she and Rob had picked up at the market for snacks later. Rob had turned quiet in the last few minutes, his eye constantly on the car or the high-banked turns out there on the track. She had talked with him and he pretended to listen, but she could tell his mind was on the car, the racetrack. He was clearly eager to get all the preparations, the waiting, the downtime, behind him, and get up to speed.

But it was over an hour later before Rob was in the race car, finally buckling up the seat belts, ready to take her out for the first true practice run of this new, hopeful season. The crew obviously shared Rob's sentiments and they all jumped to the task of making the final adjustments that Will had dictated.

Billy Winton had watched all the activity from a distance, allowing his team to work unimpeded. But then, when it was clearly time to kick off the year, he strode over to the open window of the race car and stuck his head inside.

"You ready, Robbie?"

The kid flashed a wide grin. "If I get any readier, I'll bust."

"Good. Now, don't go out there and try to win the pole position on the first few laps we run. It's a new car and a new track for you. Get comfortable with both of them first."

"I will, Billy."

"Just don't push it. We'll have plenty of time to find all the speed we need. Will thinks she'll be fast right off the truck, but we need a baseline."

"I'll find out where we are. How many laps you want me to run this first time out?"

"Will thinks we should do some short runs first, then we'll try some longer stretches once we know where we stand." Billy leaned in closer and gave his harness a couple of quick tugs. "Now, remember what Jodell told you about this place. Respect it at all times. Don't try to put the nose of the car somewhere where it won't fit."

"Don't worry, Billy. I do have a healthy respect for the place."

"Well, just remember that things happen in a hurry here. Especially if we're as fast as we want to be."

Rob looked at his boss sideways. "I'll bring her back in one piece. We still have to win a race with this thing in a little while."

Billy Winton shook the kid's gloved hand, then backed out the window. Rob cinched up the belts even tighter, then pulled on his helmet, all the while thinking about how great it would be to feel the wind as he hit full speed down that mythical backstretch. Billy's cautious admonitions didn't bother him at all. He knew Billy and Will trusted him to do the right thing with the car. They were simply coaching him, getting him ready for the mental part of what was to be over the next few days as much a cerebral test as a physical one.

Now, finally, it was time to go out and run a lap around this place for real. Rob scanned the panel of gauges before him, making sure everything connected to them was acting as it should. He was already working up through the gears, trying to build speed in the car despite the restrictor plate, as he navigated down the back straight for the first time. The hard jolts jarring the frame when the car bottomed out on the springs were nothing to him as he excitedly sailed around the track, ready to see what they had accomplished in the last few months' labor.

Rob felt as if electricity were running through his body as he pushed the car at speed around and around the speedway, lap after lap. Being able to run wide open all the way around a racetrack was every racer's dream. Rob couldn't get over being able to kick the gas pedal to the floor and leave it there. But then the raw racer in him wanted more, to have the ability to push it just a little harder and a little further into the floorboard, to try to squeeze another few ounces of speed out of the car so it was almost on the edge of skidding sideways, on the verge of losing its grip.

Will, Billy, and the others stood there, each of them timing those first few laps and comparing results. The car was fast. No doubt about that. But it was still nothing near what they were hoping for, what they would eventually need. There was work to be done and plenty more practicing to do after all.

Will radioed for Rob to bring the car in. It was a good thing the crew chief couldn't see the frown on his driver's face. He was disappointed, hoping the car was close enough that he could stay out and sail awhile longer. He was already addicted to the wide-open laps and could have stayed out there until he ran out of fuel if Will had only allowed him.

Will could read the kid's mind, even if he had not detected the chagrin in his "All right" on the radio. Rob would want to drive the tires off the car. That was why they hired him. But Will also knew the important thing now was to get the car ready to qualify, and right now, good as the car was, they were nowhere near the speed they would need to put it and its driver on the front row. And that, they all agreed, was where they both belonged.

As Rob pulled down onto the pit road, he had to carefully watch his speed. After the high velocity of the open track, the pace down the pit road leading back to the garage area made it seem as if he would never get there. Rob pulled into their assigned stall and found the crew was already armed with instructions from Will for the changes they needed to make. They immediately went to work.

Will popped open the hood and he and Billy began making minor adjustments to the cowling. Another of the crew members set about adjusting the camber for the right front tire. Then, once they were finished, the car was strung to make sure everything still lined up as it was supposed to.

The pounding of a hammer banging away at something under the hood mingled with the shouts of the crew as they compared whatever portion of the car was their responsibility. Occasionally the screech of an air wrench or the angry rumble of an engine in a nearby stall would wipe it all away.

All the while, Rob Wilder simply sat there patiently, sipping at a bottle of bright green sports drink that Michelle Fagan had passed through the window to him. She had also handed him a clean towel and he wiped his face as he waited for them to finish the adjustments, subtle or otherwise.

Finally he got the high sign from one of the crew that they were about ready for him to go give the adjustments a test. He pulled his helmet back on and tossed the empty bottle and towel back out the window. There was no time to waste in these first minutes of practice.

"Okay, cowboy. Fire her up. Maybe we did more good than harm. The ductwork leading into the cowl got bent somehow and that was restricting the airflow coming into the motor and we fixed that."

"Ten-four, Will. Want me to look for anything in particular?" Rob asked the microphone at his lips.

It seemed odd, talking to Will over the radio when he could have almost reached out and touched him. But with the motor running and the earplugs in place inside Rob's helmet and Will's own headset wrapped around his head, they would never have heard each other.

"No, just try to run as low as the car feels comfortable in the corners. And don't forget to keep it wide open all the way around."

"Hey, that's the only way! Flat out and wide open! You don't have to worry about me letting up unless they drop a boxcar in the racing groove."

"That's what I like to hear, kid!" Billy chimed in on his own radio, his voice carrying obvious excitement.

"Just go out and run us a couple of good, smooth laps. We want to see if we can see these changes on the watch," Will added.

Before Rob drove away, Will reached in through the window and reset the tachometer switch, the one that captured and remembered the highest revs that the tach measured during a run. He pulled the window net back up and fastened the clips that held it in place. Then he waved Rob out of the garage and double-timed on over to where Billy was already waiting atop the truck. Along the way he motioned to Michelle to follow along behind him and climb the ladder on up to the good observation spot.

She followed eagerly, always willing to soak up more knowledge about this loud, rapid sport which had suddenly become such an important part of her life. Maybe she didn't need to know how to adjust the camber or fix a bent duct to a cowl, but she had already decided that she needed to have more than a passing knowledge of what actually went on down there in the pits and garage. And besides, she had discovered that she actually enjoyed the racing game far more than she had ever expected she would. Truth be told, she had planned to delegate much of what she was doing now to her assistants, to soon hire someone to head up their racing sponsorship, but so far she had only managed to delegate it to herself. She no longer questioned what a young woman from Petaluma, California, a senior executive with one of the world's major software companies, was doing hanging out in the motor pits in Daytona Beach, watching grease-covered men perform mechanic magic while other wild-eyed ones drove around in circles like maniacs. Nor did she bother to question why she had quickly come to like it all so much.

As he headed down pit road, Rob gunned the car, the growl of its engine like beautiful music. Just as he headed off into turn one, accelerating as quickly as the car could, a four-car draft zoomed by him, taking the high side of the track. The restricted motor was taking so long to bring him up to speed that the bunch of cars was long gone before he had shifted down into fourth gear.

So far, Rob couldn't tell much difference in the car after the work they had done, but he kept the throttle pressed to the floor and wished it forward. With all the bumping and bouncing around the car was doing, he had all he could do to keep the thing headed in a straight line anyway. He would concentrate on trying to drive the best line he could around the track for several laps so Will could get some good times on the car. As he sailed through turns three and four on his first circuit, he worked to hold the bucking automobile low in the turns.

Then, in his mirror, he saw another closely packed line of cars, at least five of them, tucked one right behind the other in a tight draft. He crossed the start/finish line, still not up to full speed and just as the line of drafting race cars pulled alongside him.

Back atop the truck, Will clicked his stopwatch and gave its face a long look. The car had picked up several tenths of a second on its initial lap. Now it was time to see what the car and Rob would do once they joined in one of the drafts.

"Okay, cowboy, let's let her hang out a little bit here. There's a group of cars drafting up above you. When they get past you, tuck in behind them and see how the car feels in the draft."

"Ten-four. I see 'em. Man! They're moving! Are you sure I didn't drop an anchor off the back of this thing?"

"No, you're just seeing how the draft works down here. Two or more cars together run a whole lot faster than one on its lonesome. You're gonna have to take a crash course in drafting the next few days."

The five cars reeled Rob in as surely as if he had been parked, waiting for them to get by. But as soon as the last car in the pack had passed him, he tugged the wheel to the right and fell in line behind them. Immediately he felt the car jump forward as if someone had lit a rocket booster on his rear end. He couldn't believe the difference in speed between running along by himself and being dragged along in the collective aerodynamic swell of the group of cars.

The draft was a smaller factor at some of the other superspeedways, helping to pick up a tick or two of momentum or to assist in a slingshot past another car. But even then, a good strong car running alone could still hold his own against drafting competitors. Daytona and her sister track at Talladega were a different story. Two or more cars running together were always much faster than a car running out there by itself. If a car fell out of the draft, it would often appear to anyone watching that the driver had shut off the engine and hopped on the brakes. And if the unfortunate driver didn't find someone else to partner with soon, he would be at the end of the field, wondering what happened.

Rob took Will's advice and experimented. He pulled out slightly and took a peek past the Chevrolet he was tailing, feeling how the air flowing off the other vehicles affected the handling of his own car. Once he got the nose of the car far enough down on the Chevy's inside, the wind buffeted him like a strong gale. The first time he tried it, he had to struggle to keep the car from bouncing all over the track, and to hold on to the draw of the cars in front of him.

I don't remember studying this in school, he thought. But he knew he was right back in a very wide open classroom and he vowed to learn all he could before the big test coming up on race day. He watched the cars running in front of him and concentrated on mimicking what they did. Then he stepped out and tried to see the effects of attempting to get around them in various points on the speedway.

Finally Rob grew tired of following in line behind other cars. He felt as if his car was actually a tad faster than what these cars were anyway and that now was as good a time as any to let them know it. And besides, he hadn't come all the way to Daytona to follow anybody for too long.

He accumulated some courage and then gave the wheel a slight nudge to the left, swinging the Ford a few feet down to the inside. He was using the slingshot effect, the vacuum created by the turbulent wind off the cars in front of him, to try to jump down and get a good run past the car directly in front of him in line.

Whooosh! With the momentum of the sudden move, the strong yank of the air, and the powerful motor Joe Banker had built for him, Rob shot past the Chevy and then right on by the next car in line.

"Wheeeeyew!" Rob howled. "That was easy!"

Before he knew it, he was even with the next racer, the third in line, and the driver shot him a quick "what are you doing there?" look. Though Rob couldn't see through the tinted visor, he figured the guy was wide-eyed, wondering where this quick, bright red Ford had come from to challenge him. Now all he had to do was keep his foot on the floor and steer right on past the startled driver, clear the next two cars, and assume his rightful place right up there, leading the entire pack across the start/finish line and into turn one. The adrenaline shot through Rob's system, and if he had dared to move either of his hands from the lurching steering wheel, he would have pounded the dash in joyful exuberance.

But then he noticed that he was not gaining any more ground, that the third-place car was still right there beside him.

"Come on, come on!" he urged the car. "Take 'em!"

But no amount of beseeching seemed to make his car ease on past the rest of them. His foot was jammed solidly to the floorboard, the motor groaned and pulled in obedient response, answering his call. But it was like some giant hand had reached out of the sky and put a heavy thumb down hard on his back deck, holding him back and keeping him from gaining anything at all on the other cars.

Then he watched helplessly as it seemed as if the other drivers had suddenly awakened from a nap and noticed the audacity of young Rob Wilder, thinking he could actually zoom past them. It seemed as if they suddenly decided to stomp on their own throttles, and in tandem they took off. One by one, the cars he had just passed so easily rudely sailed right back past him on the outside, and there didn't seem to be a thing he could do about it but watch them. Watch them and taste their hot exhaust.

To make it worse, the cars were running so close, bumper seemingly locked to bumper, that Rob was unable to find enough of an opening to slide up and find a place between any of them. The last car flew past him and the line was running away from him, quickly leaving him behind. By the time the cars hit the backstretch, the batch of racers he had been so easily roaring past was now fifteen car lengths ahead and pulling away all the time.

Before they were completely gone, Rob slid the car up higher on the track, trying to fall in behind them before another pack came by and whipped him even worse. Fortunately, they were not so far gone yet that he couldn't still catch some effect from their draft. The strong engine stood him in good stead once again, and with the combination of horsepower and wind power, he was able to slowly close back up on them. Once he was back in the cluster, being towed along, Rob allowed himself several deep breaths and a long whistle of relief.

"Whew, Lord, that was close."

He whispered the words, then realized he had instinctively keyed the radio microphone button on the steering wheel as he spoke.

"Welcome to Daytona, cowboy," Will answered.

From their perch on top of the hauler, they had seen the entire lap developing. Each had nudged the other, knowing full well the tutoring that their young driver was about to receive.

"You, me, Jodell . . . we could all have told him, but he had to have it happen for real for him to see it," Billy said with a grin.

It was true. The kid would know exactly what they were preaching when they next told him about the quirks of restrictor-plate racing on Daytona's high banks.

They allowed Rob to tag along with the other cars for a while, drafting off them for several more laps, then they called him in. The run had been a successful one, even beyond Rob's hard lesson. Will was pleased with the way the car picked up after the adjustments and he knew he was on the right track with several more he wanted to try. Billy had another task. He wanted to pull his young driver aside and, as gently as possible, drive home the lesson the kid had just learned.

Rob coasted into the garage stall, the motor already silent, and Will, along with Tony Halsey, the engine man, immediately started popping the hood pins on the car. One of the other crew members hung a cooling fan on the nose of the car, sending cool air across the radiator, while others disappeared under the rear end, their tools in hand. Tony began tinkering in the area of the intake manifold while Will watched him work.

Meanwhile, Billy motioned for Rob to go ahead and climb out of the car. Clearly the changes they were making under the hood and to the rear suspension would take a few minutes to complete.

"Got you a good dose of the draft there, 'eh, kid?"

"Well, I suppose I did. I was going along there just fine, thinking I was going to pass them all with no trouble a'tall. Then boom! It was like I ran into a brick wall or something. The car wouldn't go for some reason. The next thing I know, the whole line of them goes sailing right back by me like I've parked the thing to take a siesta. It was all I could do to hang on to their draft and catch back up. If we didn't have such a good motor, I couldn't have even done that."

Rob's words spilled out quickly, his eyes wide. He was still rattled by the experience.

"That's what we've been telling you about. You have to be careful when you get out of line and go to make a pass. Be sure you've got the muscle before you try. It's a tough lesson to learn, even for the veterans."

Rob slid down to a seat in one of the team's director's chairs. He took a long draw on a bottle of water, then looked up at Billy.

"I know one thing, boss. I'm gonna need a lot more practice laps. That is, if I can get some of them to draft with me. You know how peculiar some of them are about hanging around rookies in practice."

"I'll find somebody who'll help you out. That's one reason I'm here. First we need to concentrate on getting you qualified. Now you see why it's so important for us to start as close to the front as we can. Passing at the back of the pack where the slower guys are won't be too hard if we got a fast car. Passing up there at the front of the field will be a different story."

Rob had a puzzled look on his sweaty face. "Why is that, Billy? The fastest cars at a big, wide track like this ought to go right to the front, no problem at all."

Billy smiled, then noticed that Michelle Fagan was standing nearby, listening as well, waiting for an answer to the question. Sometimes, when he watched the ease with which this youngster drove a race car, he forgot entirely that he was still an inexperienced rookie, that a new track like Daytona was a total learning experience for him.

"A slow car can win the race, no problem. I remember back in 'eighty-eight in the Fourth of July race. Bill Elliott won the darn thing with what most people thought was the slowest thing he'd driven around here in years. He got hooked up with the right car in the draft and the two of them running nose to tail were a whole lot faster than anybody else out there. Rick Wilson was behind him in the draft with the faster car, but he just couldn't get past Elliott no matter how hard he tried. Once he pulled out to try, he'd go backwards till he got back in the air behind Bill."

Rob remembered the race well. He had watched it on television. And he had been eight years old!

"So are you saying that out front is the place to be?"

"These days, with the restrictor plates and the kind of cars folks are bringing down here, it is. It's hard for a single car to pass anybody and make it stick. You have to have a car following behind you or you wind up running side by side with whoever you're trying to get by. Try to pull that coming down to take the checkered flag and you'll lose every time."

"Boy, this is gonna be harder than I thought. I fully expected to come down here, stomp on the gas from the get-go, and run the thing flat out all the way around. From the test we did, I figured that if I had the fastest car, I'd win the race. No problem. End of story. 'Wilder Wins.' Now you're telling me I have to do tricks? Gosh, Billy, I'm gonna have to talk with my lawyer!"

"You still have some learning to do," Billy said with a smile "Don't worry too much about it. Wait'll Jodell gets down here tomorrow and he can show you a few things. We're gonna think about qualifying in the meantime."

"I sure wish I could go out and run a bunch of laps with Jodell. I bet if I could, I'd nail down this drafting pretty quick."

"Trust me, kid, old Jodell would go out there and run laps with you all day long if he didn't think his wife would find out. Catherine's spent lots of time and effort chasing the old so-and-so out of race cars after he retired."

Billy grinned as he remembered one time in particular, right there at Daytona. Several years after he had given up driving, Catherine Lee found out that Jodell had driven some laps at Daytona in one of the preseason test sessions. She had proceeded to have a fit right there in the garage with a bunch of Jodell's friends and former opponents within earshot. That was the last time he had piloted a race car. Or at least the last time he had owned up to it.

"I'll pick his brain," Rob said.

"Good. About the only thing Jodell loves as much as driving a race car is talking about driving a race car. Now, let's see what Will's got in mind for putting this buggy on the pole."

They all stayed busy the balance of the afternoon, working on getting everything on the car ready for one fast lap. Slowly, sometimes maddeningly slowly, they began to pick up a fraction of a second here or salvaged another tick of the stopwatch there. It was often tedious work, but even the normally noncommittal face of Will Hughes cracked into what passed for a grin for him. The adjustments they were making were being reflected with every timed run they made, and that confirmed they were going in the right direction. Now they had to be careful not to go too far.

They definitely had one of the faster cars at the beach. But so many other factors could affect how they qualified. The sun could go behind a cloud and cool the track, they could draw an early slot when the track was still "green," or a late spot when it was rough and dirty. They could overlook something, leave something loose or overtorqued. Or their driver could be presented with a perfect car, make the most minor of bobbles, and lose the precious hundredths of a second that could cost them multiple positions on the start.

Everyone on the crew knew it without it being said. And they also knew they didn't need to dwell on the maybes, only on the things they could actually do something about.

That was exactly what they did as the day wore down in Daytona.

SIDE TRIP

Rob hustled from the back of the hauler, freshly showered, hair blown dry, wearing a bright red golf shirt with the Ensoft Racing logo prominently embroidered over the pocket. He stayed in the car till the session ended, getting all the practice he could. Now they were running late for an appearance he was scheduled to do some sixty miles away in Orlando. Michelle practically shoved him out to the rental car and then screeched away from the track, headed for the west side of town to pick up I-4. They only had an hour and a half for the drive. After dealing with the speedway traffic, they had to make their way across the pine flats and past the lime-sink lakes of central Florida, find the hotel on the other side of Orlando, park, and then get inside and locate the room for the event.

As soon as she pulled the car onto the interstate highway, she noticed that Rob Wilder had dozed off, ignoring the bouncing and swerving of her hurried driving. It

had been a long day already for her, too. She was tired
and irritable and dreaded the evening. But she knew that
she had not been wrestling with a stubborn old race car
all day either. She could only imagine how Rob must
feel. Yet he was still downright cheerful and had not
complained at all.

Except, that is, about her driving, the way she weaved
in and out among the other cars, the way she rushed up
to traffic lights, then slammed on the brakes.

"Drive smooth," he advised. "Anticipate the light.
You'll get your brakes all hot and use too much fuel."

She had glared at him and bit her tongue to keep
from telling him what he could do with his suggestions
about her driving. Now she actually wished he were
awake so she could have someone to talk with. Michelle
was nervous about more than the likelihood of being
late. This was going to be one of their first real appearances before such a hard-core group of key retail distributors, far more intense than simply glad-handing
from some exhibit booth or meeting a group of Ensoft
employees, and she worried about whether everything
would go right.

Would they know or care who Rob Wilder was? Were
these guys even racing fans? Would a collection of software store owners take to the kid as readily as everyone
else had? Would they see the value of the sponsorship
to which Ensoft had committed to their own low-margin,
high-volume retail businesses? Or would they pointedly
tell her the millions could have been spent in trade ads
and direct mail instead? Too late now. She would have
to count on the kid's personality and the sport's popu-
larity to carry the show.

There was a box of postcards on the backseat of the
car behind her, each one of them with a color photo of
Rob standing in front of the race car. He would use

them to sign autographs for the hundred or so people who were expected to be taking part in the session. She hoped one box would be enough. She fussed silently at herself for not having the forethought to throw another box of them in the car. Or what if nobody wanted any of them? What if they brought the whole box back with them? How would Rob handle that kind of rejection?

Likely by sleeping all the way back to Daytona, she decided.

As she zipped down the busy highway, she glanced over at Rob and wondered once again how he could fall asleep and rest like that. And how could he remain so calm when she was so nervous she was about to jump out of her skin?

The kid didn't seem to be affected at all by being the center of attention at such an important event as the one this evening promised to be. Maybe, she thought, at his age and with his background, he didn't even know he was supposed to be the main attraction. Somehow, for whatever reason, it didn't appear to bother him. He just seemed oblivious to the fact that plenty of people wanted to see him, to be close to him, to get his signature on some scrap of paper, all simply because he was a race car driver.

"One of these days, buster, you'll be as skittish about all this as I am when you figure out what all is riding on this stuff," she said, half aloud, but he didn't even stir. He was sound asleep.

As they passed through downtown Orlando, she finally reached over and nudged him awake. He groaned when he tried to stretch and grabbed a cramp in the back of his leg.

"You okay?"

"Ow! Yeah, I think so," he said as he rubbed the cramp and then wiggled his stiff shoulder. "I guess a nap wasn't such a good idea. I got all kinked up."

"Well, I hate to wake you, but I need some navigation help." She handed him a map and a slip of paper. "Looks like we're gonna be late after all."

"Aw, we'll make it. Looks like the place is a couple of blocks off the interstate."

He continued to knead the thigh, then went to work on the shoulder with another groan and a grimace.

"So, you sore from all that practice?" she asked.

"Yeah, my right shoulder is a little stiff from all the G force pushing it up against the side of the seat."

"I thought this was supposed to be an easy track for you to drive."

"It is, Chelle. In some ways. I think most of it is because I haven't hardly been in the race car much over the last couple of months. I'm just out of shape a little bit. After all the practice this week, I'll be back in tip-top form."

He said the words positively, but he was still rotating the shoulder.

"I hope you're in tip-top shape come race day. We'd kinda like you to win this race, you know. If you don't, we may need to reconsider . . ."

She let her voice trail off ominously and, out of the corner of her eye, saw him turn her way. He was giving her a hard look, as if she had blatantly questioned his ability to drive a race car.

"Don't you worry one bit about me, 'cause . . ." Then he noticed she was trying to stifle a giggle. Michelle had quickly learned how to get Rob Wilder's dander up. He shook his fist at her. "I swear, Miss Fagan. One of these days, when you least expect it . . ."

"Ooooh! Now I'm shakin'. Hey, shouldn't we be about to our exit by now?"

"Next one. Right lane. Whoa! No signal, no look in the mirror . . ."

"Hey! You drive the red car, remember? This one's mine."

Michelle took the exit and made the turn onto International Drive. She could already see the big duck logo on the top of the towering Peabody Hotel down the way and she could once again feel her anxiety swelling up inside her. She glanced over at Rob as she slowed to pull into the driveway.

"Don't you ever get nervous about doing these things? Personal appearances?" she asked.

"No. Why?" Rob answered, wondering why she would even ask such a question. He had never actually considered it. He showed up, talked a little racing, smiled a lot, shook lots of hands. So far, the groups had been small ones. He had not been called upon to actually speak, although he figured he could do that, too, if somebody told him what he was supposed to talk about and so long as it was about driving a race car.

"I don't know. If I went into some place and everyone there was sort of . . . I don't know . . . treating me like some kind of hero, it would make me nervous. Have you ever studied public speaking? Speech?"

"You kidding me? At my little bitty old high school, English was a foreign language! I don't know. I guess I never thought of how people look at me. If they want to talk about politics or . . . I don't know . . . rocket science or something, I'd be in trouble. But I feel right at home in the skin of a race car driver. That's all I ever really think about anymore. Racing, that is. I don't pay much attention to anything else."

She was quiet then, but he sensed she wanted to say something. She steered around some parked cars and came to a stop. They were out of the car then, the keys dropped with the valet, and hustling past cascading fountains at the hotel's entrance. He didn't notice the look in Michelle's eyes when she spoke again.

"Well, when you met my sister a couple of weeks ago, it seemed to me that racing wasn't the only thing that was on your mind."

Rob stopped in his tracks on the hotel's front steps and looked at her. "What makes you say that?"

"Come on," Michelle teased. "Don't tell me you were thinking about racing when we were sitting on that patio watching the sunset out over the ocean."

He started walking for the lobby again. She had him there. He had to admit that shock absorber combinations and sway bar adjustments had not been occupying his thoughts that particular evening. Still, since he had moved up from Hazel Green to near Chandler Cove, practically every waking moment was concentrated on his breakthrough into big-time racing. That is, until that night at Anderton's in Los Angeles.

"Okay, you got me there," he admitted sheepishly. "I haven't had time to think much about girls since I broke up with Sally Grainger just before I moved up to the shop. Or she broke up with me is more like it. We'd been seeing each other for almost two years, then she dumped me for a guy who worked at the local car dealership. A guy who didn't spend his Friday and Saturday nights blowing engines and kicking up the dust at some old racetrack."

"So you don't miss her?" Michelle asked as they reached the escalator at the far end of the lobby. She suspected she might be venturing into dangerous territory, but she was curious. Curious for herself as well as for Christy. And she knew no other way to find out but to ask him.

"Aw, heck no, Michelle. Since I've been doing all this

traveling and meeting people, I've realized that she probably did all three of us a big favor . . . me, her, and the grease monkey from the car lot. She always stayed focused on her own little world. All she ever wanted was a double-wide trailer, a picket fence, a yard full of young'uns, all the things old Carl could give her much better than I could. And a trip to the mall in Huntsville every once in a while was all the excitement she ever needed in her life. She never could understand why I wanted more of this great big old world. And why I was willing to risk my life out there on that racetrack to try to get it."

Michelle was disappointed that they had reached the top of the escalator on the level of the hotel where their event was to be held. The doorway to the room was at the far end of a giant mezzanine.

She seemed to have a sudden thought then and stopped again to ask him a question. "Rob Wilder, do you have any idea what a major heartbreaker you are going to be?"

"Huh?"

If she was so all-fired worried about being late, why was she stopping to chitchat again?

"If you ever get your head out of a carburetor long enough to notice, you're going to find lots of women who would do just about anything they can to get to you."

"Aw, come on, Michelle. Quit teasing me!"

They walked along a few more steps, then she stopped once more, ignoring the people who milled about around them. She seemed determined to make some kind of a point.

"And you know what else? Not a one of them will see at first that you already have a bunch of mistresses already. That your only true loves are speed and racing and winning."

Her voice broke as she spoke and her lower lip trembled. What in the world was she doing?

"I won't deny that, Michelle. Racing is my life. It has been for a long time."

"Yes, and that's what's gonna break plenty of hearts, whether you mean to or not. They'll try to win you away from your other loves, and some of them will think they have succeeded, but they won't. They'll still be there, with you in their grips just like always, no matter what they do, think, or say. And I'm scared to death my baby sister will be the next one to try to get to you and lose in the process."

She had an odd look on her face then. It almost seemed that she was angry with him about something he had said or done. Rob couldn't imagine what it might be. He looked hard at her, his head cocked, trying to figure out what she was trying to tell him.

"Christy?"

"You're all she talks about, Rob. 'Did you see Rob?' 'How's Rob doing?' 'Did Rob mention me?' "

"Really?"

"I worry about her. I know she'd always be second to some old race car. I wish you could see that there's plenty more things out there in the world besides riding around in a circle real fast. You're no different than Sally or whatever her name was. Your old girlfriend. Your world is no bigger than hers was. It's just different. Louder and more dangerous but still tiny and one-dimensional and oh, so limited."

"I like Christy, Michelle. I like her a lot. But you have to realize that this is what I have worked toward since I was ten years old. It's all I ever wanted."

Someone was coming toward them now from across

the mezzanine, two or three men in suits who were obviously some kind of a greeting party.

"I know that. But try to pay attention to what's going on around you sometime. Who else might be involved. Who else might get hurt along the way."

He had never seen Michelle like this before. Not in all the hours they had spent together on planes and at meetings and at various racetracks.

But now the men were getting closer and he didn't know what to say to her.

"Chelle, I've got to stay focused on driving, on racing, or I might miss this chance. I've got to."

She reached over and touched his arm. She looked to be on the verge of tears. "Rob, listen to me. There's more out there than racing," she said, looking up at him. "More than business and software and money, too, though I'm a fine one to talk. Don't turn your back on it all. There are other things that you might miss, too. Other things just as important . . . more important . . . than this obsession of yours."

There was that odd look again. He had a strange feeling then, a feeling that she was talking as much to herself as she was to him.

"Rob Wilder!" one of the men was saying, extending his hand and wrapping a big arm around his shoulder. "Boy, am I glad to meet you. I saw you drive that race up at Charlotte last year, and boy, when you came off that turn and . . ."

Rob turned on his smile and took the man's hand, listened intently to his story, then accepted the backslaps and handshakes of the others. The whole group had fallen into a deep discussion about the best way to drive Daytona before they even got halfway to the hors d'oeuvre table.

Michelle Fagan followed along behind them, smiling.

GETTING QUALIFIED

Rob stood beside the race car and soaked up some of the warm winter Florida sunshine. He was waiting as patiently as he could for the start of the qualifying session for Saturday's Grand National race. For once, Will Hughes seemed moderately pleased with the setup they had ended up with under the car. He stood there next to Rob and actually broached the subject of making their way down to the beach after they had finished qualifying.

Rob couldn't believe what he was hearing. For once, he was the one who was dry-mouthed nervous like Will normally would be. The car had plenty of speed. They had proved that in practice. When it was out there running by itself, the Ford was clearly as fast as any car in the garage.

So why was Rob so worked up? The only thing that was a question mark was Rob's inexperience with the track and in working in the draft. There simply had not been enough practice time yet for him to gain that experience, to assume much of the confidence that he would need to win here.

Luckily, when it came to the two-lap qualifying run, drafting would not be a factor. All he had to do was go out there and run a good, clean, and, of course, brisk second lap. The slightest blunder could mean the difference between a front-row starting position and being twentieth or worse when the green flag waved. The throttle would have to be shoved all the way to the floor for the entire run. Let off even a fraction and he would be looking at starting way back there. Or even getting bumped from the field entirely. That was how much momentum could be lost if he hesitated. And that was why the kid was clammy-skinned and distracted as he waited.

"Where's Michelle?" Rob finally asked. He had missed her earlier and now it looked as if she might be gone when they made the qualifying run. Even after the silent ride back from Orlando and the bright face she had worn during breakfast at the hotel that morning, Rob still couldn't help thinking about their strange conversation as they made their way into the Peabody Hotel the evening before.

"She'll be back before you go out," Will answered. "She said she had to run over to the airport and pick up some folks. Some of her staff that are coming in from California today."

"Who?"

"I don't know. More assistants, I guess."

"I can't believe she would risk missing qualifying. They got taxicabs here, I reckon."

Will gave him an odd look. His young driver was a bit on edge this bright sunny morning.

"Look, they're on the company plane, so it'll be on

time. As chummy as the two of you have been lately, I don't think we have to worry about Michelle missing anything you do, cowboy." Will leaned back from where he was propped up against the car and looked at Rob over the top of his mirrored sunglasses. "Anything going on between the two of you I need to know about?"

"What? No! Why in the world would you even ask such a thing?" Rob squared around and faced his crew chief, an angry scowl on his face.

"It's my job to know everything about my driver, that's all. Ever since you went out to California for that photo shoot, you've been all moon-eyed. She is a mighty cute gal. Maybe a few years too old for you. But a real nice girl."

"She is a nice girl, but that's it. She's a friend, that's all. A friend and a business associate. That's what she is. A business associate." The kid turned back around and studied the toes of his driving shoes. "Shoot fire, Will. Here I am sitting here worrying about gettin' this race car qualified and all you can do is pick on me about who I am most certainly *not* having a crush on."

Will punched the kid on the shoulder. "Relax, cowboy. It's nothing to be ashamed of. She wouldn't be such a bad catch at all for a redneck like you. She's cute as a button. Far as I know, she's got all her teeth. She's got herself a great job. You wouldn't even have to worry about working. You could just stay at home with the kids and race when you felt like it . . ."

"Will, I don't like you talking like—"

Will Hughes couldn't keep up the kidding any longer. He broke into a guffaw unlike anything Rob had ever heard escape from the man's mouth. He suddenly reached over and grabbed Rob, wrapping him up in a big bear hug.

"Gotcha!"

"Dang it all, Will. I at least thought you were above picking on me like Donnie and Tony and them do."

Then he grabbed Will around the neck and wrestled back, trying to knock him off balance so he would have to let him go.

"You just looked so all-fired serious all morning. So worried about qualifying. I couldn't help it!" Will grunted, trying to keep his feet but not releasing his hold on his driver's torso.

The two of them scuffled around the car, each of them already red-faced and pretending to be mad at each other, until several of the other crews gathered around to watch, to see if a good, old-fashioned pit brawl was about to break out. There just weren't enough good fights in racing anymore. Even a mock one could still draw a crowd. A rousing cheer went up when the two men tipped over and rolled about on the asphalt.

Will squirmed around until he temporarily had the upper hand, but he was surprised at the kid's strength, considering how tall and skinny he was. Rob didn't stay on the bottom long. He had soon thrown Will again and tried to goose him in the ribs so he would turn loose. Only when both of them were sufficiently out of breath did they call a mutual, half-grunted truce. A couple of members of the other crews tried to egg them on, to keep the wrestling match going, but Rob and Will were both ready to give it a rest.

Rob leaned against the side of the race car, trying to catch his breath, the blood pounding in his head from the exertion. Will slid to the ground next to him, breathing hard too, but trying to stifle another laugh.

"We ought to be ashamed," he snorted. "Two grown men! Well. One grown man and one skinny kid!"

Rob made a feint toward him as if he were going to

wrap him up again. Will didn't even flinch. Then they both broke into honest, open laughter.

Will's impromptu plan had worked. He had goaded the kid, got him into a tussle, had some fun, and, in the process, taken his mind off the job upcoming. Rob had been so tightly wound all morning and the wrestling match had obviously helped.

Rob had just realized what Will was doing and that he had accomplished his goal. The butterflies were no longer clog dancing inside his stomach. He was sweating from the physical effort, no longer from tension.

And he didn't care one whit about whatever burr had gotten under Michelle Fagan's saddle.

He was ready to run. It was time to see if he belonged on the same track with the legends of racing who had, over the years, tamed as best they could the two and a half miles of Daytona.

The cars finally began to line up to take their turns out on the track for the beginning of qualifying. Rob caught himself looking around for Michelle again, still hoping she would get back from the airport before he climbed in and made his laps. He desperately wanted her to see how well he was going to do out there.

Meanwhile, Will communicated back and forth on the radio with Billy Winton, who stood atop the trailer flanked by a couple of visitors. Joe Banker and Bubba Baxter from Jodell Lee's team were there, watching the qualifying session unfold. They had been busy helping to get the car Jodell owned ready for the Winston Cup race, but this day they wanted to see firsthand how the motor in Rob's car did in qualifying. Joe had spent dozens of hours over the winter getting this special engine properly cast, working like a sculptor so that every line, every nuance of his handiwork, was perfectly hewed. Banker had long maintained that building a successful restrictor-plate racing motor was more art than science. Few would argue with him.

One after another, cars rolled out off the pit lane, ready for their drivers to challenge both the clock and the speedway. Rob paid little attention to what was going on out there. So did Will Hughes. They both agreed they had no control on what was happening with all those other teams. Their only task was to make sure their own car was as fast as they could make it, then for Rob to go out and squeeze all the speed out of it that he could manage.

Billy and the rest of the crew were not quite so uncaring. They kept a close eye on each of their potential opponents, clicking their watches, comparing the times they showed to what the official timer reported, carefully writing down the results alongside each car as they made their run. Billy also made cryptic notes next to each one. "High in 3," "Motor sounded rough," "Good line," and "Sun behind cloud," were some of the memos he wrote to himself.

" 'Bout what you expected?" Bubba Baxter asked. He was a big man, though still more muscle than fat, even in his sixties, and he was notorious around the tracks for his appetite. Even now he took big bites from one of the half dozen hot dogs he had brought up the ladder with him in a grocery sack.

"Pretty much," Billy answered as the next car pulled away. "The fastest one we've seen so far was a couple of tenths better than what Robbie's been running in the last few practices."

Will was saying almost the same thing to his driver at that very moment as he finally began to take note of what was happening out on the track.

"They're about what I was expecting. Unless there's somebody left with a surprise for us and he comes out here and blasts by the rest of us, I think we'll make the field and be in good shape."

"Some of 'em are running better than our best laps in practice. You sure we're okay?"

"Oh, yeah. With the tape we've added to the nose, the soft springs bringing the tail down, and with a cool engine, we'll be fine."

"I hope so, Will."

Will smiled and put his arm around Rob's shoulder. The kid couldn't believe how relaxed Will was. In the races they had run the year before, the crew chief would have been grinding his teeth and stomping up and down the length of the pit stall by now.

"Just drive it like Jodell told you. Hold her low in the turns, then let the car go where she wants to coming out. You hang on to those reins good and tight and keep the gas pedal to the floor all the way around. If you do that, then we'll have us a good top-ten run. Top fifteen at the worst. And you start in the top fifteen, you can win this race."

"I just hope she won't buck me off!"

He could already imagine the way the car would be lunging about like a mad bronco as the soft spring setup allowed it to bottom out hard all the way around the track. He absentmindedly rubbed his behind just thinking about it.

There were a dozen or so cars in line ahead of them by now. The two of them stood leaning nonchalantly against the side of the bright red car, facing the track, watching as the cars pulled away and circled the speedway.

Donnie Kline polished feverishly on the front end of the car with a vengeance. He, too, was usually hot-wired just before qualifying or the start of a race, and he was using the useless task to keep himself occupied.

"You gonna wear a hole in my race car," Rob yelled to him over the roar of the car that was currently trying to qualify.

"When you wreck up out there, I wanna make sure we at least have the prettiest pile of sheet metal that wrecker crew ever seen," he called back, and went to work with his rag on the left fender.

Rob winked at Will, then leaned into the driver's-side window to adjust some of the extra padding they had taped to the seat. He almost didn't hear Will's sharp, admiring whistle.

"Woooeee! Would you look at this!"

"What?" Rob said as he jerked his head out the open window, cracking his temple hard on the frame railing above the window. "Ouch!" he exclaimed, and touched the spot, then checked his fingers, looking for blood.

"Who on earth is that with Michelle?" Will asked.

It took Rob a moment to focus on the two women emerging from the tangle of folks wandering about in the garage area. He caught his breath. The tall blonde walking beside Michelle was smiling broadly and waving to him. Then she broke ranks, trotted over, and gave Rob a quick hug and a kiss on the cheek, while Will, Donnie, and the rest of the crew let loose with whistles and catcalls. He didn't care. He hugged her right back.

"You best check his blood pressure, Will. I ain't never seen nobody turn that red before," Donnie said.

"I think we need a fire extinguisher," another crew member kidded. "I believe the boy's on fire."

"Somebody better grab the radiator fan. We may need to cool old Robbie off before we can get him in the car."

Rob never heard a word of their nonsense. He stood there holding Christy Fagan's hands, smiling, looking into those blue eyes. She seemed just as glad to see him again as he was to see her. Her lips were moving and it took him a moment to realize that she was speaking to him, saying hello.

"Well, hi!" he finally managed to get out. "You look . . . that is . . . uh . . . it's so good to see you. What in the world are you doing here?"

"I wouldn't miss it for the world. When Michelle called and said the plane was coming this way and asked if I wanted to help out for a few days, I accepted the offer. I hope you don't mind. You said I could come watch a race anytime."

"Mind? I'm glad you're here. I wanted to call and see if you wanted to, but . . ."

His voice trailed off and he was quiet then, too embarrassed to admit he had simply been too bashful to make the call. Too afraid she would turn him down. That she would have no interest in seeing him at all, let alone fly all the way across the country to do so.

Will shooed everyone away so they would quit gawking at Rob Wilder's gorgeous friend with the long blonde hair and the perfect tan. Will knew at once that this must be Michelle's kid sister, the one Rob had the high-octane crush on whether he realized it or not. He also knew he wouldn't have to wrestle his driver anymore to help quell his butterflies. But he might have to hog-tie him to get him to leave the girl and climb into that old race car for a couple of laps.

Rob was pointing out the features of the car to her as the crew shoved it up another spot in line. She seemed genuinely interested. Now there were only five cars left to go in front of them when Will walked over to where Rob was showing Christy the netting on the driver's-side window.

"Will, this is Christy Fagan, Michelle's sister."

"Pleased to meet you, Miss Fagan."

"I met her when I was out shooting those commercials. She's interested in racing. How the car works and all."

"I can tell. I hate to interrupt the tour," Will said politely as he shook her hand. "But our driver here has got to get in the car and go out there and get us qualified for the race."

Christy touched Rob's arm. "Good luck," she said.

The car qualifying out on the track roared by them at nearly two hundred miles an hour. Her eyes grew wide when she realized how fast these things went. And that Rob was about to try to drive this bright red automobile equally as dangerously.

Rob smiled back at her, his lips forming the word "Thanks," though she couldn't have heard him over the thunder of the other car. Then he turned away, climbed into the Ford, and began getting himself set.

His head was spinning as he pulled on his helmet. He could still feel her touch on his arm, still see that wonderful smile of hers. But somehow, Christy being here was not actually distracting him. Her presence had merely intensified his determination to drive on out there and do well, to show her, her sister, everyone at Ensoft, even his own crew, that he was ready to drive Daytona.

"You ready to go, cowboy?" Will's words crackled in the radio earpieces he'd just taped into each ear.

"Let me at 'em!" Rob responded. He pounded the wheel with the palms of his hands.

Will grinned as he snapped the net in place. He didn't know if having his girlfriend at the track was a good thing or a bad thing for his driver. But it sure seemed to have turned up the kid's wick a notch or two. Wilder had been eager to drive a race car the first time Will had seen him, at the test run at Nashville. And it seemed he had grown even more determined, more driven, ever since. Now he was so ablaze Will could only hope he didn't go out there and overdrive the car. He only needed to keep his head and drive a good, solid lap and they would be in fine shape for the race. Maybe not on the pole, but in good shape. Push too hard and it would be disastrous.

Michelle and Christy retreated behind the pit wall and watched as the crew shoved the car closer to the front of the line. From atop the trailer, Billy Winton had watched the arrival of his driver's friend with more than passing interest. He had actually encouraged Michelle to extend the invitation to Christy to make the trip to Daytona. Billy knew how easy it would be for his driver to be sidetracked by the women who typically hung out just outside the garage at every track, each of them trying to hook up with a real, live race car driver. If he got involved with one of the "racer chasers," there could be trouble, for the young driver as well as the team. Such distractions could muddle the carefully cultivated chemistry that was so vital to a successful effort.

Billy glanced over at Joe Banker. Racer chasers had been Joe's weakness, too, and Billy had seen the strain Banker's womanizing had put on Jodell Lee's team at times. Even though he was married and had grandkids now, Joe still bore watching. Even now, he was concentrating more on the two young women down there in the Winton Racing pits than he was on the car Casey Atwood was at that moment attempting to qualify out there on the track.

For some crews, it was drinking that caused debilitating tension. Especially in the early days when drivers like Curtis Turner and Joe Weatherley seemed to drink and party with the same dedication they showed for driving race cars. For others, it was ego, plain and simple. Or greed. Wanting more than a fair share of the winnings.

But whatever it was, it could ruin the balance that was necessary for a team to function. Billy had vowed that whatever happened in his racing effort, he would not let such foolishness keep him from building a championship team.

The two sisters watched as Rob's car sat there, waiting at the head of the line while the car that was already out on the track completed its own run. That car zoomed past, getting a white flag, signaling one more lap to go for him to finish his run.

"I didn't realize they went so fast," Christy said, her eyes still wide and a worried look on her face.

"Wait till you see a whole bunch of the things go by, all of them going that fast but they're only six inches apart." Michelle held out her hands to illustrate how ridiculously close that was.

"I can't imagine."

"Just wait. Once you see it firsthand, you won't believe it. And you'll see why people love this stuff so much."

"Well, it kinda scares me," Christy said as she followed the howling race car as it went out of sight through turn two.

Billy smiled as he watched Michelle, gesturing, talking animatedly to her sister. It seemed like only days ago that he and Rob had gone out to talk with the Ensoft folks about the sponsorship. Michelle, as head of marketing, had been pushing the rest of the company's management to take the plunge into motor sports as a marketing ploy. She had never even been to a race, but in watching Jeff Gordon, Tony Stewart, and some of the other young drivers on television, she had quickly determined that the sport was now attracting the same people they wanted to reach for their software systems. Her research backed up the theory, and so did the facts and figures she received from Billy Winton in a well-documented presentation.

Now he could only imagine how exciting this all must be to her, and to her sister as well. And he had to admit, it was still quite stimulating to him, too. Sure, he had been at this historic track many times before. But this was his first real effort as the owner of a serious, contending, well-funded team. And with a young driver who could, just maybe, be the most talented racer to come along in years. All that was now suddenly making him pretty darn nervous, but he tried not to let it show.

"Don't worry, Billy. It'll be over in a couple minutes."

Bubba Baxter had seen right through his calm façade.

"I know. But we've spent more time on that car than any I've ever been around. If it's not perfect, it's because we messed it up trying."

"What does Will think?"

"Funny you should ask. He's usually the one that's never satisfied, but he pronounced this one ready this morning. I nearly dropped my cup of coffee!"

"Then she is, Billy. You'll be on the front row," the big man said, as if there was no doubt now. Then he took half a hot dog in one bite and chewed contentedly as the Billy Winton Racing Ensoft Ford began to roll away down there below them.

"From your lips to God's ear," Billy said in a near whisper.

Will had radioed for Rob to start the engine as soon as the car on the track took the white flag. The engine idled like subdued thunder as the kid waited for the signal to go. Then, finally, the speedway official standing at the head of the line waved Rob off pit road and he was pulling out.

Things would happen fast now.

He didn't hesitate. He gunned the engine and was gone. It was time!

Up in the television booth, the commentators watched with interest as the red 06 rolled off pit road. They, too, knew the young driver was a potential story in the making. The lead announcer couldn't wait to recap Rob's quick climb for his viewers.

"Here goes the new, young driver, Rob Wilder, up next to qualify in the oh-six Ensoft Ford. He's the one who shocked everyone with that surprising weekend last fall at Charlotte when he finished second in the Grand National race. But that's not all. He then drove the car owned by famed driver Jodell Lee to a respectable fifteenth-place finish in the Winston Cup race when he was substituting for an injured Rex Lawford, the Lee team's regular driver."

The color commentator breathlessly picked up the story.

"I tell you, for all our new fans out there, this is one kid to watch. Not quite twenty years old, but he drives like a veteran. Lots of the old-timers say he looks just like a young Joe Weatherley, or like his mentor Jodell Lee. On the track he is relentless, always attacking, always pushing the car, yet he drives smooth as silk."

"And there's more to the oh-six team than its exciting young driver, too. Billy Winton, who was chief mechanic for Jodell Lee during the heyday of his career in the seventies and early eighties, owns this team. The crew chief, Will Hughes, was a part of the Lee team for a while, too. Famed engine builder Joe Banker is supplying the motors, so you know there will not be any problem with them finding the horsepower to be competitive. This team has high hopes heading into this, their first full season on the Grand National circuit."

"High hopes indeed. I spoke with Will Hughes yesterday. He's one of the most talked-about young crew chiefs in the garage, and he felt confident that they had a car that was capable of starting up at the front. The chemistry between driver and crew chief is definitely in evidence. We even witnessed a little good-natured scuffle between Hughes and Wilder down in the pits earlier today. They were definitely loose and supremely confident."

"Well, let's see if that confidence in what the Ensoft Ford can do is justified. Rumor in the garage area has this as one of the top sponsorships in the Grand National division. Let's watch together now as he exits turn four, coming down to take the green flag."

The camera picked up the Ford as it set the line out of the fourth turn, the young driver pointing toward where the flagman already held the green flag, ready to send him off on his first timed lap.

"The car has been fast in practice, but breaking the current pole time at sixty-two hundredths of a second is going to be tough. There are also a couple of cars behind them that are capable of running in the forty- or fifty-hundredths range. My bet is that it is going to take a speed in the thirties to get the pole, maybe even better than that."

The announcer joined in with a prediction.

"Whatever the time, it's going to take nothing short of a perfect lap for this youngster to have any shot at the pole. Frankly, as good as he is, I'm not sure he has the experience. Not just yet. It's his first trip to Daytona, you know."

The commentator's microphone picked up the howl of Rob's motor as he begged to differ.

"I don't know. I don't think I would dismiss this kid's chances. He's already surprised a lot of people."

"Well, we'll see in a minute, won't we? Wilder's just

now taking the green flag, and as you know, with the restrictor plate, he'll still be coming up to speed this lap. The second lap will be the money lap, and that's where we'll see what he and the Winton team has today."

Rob felt his heart quicken as he steered for the first turn after getting the green flag. He had had the throttle floored since bringing the car off pit road, working quickly up through the gears. He kept the car low on the track as he made his way through turns one and two and shifted down into fourth gear as he hit the straight. He pressed even harder on the pedal through the long backstretch, but there was no more power available. He let the car have its head, like an experienced racehorse, and drifted up high through turns three and four so he could keep the revolutions up in the powerful motor. His foot never lifted as Rob roared down through the short chute, through the D-shaped turn, and underneath the waving green flag.

Rob felt another sharp bump as the car bottomed out on the springs. The steering wheel jerked, trying to tear loose from his hands, but he held on, fighting to keep the car under control. He had to remind himself to be smooth as he wrestled with the wheel, to keep it on a straight course, and was thankful again for the weight-lifting regimen that Billy had put him on since Thanksgiving.

Then he roared down the back straight, setting his line for turns three and four. The car sat low in the back end as it flew into the corner, bottoming out several times, but Rob held on, keeping it smooth and as straight as he could.

Now, at last, he roared off of turn four and looked ahead to see the flagman already brandishing the white flag.

Will Hughes clicked the stopwatch as their race car

passed beneath the flag stand. He couldn't help smiling broadly. He could tell it was a good lap. If the car picked up the usual tenths on the second lap, and if Rob drove the same consistent lap, then they were definitely looking at a top-five starting spot.

"A seventy-three," Will mouthed up to Billy as Rob disappeared down into turn one. Michelle and Christy stood on tiptoes and watched him disappear into the high-banked corner. They assumed the grin on Will's face was a good sign. All they knew was that the car seemed to be a captured rocket, and that it was painfully loud.

Back up in the television booth, the announcers followed the run closely. They told their viewers that, at seventy-three hundredths, it was one of the best first laps of the qualifying session.

"Wow, did you see that time? It looks as if . . . yes, it is the second fastest first-lap time for the day so far. Barring some kind of problem, this kid is about to get everybody's attention."

The camera followed the car off into the first turn, already setting sail for its second lap, the one that would actually determine their starting position.

"We could be looking at the pole sitter right there in that bright red car. With only a couple of people left to go who might have the speed to challenge, he's assured of a good starting spot if not the pole. But lots can happen in a lap here at Daytona."

"Well, looking at his times through turns one and two, I'd say he's smoking this lap."

"As fast as he's running, you have to wonder if maybe he has one of those rocket engines they make down there in his hometown of Huntsville, Alabama," the color man said, his eyes glued to the monitor in the booth.

"Whatever time he turns, this is certainly a phenomenal run for a rookie at this track. And such a young one, too."

"Trust me, this kid may be nineteen, but he drives like a ten- or fifteen-year veteran. He can get around this track as good as anybody I've ever seen run down here. And that includes the great ones like Petty, Pearson, and yes, our sometime colleague Buddy Baker."

The camera zoomed in on the car as it raced through turns three and four. The car hit bottom once more, but even harder this time and it bounced noticeably.

"Did you see that car bottom out there?" the television announcer asked.

"I sure did. I'll tell you what. If you don't think this kid is a whale of a driver, then you need to take another look at that right there. How he held on to the car is amazing, but he did it without cracking the throttle one bit. That is something else!"

"Let's watch him as he brings the Ensoft Ford down to the line. This looks like an outstanding lap, all right, but is it going to be fast enough?"

"It looks real good to me. We'll have to wait and see what the official time is. I don't think there's more than a car or two left to qualify that has anything near the speed of this young kid out of Alabama."

The two men paused then as the camera followed Rob and the red car on into the pits. Then the director cut to a shot of the official scoreboard in the infield.

"Well, there it is. A forty-seven twenty-nine. That's better than twenty-one hundreds of a second faster than the second-place car."

"That was an incredible run you just saw. Maybe he did have one of those Huntsville rockets strapped to the Ensoft car after all."

"I wouldn't doubt it! If this time holds up, I think we can look back on this day and say we were there when

'Rocket Rob' Wilder blasted onto the scene here at the Daytona launching pad."

The color commentator laughed out loud.

"Rocket Rob Wilder is exactly right," he agreed.

The name did have a certain ring to it.

FRONT ROW, INSIDE

The newly dubbed "Rocket Rob" Wilder cut his jets and coasted the race car to a stop. He really couldn't tell for certain what kind of a lap he had just run. He knew fractions of a second could make a considerable difference in where the eventual starting spot fell. It felt good. He was reasonably certain he had made the field. But whatever, it was done.

Rob did exactly what he had intended. He stood on the gas all the way around the track from the time he pulled off the line until he roared beneath the flagman waving the checkered flag. The ride was rough and he had worked hard to hold on to the wheel, to keep the car going straight. In the center of turns three and four, the car bottomed out badly as Rob tried to hold her down low, skirting the white line that marked the edge of the racing surface before it became the flat of the apron. That was where he needed to be. He knew that and he kept her there, no matter how desperately she wanted to climb higher on the track. Then, out of the turns, he had allowed her to drift higher so he could keep the throttle depressed, the engine at full tilt.

It had been as wild a ride as he had ever had at a track. On the last lap he felt as if he was hanging on for dear life. The fact is, he had been. The slightest bobble and he would have killed his chance for a top qualifying slot at best and quickly taken a direct route to the outside wall at worst. As he dug in and hung on, he gritted his teeth so severely his jaws ached, but he ignored the hurt. For an instant, an image of Christy Fagan waiting for him at the start/finish line flashed through his mind, and that, somehow, helped him keep up the hard stand on the throttle, maintain the most speed he could coax from the engine, and hold the lunging machine where he wanted her.

Now he could only hope that what he had done would be good enough. He was satisfied he had done all he could. He sat there in the car after it had rolled to a stop and waited patiently for Will to radio him his time.

And it was beginning to worry him that the frequency remained eerily silent.

He didn't know this track. Maybe the run had not been as good as he thought it had been.

As soon as the car zoomed past the start/finish line, Billy Winton led the entourage back toward the garage. Will Hughes' feet hardly touched the asphalt. He was certain they had just turned in a speed that would put them on the pole, but he also knew a couple of faster cars still had a chance to bump them, including one driven by one of the Winston Cup regulars. Still, he was so elated at the effort he forgot to jump on the radio and tell the kid.

Michelle was worried. Billy had come down from atop the trailer in such a hurry she had at first been afraid something was wrong. He waved to her and Christy to follow them to the garage without a word and then he jogged away at a clip that was quite impressive for a man his age.

"What now?" Christy asked. "Did he do well?"

Michelle shrugged and fell into step behind Will and Billy.

When she finally caught up with the long-striding Will Hughes, he explained that they had run even better than he could have hoped, but they would just have to sweat out the dozen or so cars left to qualify. Pole or not, that had been the run of a lifetime for this young team.

Michelle looked back to where Christy jogged along behind the group and gave her a thumbs-up. And then she began planning already how she would break the good news to the executive team back at Ensoft in San Jose.

Christy was relieved that things had apparently gone well. Rob had told her how important it was for them to begin the race somewhere near the front of the field. It made sense. He had also told her that winning the pole got them more coverage in the media, and that would be good for the new sponsor. That, too, made sense. Her sister had made her very aware of the gamble they were taking with this totally new team with the totally inexperienced driver, and that the whole idea had originated and been sold to the rest of the executive staff by her.

Christy was fully aware that this car-racing stuff was big business, with plenty of money at stake. And it hinged so much on the skills of one young, handsome, blonde man with the soft, self-effacing southern manners and innocent blue eyes. One thing was for sure. The atmosphere around this sport was far more electrifying than she could ever imagine from the few bits of races she had seen on television. And she had only been at the track for a good hour so far!

Rob still sat in the car, perplexed that Will had still not radioed him his time. Was there a problem? Maybe something with the clock? Or were they so far off the pace that they were embarrassed to say the numbers out loud so all the fans with scanners in the stands could hear them? Already he was trying to think back to where he might have lost some momentum out there.

Then Billy and the others came running up beside the car, and the looks on their faces immediately eased his mind. Wide grins everywhere. And as he began to unbuckle to get out and see just how good it had been, a television crew appeared from nowhere, stuck a camera halfway through the car's window, and thrust a microphone in his face.

". . . reporting here from the garage area," the reporter was saying. "I have young Rob Wilder, driver of the Ensoft Ford, who has just posted a tremendous lap on his qualifying run here at Daytona. Let's see if we can get a comment from him."

The pit reporter waited as the kid reached out, grabbed the roof rail with both hands, and pulled his lanky frame out the open window. Will, Billy, Michelle, Christy, and a sudden sizeable assemblage of bystanders joined in a rousing, wild cheer. Rob acknowledged them with an offhand wave and a sheepish grin.

Then the reporter was yelling something to him over the cheers and the passing clamor of another qualifying car.

"That was a superb lap you just posted, Rob. Good enough for the provisional pole."

Then the microphone was back in his face while the television guy waited for a reaction.

"It was?" was all Rob could manage. He was still

mostly out of breath from the excitement of the moment and the wild ride he had just completed. A trickle of sweat ran down his forehead and threatened to drip off his nose, right there on national television. He wiped the sweat away with the sleeve of his driving suit.

"You were several tenths faster than the next closest car. Explain to our viewers how you drove out those laps and what made the car so strong."

"Well . . ." Rob hesitated as it finally sank in that he had actually posted the fastest lap so far in the qualifying session. There had been some good times out there, but theirs had been better. Now he smoothly moved into his interview mode, exactly the way Billy had coached him. "I thought it might be a good lap, but I couldn't be sure. Will Hughes and the rest of the Ensoft crew did a great job getting the right spring setup under the car to run in qualifying. It made for a very rough ride and it was quite a job hanging on to the Ensoft Ford, even for two laps, but she certainly was fast out there. I can't say enough about the guys in the crew and all the work they've done over the winter getting us ready to run here."

"Well, Rob, you did a lot more than hang on. The car looked like it was driving perfectly through the corners."

"That's what Will, our crew chief, and Billy Winton, the team owner, and the rest of the boys worked on. We wanted to get the car right. We knew we had a strong motor with a Joe Banker power plant under the hood. We just needed the kind of car setup a good motor like that deserves."

"How did the connection between your owner and the people over at Lee Racing help in your setup for today's qualifying? There is a strong connection there, right?"

"Very much so. Billy Winton spent hours working on the suspension and body work, and a lot of the setup came from wind-tunnel information from Bubba Baxter and Jodell Lee."

"So did Jodell give you any tips on how to get around this place? With all the poles and wins he has here, he and a few others like Richard Petty and David Pearson are like walking encyclopedias on how to drive Daytona."

Rob could see Billy Winton standing there, still grinning. And Joe Banker and Bubba Baxter were standing right behind him, looking almost as pleased as his boss did.

"Jodell has helped me a lot here and at a lot of other places as well. He gives me tips, how to set the car up for the corners and such. You know I wouldn't be here without him."

"So what sort of advice did he give you for qualifying here? Whatever it was, it sure seemed to work for you."

"Aw, all he said was to mash the gas to the floor and hold on tight so I wouldn't fall off!" the kid said, grinning mischievously.

The reporter started to turn away and wrap up the interview but seemed to have another sudden thought.

"By the way, Rob, can you confirm all these rumors about you replacing Jodell Lee's driver in the Lee Racing Winston Cup car this season?"

Rob looked blank, then a scowl broke out on his face. "That's the silliest thing I've ever heard. Rex Lawford is a fine driver. They had a good year last year and they have big plans for this season. I helped out at the end there when Rex got hurt. But . . . gee . . . anything like that is the craziest blame thing I've ever heard!"

The anger was evident in his voice by the time he finished speaking. The interviewer sensed it and closed out his interview quickly. First, the rumor was totally unfounded. Secondly, such gossip could only hurt Jodell and his crew. And Rob wanted no part of such guff.

"That's what they get paid to do, young'un. Ask questions." Billy Winton stood there, still grinning, then he grabbed his driver and gave him a big hug. "Congratulations on a mighty fine run. We got a few more that could bump us off the front row, so I'm not gonna break out the champagne quite yet. But hey, I think there's some other folks here you'd rather hug on than me."

Sure enough, Michelle grabbed him and gave him a quick embrace and smiling congratulations. Then Christy wrapped her arms around his neck and hugged him hard, maybe lingering a second or two longer than her sister had.

Will and Billy and the rest of the crew had already turned their attention back to the track, so much so that none of them even bothered to hoot or whistle at all the hugging that was going on behind them. One by one the remaining cars headed out for their run while the Winton crew and their visitors exchanged glances, shifting restlessly as car after car registered their times.

Billy clicked the stopwatch on each race car as it passed in front of them to end its second lap. Then he would hesitate before finally glancing down quickly to check the time, as if he was afraid the news would be bad and he wanted to postpone it as long as he could. Only one of the several Winston Cup drivers who were trying to make the field was left to qualify. He was the major threat to remove them from their slot. His practice times had been good enough to demonstrate that. And he had far more experience qualifying at Daytona than Rob had.

Donnie Kline announced loudly that he didn't even want to watch "Mr. Big Time" try to qualify, that he and his crew had work to do in buttoning down the car for the night. He waved the rest of the crew back to the garage and they followed reluctantly. Rob, Christy, and Michelle walked over to join Will, Billy, Joe, and Bubba as the last couple of cars prepared to make their runs.

Rob was already laying out the possibilities to Christy and she listened attentively, apparently deeply interested in how he had driven the course, how the other cars were likely set up for late-session qualifying as opposed to the first ones to run, and why a Winston Cup driver would be running in a Grand National race.

"Don't they risk getting hurt?" she asked. "Or just getting tired driving two races in two days?"

"Yeah, but some of them own Grand National teams with sponsors and a whole other different crew from their Cup team. It's like a side business. Some of them run just the Grand National races that are the same weekends as the Cup races. They see it as getting a ton of extra practice time, and especially on the tracks they don't get to drive often, like Texas and Las Vegas. But some of them do it just because it's a chance to race. Kinda like the old days when they ran somewhere about every night of the week. I think some of these guys would run every day if their owners and sponsors would let them."

Christy nodded, then smiled. She suspected Rob Wilder might fall into that category himself. She had noted the spark in his eye as he talked.

And he took stock of that wonderful face, that smile of hers, and remembered all over why he had thought about her so much the last few weeks.

The Cup driver was now at the head of the line, next to last to go out. The Winton entourage fell silent now as they watched the car pull away confidently, with a smoky screech, as if its driver was anxious to get the formality of winning the pole over with so he could come on back in and get his interview done.

Rob still wore his driving suit, the top unzipped and the sleeves tied about his waist. His arm lightly brushed against Christy's as she stood next to him, stretched up on her tiptoes so she could follow the car as it grumbled irritably off into turn one. Rob tried to maintain concentration on the threat of the brightly painted competitor out there trying to claim what he had earned, but her touch, the aroma of her perfume, the sheer dazzling beauty of her standing there in the Florida sunshine, made it difficult.

"How's he doing?" she asked, almost in a whisper. He leaned down to hear what she was saying and felt her breath on his cheek.

"Well, this won't be his fast lap. He's still getting the engine wound up to full speed. The next one will be the one that matters. That'll be the money lap."

"Okay. Is it bad form to hope that he has a bad lap?" Everybody in this sport seemed to be so darn polite when they talked about each other before the race, then went out there and tried to run all over each other. She wondered if it was acceptable to wish bad luck on a competitor.

"No! Hope all you want to!"

He laughed and made an X with his crossed index fingers in the direction of where the Cup driver had headed, as if to put a jinx on the circling race car. She laughed, too, crossed her own fingers and closed her eyes, obviously trying to conjure up some bad spell.

Rob felt as if his head was spinning as he struggled to maintain focus. He could feel himself falling, losing control of his emotions. It was something he had never had to deal with before. Falling head over heels in love? Never an issue before. But he knew instinctively that that was exactly what was happening to him, and he, quite frankly, didn't care. He did wonder how he was going to maintain concentration if she was going to be around all weekend. But he definitely did not want her to go. No! Not having her there, close by, where he could see that face and hear that laugh would be infinitely more distracting.

The thunder of the car barreling out of the fourth turn dragged him back to reality. Billy clicked the watch as the Cup driver brought his racer past the start/finish line to take the white flag.

"A sixty-eight," he said, and showed Will the watch to verify it. The speed was a couple of hundredths of a second faster than Rob's first-lap time had been. If he picked up the usual speed on the second lap, then he stood a very good chance of yanking the pole position right out from beneath them. They all suddenly wore glum expressions.

"It's gonna be close. I don't know," Will said, then he glanced over at his young driver, watching the pole thief zoom off into turn one with a contented look on his face. The kid seemed unfazed by any of this, the pressure apparently no factor at all. Will wondered once again how he did it. Nothing ever seemed to put the kid on edge.

Will had no idea that, at that particular moment, Rob Wilder felt exactly as if he were on the edge, all right. On the edge of a cliff, about ready to plunge right over. And Rob had absolutely no desire to do anything to regain his balance.

Now they all watched the yellow and black race car charge off through the center of the turn. The car bottomed out hard, just as Rob had, but Billy thought he saw something, a slight wiggle of the vehicle's rear end. Or was he mistaken? Maybe it was only the shimmer of

the heat rising off the track. But he couldn't help himself.
A tight smile broke on his face and he covered it with
his hand so as not to give the others any false hope if
he was wrong.

The car echoed around the back side of the course,
exploded out of the third and fourth turns, raced down
through the dogleg, and seemed on the verge of becoming airborne as it took the wildly whipping checkered
flag. Will glanced down to check the time on his own
watch. Billy didn't even bother. He knew already that
the Cup driver's car had come up fractions of a second
short. Years of experience, decades of watching speeding
cars running rapid circles, gave him the unique ability
to sense the slightest variation in velocity.

The announcer in the television broadcast booth
called it as the hornet-colored car took the flag.

"No doubt about it. That looks like a strong run, but
that slight bobble in the center of the corner may have
cost him the pole." The announcer paused to gaze at
something in the booth. "Here comes the time and let's
see . . . it's going to be a tenth of a second short. It looks
like the young driver Rocket Rob Wilder is going to hold
on to the first pole position of his fledgling career." Then
he seemed to remember something. He needed to keep
his audience from tuning out before the last car had run.
It still was not official yet. "That is, unless this final car
to qualify has found some major speed since the last
practice."

The color man joined in then, his voice showing his
own excitement, even lapsing back into a twang he had
worked long and hard to alleviate for his broadcast role.
After all, he had once raced against most of the men
who were responsible for a good part of this rather remarkable achievement.

"I'll tell you one thing. I bet there'll be some celebratin' goin' on in the pits of both the Billy Winton and Jodell Lee teams. It's been quite a while since a Joe Banker–powered machine has sat on the pole at Daytona, and this has got to bode well for Rex Lawford and the Lee team in their own effort this year. It almost takes me back to when I used to run against that bunch more years ago than I care to think about. They were always the hardest-working bunch in the garage. Strong but fair competitors. I know this has to be a proud moment for Billy Winton, especially after coming back from several years' retirement to build up this team and take a chance on an unknown driver. Then, seeing his car sitting on the pole at Daytona! Man, that's gotta make old Billy feel great! Billy, I'm proud of you!"

The old driver doing the color commentary sounded almost as thrilled as the Winton team had to be, as if he shared in the excitement as one of his contemporaries enjoyed success at one of the toughest venues of them all.

Michelle sensed from the expressions on Will's and Billy's faces that they had, indeed, won the pole, even before the reverberating voice of the public address announcer confirmed it for those who couldn't make sense of all the numbers on the scoreboard. But why was everybody so excited when there was still one more car to run? And shouldn't they save some of the commotion for the race itself? Was qualifying at the front such a big deal as they made out? Still, she mimicked her sister and crossed her fingers as that driver steered out onto the track. It seemed to take forever for him to do two laps, although she knew it was less than two minutes.

Will could tell the last car wasn't even close, but he tried to contain his excitement until the figures were on the scoreboard, all but official. Then he suddenly erupted into a loud fit of whoops and hollers and danced

a wild buck dance around the pits. Billy Winton didn't
know whether to join in or keep out of the way of his
crazed crew chief. He had never seen Will Hughes act
such a way. Donnie Kline was the first to come running
up, grabbing Will and dancing right along. The sight
might have been comical, but none of the rest paused
to watch now. They all joined right in with the celebration.

When Christy grabbed Rob around the neck and gave
him a kiss on the cheek, it felt like an electrical shock
had coursed through his body. But he ignored it and
hugged her right back, then let her go so he could dance
over and hug Michelle, Billy, and a whole bunch of folks
he didn't even know who had joined the party.

From the broadcast truck beneath the stands, the director ordered the cameras to zoom in and capture the
jubilation. It occurred to the veteran television man that
this footage might be valuable someday when the youngster at its center was a major star in the world of racing.
He took extra care to pick his shots and to be sure Rob
Wilder was the focus of each one. As the camera moved
in, the tall blonde woman who had been next to Wilder
grabbed him and gave him a kiss on the cheek.

Perfect, the director thought. Handsome, daring
young race car driver, all wrapped up with a beautiful
girlfriend. Women viewers and young people were flock-
ing to racing telecasts nowadays. They would love this!

Now he saw his pit reporter edge into frame left and
poke the microphone in Wilder's direction.

"Congratulations on winning your first pole, Rob."

"Thank you!" The kid was breathless from all the
dancing he had been doing, but he quickly fought to
calm himself down so he could remember everyone he
had to thank. "I'd like to recognize all the people who
worked to put this deal together with Ensoft and all the

guys at Winton Racing who deserve the credit for giving me such a strong car today. I can't wait till Saturday. Reckon we could go ahead and run the race right now? I love this place!"

Rob grinned and raised his arms in triumph, the crew cheering him along in the background, but then his right arm went back around Christy Fagan, framed perfectly in the camera shot, her smiling face right there next to his. Cameras clicked all around them as the photographers recorded the moment. Most of them were already thinking about how great these two attractive young people would look on their sports pages the next morning or in next week's *Winston Cup Scene* or on one of the many World Wide Web sites devoted to racing.

Twenty-five hundred miles away, a young man wearing a Bugs Bunny T-shirt, short cargo pants, and sandals sat in an executive chair in the boardroom of one of the top software companies in the world. Toby Warren had a broad grin on his deceptively young face as he watched the cable channel that was being beamed to his television set. As CEO of Ensoft, the young entrepreneur had more than a passing interest in the happenings at a particular speedway all the way over on the nation's other coast.

His driver had just won his first pole position at the storied track, despite the odds of an inexperienced rookie doing so. His vice president of marketing, Michelle Fagan, had set him up for disappointment.

"Billy says not to expect much just yet," she had told him that very morning, her voice totally sincere over the telephone. "He says it's a strong field out here. Rookies don't have a shot at much at this track. We'll likely make the race, but that's about it. That gets us a little bit of TV time. Maybe we'll even finish if we're lucky, but that would be an upset," she had babbled on.

He shook his head and slapped the desk excitedly, then reached for a brightly painted Dick Tracy walkie-talkie that rested there in its charger.

"Java Man to Web Rider. You copy?" he spoke into the face of the radio.

"Ten-four, Java Man. You see it?"

It was the voice of Martin Flagstone, Warren's former college roommate, now president of the company and one of the wealthiest twenty-eight-year-olds on the planet. His radio signal came all the way from the office right next door, fifty feet away inside the headquarters building of Ensoft Incorporated in California's Silicon Valley.

"Sure did. That Michelle is a genius."

"Yeah, you see the logo? It was up there on-screen for just about all of both interviews."

"Not only that, did you see Christy?"

"Oh! I see what you mean."

"We could have done focus groups and written copy and produced a hundred TV spots and magazine ads, but we'd never get anything that would reach our target customer better than that minute or so just did."

"You're right, bro! Wanna celebrate over fajitas at El Toro?"

"You're on."

Toby Warren shoved back from his desk, stood, and looked outside for a moment at the brilliant sunshine.

"Maybe this stock car racing thing is gonna work out after all," he said to the blinds.

Then he turned and gave the die-cast model of the 06 Ensoft Ford on his desk a nudge, imagining how the real thing had rumbled and roared the year before. He had actually flown back east and watched a race in person then and he had been sucked right in.

Who would ever have thought it? A software entrepreneur hooked irretrievably on stock car racing!

He bounded for the door, already wishing, like the young driver of the car he sponsored, that the race could be run right this red-hot minute.

THE WALK

Rob gave the car one more gulp of gas as it crossed the finish line, pretending he was nosing out the Chevy to his right for the win. It was actually only the last lap of practice and the flag in the official's hand on the stand was red, signifying the end of the session, not checkered for the last lap of the Grand National race. It had been a productive session, for Rob as well as for Will and the crew. The rookie driver had been working on mastering the draft, nosing up behind anybody he could find to race with, testing what would happen with a wide array of different moves he might want to try when it was all for real. And Will wanted to see how the race trim would work with a track full of cars. The setup under the car appeared to be perfect. She had plenty of horsepower and seemed to be handling as well as they could have hoped for when they had been plotting strategy all winter back in the shop.

Normally they would have parked the car early in the

"happy hour" practice session if they had been this happy with it. They would have wanted to avoid some silly accident messing up a good race car. But with Rob's lack of experience in the draft and on this behemoth of a track, they were willing to take that risk and let him run every lap they could. Rob was well aware of why they were still out there running when the last of the cars were waved off at the end of the session, but it didn't bother him at all. He welcomed the chance to learn all he could.

He only hoped he had made the most of the opportunity. And he did feel he had absorbed, sometimes rather harshly, many of the finer points of life in the draft. Jodell Lee even got on the spotter's radio and talked him through some maneuvers. It would have been difficult to find a better professor to tutor him on the best ways to race in the big packs of cars that inevitably formed when the competitors all ran the restricted motors.

Still, as he brought the car around and found the entrance to the pits, Rob wished they could run another hundred laps. He needed the experience, sure. But more than that, he simply loved driving in this place.

"Okay, cowboy. Let's quit while we still got a car in one piece," his crew chief ordered over the radio.

"Think they'd mind if I sneak in a few more laps?"

"I think we'd get caught on that one. We're good to go. A few more laps won't do us any good today. You'll get plenty of laps once the green flag waves."

"Roger!" Rob answered as the car rolled to a stop at their garage stall, the engine already silent.

The crew immediately went to work on the car, even as its driver was getting unbuckled and was climbing out. Will barked orders as Donnie Kline shoved the jack up underneath and the others placed jack stands under the car.

Michelle was standing there as Rob set foot on the ground, handing him a wet towel and a cold drink. He accepted them gratefully and then looked around for Christy. She was sitting in one of the director's chairs over by the toolboxes, trying to stay out of the way of all the frenzied activity. Rob ambled over and eased down into the chair next to her. It had finally dawned on him how tired he was from wrestling with the car for the last little while, and the chance to actually sit without a wildly jerking steering wheel in his hands felt wonderful.

"Whew! What a run!" Rob said, then took another big gulp from the bottle of Gatorade.

"You sounded like you were having fun out there," Christy said, and nodded at the earphones hanging on the back of her chair. She had obviously been listening to the exchanges between him, Billy, Will, their regular spotter, and Jodell.

He answered her back in a shout to be heard over all the banging and clanging going on around them. Some of the last-minute adjustments being made by the other teams were not so subtle.

"I wish I could stay right there in the car until the race is over. I hate to have to get out and spend the night waiting for everything to start up tomorrow."

She looked at him with a playful look in her big blue eyes. "You mean you'd rather do that than have dinner with Michelle and me?"

Rob blushed. He'd been looking forward to tonight's dinner with Michelle and Christy ever since he'd found out that there would be no other sponsor obligations this evening, that it would be only the three of them there. Everyone else had plans for dinner with a bunch from the Lee Racing team. Rob had already begged off, explaining he needed a quick meal with his sponsor representative, then an early bedtime.

Once he had caught his breath and changed out of his driving suit, Rob followed Michelle and Christy to their car and allowed them to chauffeur him back toward the hotel on the beach. He had checked with Donnie and Will first to make sure they didn't need him to stay and help. Even Donnie was serious when he told him to go on, to get a good night's rest, that they needed him fresh in the morning. But the big man couldn't help it. He took one look at the two exceedingly good-looking women waiting across the shop for the driver and gave him a broad wink.

"You sure you don't need some help? Looks like they got you outnumbered."

Rob hit him in the face with an oily rag and scatted out of range before Kline could retaliate.

Rob chose the backseat so he could uncoil his long, aching legs. They were hardly in the car and pulling away from the infield when Michelle's phone yodeled. She spoke quickly but mostly listened to what the caller on the other end was saying. She winced a couple of times, her demeanor changing as she listened. They were almost to the hotel when she finally clicked the hang-up button on the phone. She had a scowl on her face.

"Well, so much for a nice relaxing dinner. I've got to hook up with another bunch of folks who're in town for the race. You two go on and maybe I can catch up with you later on for a nightcap."

"We'll wait on you, Michelle," Rob offered while Christy nodded her agreement. "I need to take a shower and maybe rest up a bit anyway."

"I'm not sure how long I'll be gone and I don't want to leave the two of you hanging around the hotel waiting on me. I promised Billy you'd have an early evening anyway, Rob. I don't want Mr. Winton mad at me. Go on out and have a nice meal."

"Are you sure?"

"Go ahead. Don't worry about me. It goes with the territory."

"Okay, Michelle."

Rob couldn't keep the disappointment from his voice. Already he had been positioning this night as something of a re-creation of their magical evening together in California. The three of them together. And he still had thoughts of that evening almost every single day.

Billy Winton grinned as he hung up the phone with Michelle, but he felt a tiny twinge of guilt, too. He didn't like playing tricks on his young driver. But now Michelle could have dinner with the crew and him as she had wanted to in the first place. She had already complained about feeling like a third wheel with Rob and Christy. And her sister and his driver would best be left alone to get better acquainted with each other. Besides, he would know exactly where his young and innocent driver was this night before a big race and with whom. At least it wouldn't be some hard-living crew members dragging him from party to party, or a "racer chaser" enticing him into Lord knew what. Billy figured he was much too old to have to live with such worries.

An hour later, Rob fidgeted nervously in the lounge chair next to the pool as he waited for Christy to come down. His head was full of questions. Where should he take her? What sort of food would she like? Would he make some sort of crucial mistake in etiquette that would send her running off, disgusted?

He realized now how much he had come to depend on Billy or Michelle to make even the most basic decisions for him. There had been no such weighty things to worry about back in Alabama. When it came to a date, there was the Dairy Queen, the twin theaters, or a ride down to the really bright lights of Huntsville. Rob had gotten very comfortable with having someone tell him where to be and what time to be there, to pay the tab and tip the wait staff, but this night he was on his own. And he was as lost as he might have been if someone had sent him out onto the speedway at Daytona blindfolded.

He stood and walked to the back of the pool deck, trying to shake off his nervousness. It was a beautiful evening. As he leaned casually against the railing, he could see the ocean glittering and sparkling in the light of a half moon, with only a few clouds along the far horizon. As the breakers rolled up the wide white beach, they seemed to glow as if they were phosphorescent, and the first of the evening's stars had begun to dot an oil-black sky. There was so much wide world out there, he realized once again. So many strange, distant places that he had never seen, never even thought about before he had embarked on this sudden, wild ride he was on.

And the feelings he had been experiencing lately were just as foreign and unfamiliar, too. Feelings just as strange and unknown and frightening as that vastness out there beyond the circle of moonlight.

Then his thoughts were interrupted by something tickling the back of his neck. He jumped and turned and there she was. She had changed into a filmy black top and dark slacks, her long, blonde hair glistening in the multicolored lights of the poolside bar. He caught his breath when he saw her and was momentarily speechless. She was the most beautiful thing he had ever seen. And up until that very moment, that distinction had belonged to a bright red Ford race car.

"What are you looking at out there?" she asked as she

slid her arm into his, letting him off the hook. They both turned back to the beach and the ocean beyond.

"The ocean. The moon and stars. We've got the moon and the stars and the Tennessee River back home. But it's nothing like this. Or like the Pacific Ocean."

"It is beautiful, isn't it?"

"I never get tired of the ocean. I could stand here and watch it all night. After listening to the roaring of those engines all day and all the pounding and banging that goes on in the garage, the sound of the surf is positively soothing."

"I love the ocean myself. I practically grew up on the beach. Back home we have beach parties all the time. We just find a secluded stretch of beach, build a fire with a little driftwood, then sit back on our blankets and enjoy the solitude and the stars overhead and the sound of the waves. And the company of good friends, of course," Christy said softly, looking over at him.

Then, as the cool sea breeze blew in their faces, she nestled even closer to him.

"That all sounds good to me right about now, Christy. Especially the 'good friends' part," Rob said, then blushed. He hoped she didn't think him forward. He had to remember this was Michelle's sister, and Michelle was the primary contact for the multimillion-dollar sponsor of his race team. And besides, his southern upbringing dictated that he always be the perfect gentleman. She let it go.

"You nervous about tomorrow's race?" she asked, and looked up at him to watch his face as he answered.

He found himself getting lost in her eyes again. They were so deep, so blue, so all engulfing.

"No. Not that. I don't get nervous. I get anxious. I want to go run it right now and then come back to-morrow and run it again."

"That is nerves!" she said emphatically, but with a smile. "You need to learn how to relax between races. You can't be in a car on a track all the time, you know."

"Sometimes I wish I could. For me, racing is all I know how to do. Except for building cabinets, that is. And I don't think cabinetmaking would have ever gotten me on the pool deck of a luxury hotel in Daytona Beach, watching the moonrise, standing next to a . . . well, standing next to you. All I've ever wanted to do was race. Nothing else. But it has nothing to do with the money or the travel or the people I meet. I want to win. That's it. I live to finish first. I'll never be satisfied with second or third or any other place for that matter. That's why I'm driving a race car all the time, even in my sleep. It's always in the back of my mind somewhere."

"So are you driving a race car right this very minute?"

The question surprised him and he stammered when he answered. "Uh . . . well . . . of course not."

"Just checking. I don't care much for second place either." There was that impish look in her eyes again, clearly visible even in the moon- and starlight. She squeezed his hand. "But I guess I'm the same way about school. If I'm not thinking about it, I feel guilty." She paused for a moment, then went on. "Do me one favor tonight."

"Sure."

"You don't have to be to the track for at least twelve more hours yet. Since it's just you and me, let's only think about this evening. Let's enjoy it together. And then we'll win the race tomorrow."

"Agreed!" he said at once. But he wasn't sure that this was right somehow. Shouldn't he be consumed by the biggest race in his career so far? Shouldn't he be in his room right now, tossing nervously, driving the laps over and over in his mind? What made him think he deserved a night out with this beautiful woman when there was a race to run the next day? He had another thought. "But if I do, you have to promise not to think about your classes, too."

She hesitated for only a moment. "I promise."

He smiled, then looked at his watch. "Look, let's go get the car and we'll find a place to eat. After that, I'll show you around town. How about that?"

"Do you mind? With all the traffic out on Highway 1, why don't we take a walk down the beach to the pier? They've got lots of places down there. I'm sure we can find some place to get a quick bite to eat."

Rob quickly agreed. He didn't mind her taking charge at all. He needed an easy night out. The walk would do him good, too. He didn't relish fighting race-week traffic or running into fans who might recognize him or waiting for hours for a table at some fancy restaurant with stuff on the menu that he couldn't begin to pronounce. He'd only assumed that would be what she expected him to do.

He reached for her hand then and guided her across the boardwalk and down the steps to the hard-packed sand of the beach. They walked toward the twinkling lights that marked the spot where the pier stretched out into the ocean. As the waves lapped the sand down the beach to their right, they ambled along slowly, clearly in no hurry, talking softly of oceans and skies and moons they had seen.

On some level, Rob suddenly realized that the race-track and the car and the Grand National contest the next day had been shoved back to the far reaches of his mind. And he was no longer feeling one bit guilty about it.

Nor did the track intrude again on his thoughts over the next few hours. Rob felt like a kid again, carefree as he spent most of twenty dollars at a carnival booth, trying to win Christy a five-dollar teddy bear by tossing baseballs at a stack of milk bottles. She laughed uproariously at his feeble efforts, then scoffed at his claim to have once been a decent pitcher on the high school baseball team back home. Then she tried and did no better, though she claimed she had three years of varsity softball experience herself. Neither of them ever managed to knock all the bottles down and he only won for her a foot ruler that had DAYTONA BEACH, FLORIDA stenciled on its side. Christy promised, with a giggle, to keep it always as she held it clutched to her chest like some rare, precious gift.

They did no better at tossing pennies at plates or trying to maneuver a set of claws to pick up something glittery inside a glass-encased pile of prizes. Skee-ball netted only a souvenir drinking glass, but neither of them cared. Christy awarded it to a passing kid who was as happy as if he had won the lottery. They laughed and played with total abandon, each of them forgetting the pressures of school, of winning a race, of trying to impress the other.

Then they laughed some more over shrimp po'boy sandwiches and French fries and milk shakes as they sat together in a booth overlooking the water. It wasn't nearly as fancy as the restaurant at the end of Sunset Boulevard, and Christy chided him for eating so unhealthily. Then Rob pointed out she had wolfed down her own sandwich and most of his fries and still had ketchup on her mouth as incriminating evidence. Finally they both admitted that they had enjoyed the food and the atmosphere just as much as they had that night on the other coast. And even with Michelle missing, they had enjoyed the company as much, too.

They held hands again as they strolled along slowly

back toward their hotel, neither of them especially anxious to get there, to end this evening.

"Rob, I've had a good time tonight. The best time I've had in a long time."

He couldn't imagine such a thing. With her beauty, her circle of friends back in California, she likely had boyfriends galore. Boyfriends who could take her to far nicer places than a cheap amusement park or a fast-food joint perched on the end of a pier.

"That's hard to believe. I'm sure you—"

"Have lots of boyfriends?" she interrupted. "Most men I know are only interested in themselves, in surfing, making money, or having a . . . how should I put it? A fling." She looked up at him. "I like being with you, Rob Wilder. You're . . . the real thing. You're a paradox, too. A real challenge for me to figure out. So intense, so cocksure, when you're in that race car. So unassuming, so modest, when you're not. And I know so little about you. Where you come from. How you grew up."

She couldn't see in the semidarkness how he reddened at the praise. But he was relieved when a group of fans passing them going the other way recognized him, darkness or not, and interrupted them for autographs. They were nice enough, wished him luck in the race the next day, got their autographs, and then went happily on their way, looking for other drivers.

And the lights of Rob and Christy's hotel were in view now.

Their slow stroll ended as they climbed the wooden steps up to the pool that overlooked the water. Before she had an opportunity to tell him good night and disappear, Rob dragged over a pair of chairs, suggesting that they could sit and rest up from their walk across the sand, that they take a few minutes to gaze out at the ocean. It was still early, after all, the beach still busy with couples walking in the moonlight, the bar behind them full of loud drinkers trying too hard to have a good time. But as they sat close to each other, holding hands and watching the waves roll gently up onto the white sand of the beach, they might just as well have been the only ones left on the planet.

It occurred to Rob Wilder that he was the most at peace that he could ever remember being in his short life so far. His had been a tough, lonely existence before Jodell Lee and Billy Winton and the others had dropped into it and snatched him away. And it had only become more hectic, more filled with unnatural pressure, since then. He was ready now to concede that Michelle had been correct when she had told him in Orlando that he needed to learn to see the other things that surrounded him. That he shouldn't be so totally enclosed by the race car that he missed all the good things that were zooming past right outside his window.

He would have to remember to thank her for that bit of advice.

As they sat there, they talked easily of music, television, movies, and the like, the few things they had in common. Christy told him of the things she loved and disliked about California and asked him questions about growing up in the South, about the inevitable stereotypes. She laughed when he tried to do his "surfer dude" impression. And he took great delight in trying to teach her to say "y'all" and "school" and "swimmin' pool" and other words the way a true southerner would.

The subject of the next day's race or the psych paper Christy was supposed to be writing never seemed to come up.

They did agree they needed to spend more time in each other's environment.

Christy finally stifled a yawn and tried to see the hands on her watch in the dim light.

"What time is it getting to be?"

She knew she would have been perfectly content to talk the rest of the night, to see if the sunrise was as spectacular on this side of the continent as the sunset was on the other. She vowed out loud to find out someday, and to do it with Rob Wilder. But Michelle had made her completely conscious of her duty to make sure he had an early evening with as few distractions as she could manage.

"It's almost eleven."

Rob wondered where this evening had gone. It seemed only minutes ago they had struck off, hand in hand, for the pier, and now it was time to break up and go their separate ways. There was no telling when they would have the benefit of each other's company again.

"I guess we do need to call it a night. Michelle will shoot me if I keep you out too late. And if she doesn't, Billy Winton will."

"She knows she can trust you with me."

"Can she?" Christy asked with a grin. Rob hid his eyes with his hand and reddened yet again. She seemed to enjoy making him squirm. "I could sit here all night, Rob, listening to the ocean, talking with you. I feel like we are just now getting to know each other."

"Me, too."

"I don't want to be the reason you don't win that race tomorrow, though. You need to be rested. I don't want you falling asleep at the wheel or something."

"You're right and I hate you for it." He smiled at her. "I had a wonderful time tonight, Christy. Promise me we can do it again soon and I'll promise to go upstairs and go right to sleep."

As he stood and helped her to her feet, their hands

still linked, she whispered, "I promise." Then she had another impish thought. "But you'll have to go to sleep without that teddy bear we couldn't win!"

"It was rigged! Those bottles were full of cement or something."

As they laughed, he found himself standing there, close, face-to-face with her. He tried to say good night, but nothing came out. He dropped all caution, took her other hand in his, and pulled her close in a tight embrace. He could smell the faint scent of her perfume on the soft wind from the ocean and he could see in the moonlight that she was looking up at him with those wonderful blue eyes of hers. Her face was inches from his, and without either one planning it at all, their lips met. It was like he was fourteen again, experiencing a real kiss for the very first time, awkward, wonderful, frightening, mysterious, unforgettable.

Rob saw her off the elevator on her floor, then headed quickly to his own room, hurrying before he changed his mind and asked her to go sit till dawn on the deck with him. Surprisingly, he had no trouble at all falling asleep, the aroma of her perfume still lingering. It would be the next morning before he realized that there had been none of his usual night-before-a-race tossing and turning.

And there had been no need to dig out that old scrapbook that was his usual pre-race-night companion either. The yellowed newspaper clippings it contained, its unanswered questions and tenuous connection to his past, were usually his only ticket to sleep on such long evenings.

No, that night he slept more soundly than he had in years.

RACE DAY

Rob was resting on the hood of the rental car when Michelle and Christy exited the hotel together. They looked as if they had stepped from the pages of a fashion magazine, decked out in their matching red Ensoft Racing team golf shirts and slacks. They were clearly ready for a race.

He wished he could prolong the moment, maybe talk them into a leisurely breakfast in the hotel restaurant that faced the beach, but there was no time for that this day. They still had stops to make and they needed to stay ahead of the early morning traffic to the track.

Michelle gave him a sisterly hug, then whispered in his ear. "Have fun last night?"

"Yes," he said, proudly and out loud. Christy guessed the question and smiled at his enthusiastic answer. "As a matter of fact, we did."

Christy's embrace was for longer and he loved the feel of her softness next to him. He hated to let her go, but she crawled into the car's backseat and let him ride shot-gun. Only then did he begin to settle into his race-day role. He and Michelle had things to do.

The first stop was a fast-food restaurant drive-through. Christy fussed at their culinary choices but went ahead and ordered a steak and biscuit for herself and pro-ceeded to finish it right down to the crumbs.

"You guys are going to put ten pounds on me," she stewed. "I'll have to eat tofu for a month to make up for this weekend."

Next they pulled to a stop in front of a twenty-four-hour market near the speedway. Some early-bird race fans were already filling their ice chests with beer and sodas, getting ready for a full day, but the three of them headed directly for the coolers in the back. They picked up plastic containers of Gatorade, soft drinks, and bot-tled water, then stopped at the candy counter. Christy carefully selected high-protein power and granola bars, but Rob sneaked a few Snickers into the batch.

The clerk, obviously tired from pulling the graveyard shift, was less than friendly, almost surly, hardly looking up from the register as he stabbed the keys. But then he noticed the two beautiful women standing there across the counter from him. That was when he broke into a huge smile and said a most pleasant "Good morning" as he continued to ring up their purchases.

"Y'all headed for the races?" he asked, suddenly quite friendly.

"We sure are," Michelle answered. "This is the fellow who will be on the pole this afternoon for the Grand National race."

The old man couldn't seem to figure out which to look at, the lovely ladies gracing his store or the real, live pole winner who was just then surreptitiously adding some peanut M & M's to the candy stack.

"You Rocket Rob Wilder?" the old clerk wheezed, his eyes wide.

Rob paused for a moment. He had not yet heard the moniker the television commentator had hung on him the day before. But he liked the sound of it.

"Yessir."

"Here. Would you sign my inventory sheet? Dave Marcis comes in here sometimes race weeks. Michael Waltrip bought a sody pop out of that very cooler right there once. They say old Fireball hisself used to get his chewin' tobacco here on the way to the track."

Rob signed the paper the old man had thrust his way, remembering to add the "Rocket" part, accepted his good-luck wishes with a grin, took the grocery sack, and headed for the door. The clerk's head was still on a swivel, pivoting from the girls to Rob as they left the store.

"Being with a big-time race car driver could hurt a girl's ego," Michelle remarked as they drove away, but she was grinning.

They were soon back on the highway, dealing already with thickening traffic headed for the track. Christy and Rob told most of the details of their night out, carefully leaving out the part about the kiss. Michelle finally admitted that her dinner with the "folks in town for the race" had actually been with Donnie Kline and the rest of the Billy Winton crew.

"I knew you would have insisted on going along, Rob," she explained. "And we would have talked all night about changing the oil in the framish and adjusting the gizmo gears or something. Billy figured you needed a few hours away from the car and the track and racing in general. And I really wanted to spend some time with those guys, too. At least I thought I did."

Rob might have been irritated at being tricked had

he not actually been so grateful. He couldn't even conjure up a scowl.

"Well, thank you, Michelle," he said with a glance in the mirror at Christy's eyes. She was smiling, too, obviously in on the plan all along. He glanced over at Michelle again. "You mean you went clubbing with those guys and lived to tell about it?"

She rolled her eyes and then squinted, as if to erase the memory, then told the sad tale. What had started out as a casual dinner at a place that served fried shrimp and oysters by the bucketful quickly turned into a wild night on the town before she could climb off what she called the "Donnie Kline steamboat." Kline's massive frame and shaved head were immediately recognized wherever they went in the course of the wild evening, by other crews also out on the town and race fans alike. And he was proud to show the crew and its lovely California guest what it was like to properly "do Daytona" on the eve of a race.

That led to lots of wild greetings, semiserious wrestling matches, quick trips from one watering hole to another, tearful bear hugs from old friends they hadn't seen since all the way back in November, loud arguments about who would win the weekend's races, who had the best car, who had the prettiest car, who had the ugliest car, raucous sing-alongs at every place that had a karaoke machine and a few that didn't, plenty of tropical drinks and pitchers of beer and raw oysters and hot wings run up on other people's tabs, most of them total strangers who had long since surrendered their credit cards in the spirit of the party, and a general untamed time for all who dared to swim in the big man's wake.

At one stop, Donnie bet some of the boys he could play the piano better than the keyboardist in the band that was performing. The club owner didn't take too kindly to his storming the stage while the band was on a break, but when he broke out, hamlike fists flying across the keyboard, banging out a genuinely fine ragtime, the crowd wouldn't allow him to be stopped. Still, the owner persuaded him, his musical talents, and his loud entourage to kindly move on before he summoned Daytona Beach's finest to urge them along.

"Thank God we passed the hotel on one of our sweeps about three o'clock," Michelle said. "I jumped out before they could stop me and I can honestly say that I am lucky to still be here and able to tell these tales."

Rob wondered how Kline and the rest of the boys could do it. They were almost certainly at the track ahead of them already, working away as if they had been comfortably tucked into their beds early the night before. They seemed as indefatigable having a good time as they often did working long, arduous hours in the shop or at the track. But he was also sure Will Hughes would tolerate no slouching around from a bunch of hungover race crewmen this morning. It was too big a day.

And Rob was thankful again that he had spent such a sedate evening. Such a wonderful evening.

He couldn't imagine how some of the old-time drivers had done it either. Stories of prerace partying were often related around the shops and garages, passed on like myths and folk tales. Driving a racetrack like Daytona was hard enough without having to carry a pounding headache and the cold sweats of a hangover.

Rob carried the sacks from the market into the garage. He couldn't help but notice the stares Christy was drawing as they walked past all the stalls. Then someone was waving at them, calling Michelle's name from over near one of the other team's cars.

"Stephanie!" Michelle yelled, and ran to embrace the slender brunette with the big sunglasses.

Michelle had met Stephanie Howell the previous season at Charlotte. She was a public relations rep for a grocery store chain that sponsored the car she was standing next to. Stephanie had been kind enough to take Michelle under her wing and show her around the pits and garage and had introduced her to some of the things sponsors and their representatives were expected to do during the races.

"I'm glad you survived last night. How you feeling this morning?" Michelle asked. Stephanie had apparently been a part of the Donnie Kline tsunami the previous evening.

"I'm just glad not to be in jail or the hospital!" Stephanie moaned, holding her forehead with one hand. "You were a smart girl to bail out when you did, Chelle. The bad thing is, I know better. Or at least I thought I did."

"You need an aspirin?"

"Already covered that. I'll be okay by race time."

"You sure?"

"Yeah, if I don't die." She gave Michelle a pained look, then grabbed her ears with both hands as an engine was suddenly revved two stalls down. The steel of the building vibrated right along with the din of the motor. Stephanie leaned back against a support post and shook her head slowly from side to side. "If I don't die, I'll be fine." Then she looked sideways at Michelle, grinned weakly, and said, "But we sure did have ourselves some fun, didn't we?"

"Yeah, we did," Michelle answered through a grin of her own.

"So what about tall-blonde-and-good-looking there?" She nodded toward Rob, who was still standing there, holding the sack of goodies. "He looks nice and rested and I don't remember seeing him last night. Though there's a whole bunch of it I don't remember."

"He and my sister walked up to the pier and back."

"The pier? Is that all?" Stephanie said. She winked at Michelle and leaned in closer to whisper. "That walk to the pier has gotten lots of folks into trouble, you know."

"Well, if you ladies are going to talk about me as if I'm not here . . ." Rob said, and turned on his heels to walk on toward the garage. Christy Fagan was right in stride with him. "We've got a race to win!" he called back over his shoulder.

Michelle and Stephanie winked at each other.

Rob and Christy had not even turned in to the 06 stall when one of the pit reporters from the network headed them off. Christy stood aside to allow Rob to talk with him.

"Mind if we record a quick few seconds for our opening spot?"

"Not at all."

Rob set the sack of groceries aside, ran his fingers through his longish hair, and adjusted his jacket so the Ensoft logo on his shirt would show.

"Young Rob Wilder, the pole sitter for today's race . . ." the reporter sang into his microphone as his cameraman zoomed in tightly. He made certain that the lovely blonde lady who had been walking with the driver was also in the frame. The producer in the truck made sure he kept that shot, too. Handsome young driver, his beautiful girlfriend. A million-dollar shot! "Rob, how do you like your chances?"

"I think we have a good car and if I can drive it to its potential, then I think we'll be talking later on this afternoon in victory lane."

"You feel that confident about winning this afternoon?"

"If I didn't feel that confident, then I wouldn't be

about to climb into the race car. We came down here to win."

The last words were delivered emphatically, with a forceful gaze directly at the camera lens. It would be the first thing viewers would see when the race telecast began that afternoon, Rob Wilder's words underscored by roaring guitars and his image backed by shots of him winning the pole position in the first place.

All the while Christy stood behind him, a slight smile on her face, and she nodded when Rob delivered the confident statement right into the camera. At the same time, the producer was ordering someone to find out who she was. If she was the driver's girlfriend, he wanted to make sure she was within reach of a camera throughout the race for reaction shots. Shots every woman viewer out there could identify with as the beautiful young lady went through various emotions, watching her boyfriend run the biggest race of his young career.

"Thanks, Rob. 'Preciate it," the reporter was saying. "Good luck out there today."

"No problem," Rob said, shaking the man's hand. "And I'm serious. I intend to see you in victory lane in a few hours."

There was no reason to doubt the young man's sincerity.

Billy Winton was standing in the front fender well of the race car as Will Hughes leaned over the radiator, up to his waist in the engine compartment. Billy, a measuring tape in hand, was checking the geometry on the front end as if it might have radically changed overnight. Will was reviewing the changes they had decided on the night before. There was a reason for their recalculations. There had been a subtle shift in the weather, not enough to cause a single fan to reevaluate his wardrobe for the race, but plenty enough of a change so every race team in the garage was rethinking its setup.

Christy took the sack of groceries on back to the hauler to stow them in the fridge while Rob surveyed the sheets clamped together on Will's clipboard. These were the changes Will and Billy had decided were needed. The three of them quickly went into a huddle, working their way down the list and the reason for each entry on it, what they expected the track conditions to be at the beginning and how they would likely change as the day wore on.

Will and Billy both noticed something different about their boy. There seemed to be an edge to Rob's voice, an obvious confidence in his manner that had not been there to this degree before. Rob had always been quietly confident, from the first time they had met him in Nashville at the driving test. But today he seemed more willing, even eager, to take more control of all that was going on around him. Maybe it had come with the experience he had gained driving on this track for the last few days. Maybe it was simply more maturity that only time and proper seasoning could buy. Or was there something else going on with him?

Finally it came time for the crew to push the car toward where the Grand National officials waited to do their final prerace inspections. Rob walked over to the truck and climbed up into the crew lounge. Michelle was there, chatting on her cell phone, making sure her assistants were keeping their corporate guests happy at the hospitality tent. Rob was scheduled to make a quick stop at the tent an hour and a half before the race to shake as many hands and sign as many autographs and have as many pictures made as he could manage. He would be very popular this day, having won the pole his first try at Daytona. Everyone would want to know how he did it. And would want to tell everyone back home that he had an audience with the young driver who led the field off at the start. Maybe even with the eventual race winner. And the driver of the car that was sponsored by Ensoft, whose products they sold, distributed, or had helped develop.

Rob actually looked bored as he leaned back on the couch and sipped a bottle of water. Christy eased down next to him, wondering how he could be so relaxed with so much going on around him, with such a dangerous task awaiting him in a short while. Did the pressures of this wild and woolly sport ever get to him?

"Tired?" she asked him, touching his arm. Maybe that was why he appeared so relaxed.

"No. The race just never comes fast enough. I don't like all the waiting. I wish they'd go ahead and line all the cars up and let us go right now."

"Waiting would make me nervous."

"It's not really nerves. I'm itching to get in the car. I've been waiting all my life to race at this place."

"It must be exciting for you then."

"It will be when we finally get to racing."

He pantomimed steering the car, shifting gears, hunkering down to watch someone in front of him on the track as he drove up on his tail, ready to put a lap on him.

"Would you like something to eat or are you going to get something in the hospitality tent?" Michelle asked him, covering the mouthpiece of the phone with her hand.

"I'll take a big old baloney and cheese sandwich with double mayo and lots of onion." She ignored him, handed him one of the power bars instead, and he ate it as if it were actually what he had ordered, a look of mock bliss on his face. He glanced down at his watch. "What time do we need to go over?"

"Another half an hour or so. Enjoy your 'baloney sandwich.'" Then she was jabbering away at whoever was on the other end of the cell phone.

Rob turned to Christy. "You know what else I'd like? An RC Cola and a Moon Pie."

"I don't think I have that . . . whatever it is . . . in the sack here. How about carrot sticks and sprouts and some mineral water? Now, that's some fine California food!"

At last things were moving. Rob made his appearance at the hospitality tent. Then driver introductions were completed and he and the rest of the crew were standing idly next to the car on pit road, more than ready to get the show going.

Christy stood back out of the way, wide-eyed at all the flurry of activity, the masses of milling people all around her. How in the world would they ever get all these people out of the way so they could get a race run? Meanwhile she hid behind the tool chest, the big box the crew called the "war wagon." Michelle was busy organizing the drinks they had picked up that morning, getting them ready for when Rob would need them on his pit stops.

The young driver was quiet now as the crew carried on their tension-breaking banter. Will had finished going over the planned pit strategy with him, and Rob had recited back the whole plan perfectly. Now Will sauntered over, put his arm around the kid's shoulder, and surveyed the enormous crowd with him.

"All these folks for a Grand National race!" Will remarked. "Who would have thought it a few years ago when folks thought of this whole division as the minor leagues."

"I suppose they heard I would be driving," Rob said,

first with a straight face, then he broke into a broad grin.

"You just go out there and drive like you know how," Will ordered. "Like my old grandma used to say, 'Patience is a virtue.'"

They certainly didn't need for him to try and force his way into somewhere he didn't belong, finding himself outside the draft without a partner to help him along. In the early part of the race, he could easily find himself being drop-kicked backward to the rear of the field before he even realized what was happening. And such a happenstance could leave him in a hole so deep he couldn't climb back out of it by the end of the race, no matter how fast the car or how perfectly he might drive from then on.

"I know, Will."

"Look, I know you get tired of me preaching the same sermon before every race, but at this place, patience is especially critical. Seems like drivers get so excited running around out there with their foot jammed through the floorboard and whistling along so zippy-like that they think they're invincible. Next thing you know, you're out there by yourself and everybody else is driving off and leaving you."

"I know, Will. I also know what I don't know. And I don't plan on letting that beat me."

"Of course you won't. I just have to say it, though," the crew chief said with a grin. The kid was, he realized, demonstrating admirable patience simply by not bucking up at him for all his constant fussing.

"Will, I can't wait to get this car out on that racetrack. There's only one thing I want worse."

"What's that?"

Rob looked at Will with a deadly serious look on his boylike face. Hughes couldn't help but wonder if the kid even had to shave every day.

"I want to park it in a few hours over yonder in victory lane, that's what."

"Run a smart race and you've got a blame good chance." Now it was Will's turn to go serious. "You know, I've dreamed of wining a race at Daytona since my daddy brought me down here and I watched Richard Petty win one of his seven Daytona Five Hundreds. Victory Lane here would be sweet. Real sweet."

Will's dad had been a struggling small-time racer, showing promise but never really tasting much success before he had died much too young. In a short time, though, he had instilled a love for the sport in his only son, an intense desire to win that sometimes bordered on the fanatical. And that hunger had sent Will Hughes off on his carefully planned career path, first to engineering school, then to Jodell Lee's team as an engineer, and now to the 06 team as crew chief on Billy Winton's fire-engine-red Fords. Winning this race at this sacred place was only the next step in what he considered his ordained march to the top of big-time stock car competition. He, too, craved much more, including his own team someday, a team where his innovative ideas and passion for perfection would let him taste the sweet fruit his father had been so cruelly denied.

The clock was still progressing in slow motion, but winding nonetheless toward the start of the race. Rob sauntered over to chat for a moment with Christy. Then, when Will gave him the high sign, he quickly gave her a good-luck hug, a wink, and he turned and was gone.

As he walked away, Christy noticed how different he now seemed from even an hour before. He was distant, distracted, as if his mind was far, far away from her and their idle conversation. Was he simply nervous about the race, preoccupied with his plans for how he would drive the car? Or was it deeper than that? Was he having second thoughts about the night before? Maybe regretting that he had opened up to her, that he had kissed her, that he had allowed himself to show interest in her?

She decided to assume he was only concentrating on the race until she found out to the contrary.

Then he stopped in midstride as if he had just thought of something that he had forgotten to do. He turned back to her and quickly stepped to where she stood. He hugged her again, then looked into her eyes.

"Would you kindly accompany me to a victory celebration dinner tonight, Miss Fagan?" he asked.

"On one condition. That you go out there and show everybody how fast you can drive that car."

"Deal!"

"Then you better win that race, 'cause I know where I want to go already."

He almost kissed her then, but he didn't want the crew to see that. They'd carry on like a bunch of high school sophomores and have the whole garage area hooting at him. And besides, he didn't want any of them to think he wasn't concentrating totally on the job at hand.

But before he knew what hit him, Christy leaned up and kissed him quickly on the lips.

"That's for good luck!"

Then she let go and flashed the most beautiful smile he had ever seen before as she shooed him on to the car. He listened for the silliness to erupt from the crew, but they must have missed it. Thank goodness!

But Rob had not noticed someone else watching them. A camera crew from the network had been shooting away. The touching shot of the young driver and his girlfriend, sharing a sincere embrace before the dangerous contest began, the beautiful young woman's lips obviously forming the words "That's for good luck" after the kiss, the handsome young driver walking away to crawl into his machine. It would all make for wonderful television as the coverage of the race on national television began. Men and women alike would envy the two attractive youngsters, and would stay in front of their sets all afternoon to see how the story played out.

Rob hardly remembered walking to the race car. He realized that he was there when he got there and began zipping up the red driving suit with the blue Ensoft design stitched across the front and back. And he was aware of Will Hughes, whispering to him, reminding him yet again of the strategy they had already gone over a good dozen times.

"Remember, you don't have to win the race in these first few laps. Just settle into a rhythm and we'll worry about winning when we get down to the end."

"Don't worry, Will. If anybody does, I have a healthy respect for this place. Jodell and Billy have made sure of that."

"I know you do."

"Where is Billy?" Rob asked.

"He's over talking to Jodell in the Cup garage. Look for Jodell to be on the radio some."

"Great, I could . . ." Rob started, but the network camera crew was easing around the car, the cameraman moving his camera alongside the vehicle, following its lines, up and down, over the hood, and stopping with a close-up of Rob and Will as they talked. The reporter was once again telling viewers about the unlikely capture of the pole position by this young slender upstart, this amazing young driver from Alabama who had already been christened "Rocket Rob Wilder."

As the man talked, Rob climbed through the car's window and settled down into his seat while Will reached through the window and helped him buckle up the belts and checked the radio hookups. He caught a glimpse of Christy moving to the back of the pits to watch the race from there, but he could only grin as he finished adjusting his helmet. He was so engrossed in running the race in his head that he was actually surprised when the command he had been so impatiently awaiting finally came.

"Gentlemen, start your engines!" echoed throughout the giant speedway.

Rob reached up with his gloved left hand and flipped the starter switch. The starter ground away for a full second, then the powerful engine coughed once and rumbled to life. Rob loved that sound, the deep bass of the powerful engine that sat out there in front of him, waiting for his command to engage and race away, its throaty growl ominously threatening even though it was muffled by the earplugs and padding of his racing helmet. And he loved the vibration the motor's sheer kinetic energy set loose up the steering wheel shaft and through the wheel to his hands, through the frame of the race car and up his body. It was as if the engine were trying to reassure its driver that it was ready to go, ready to drag him around as rapidly as it could.

He goosed the throttle gently, more ready than ever to guide the car out onto the track.

"Come on, come on . . ." he said out loud, wishing the official standing in front of them, blocking the way, would finally step aside and wave them past. Once the engines had been started, he could figure no reason for them not to be set loose. "Wastin' gas. Wastin' time," he said, almost in a singsong, but he could see a couple of the other crews had been slow to leave pit road and the entire field was left idling, waiting for them to clear the area.

Will listened to his own motor with a practiced ear,

like a piano tuner trying to detect the slightest disso-
nance. But he was satisfied. He could at least send it
away knowing the mill was as perfect as he could make
it. It was ready to race. It might blow all to pieces when
the kid showered down on it out there to lead the pack
to the green flag, but for now, it was as ready as he knew
how to make it.

He grabbed the window netting, pulling it upward,
then pushed one edge into its slot and snapped it to
fasten it. Then he locked his fingers and gave the net a
sharp tug. It held.

Rob reached his hand out the window to shake Will's,
then flashed a thumbs-up to the rest of the crew where
they stood next to the wall, watching expectantly, clearly
as anxious to get this thing under way as their driver
was. The fastening of the window net was the unspoken
signal for the boys to head down toward the team's pit,
farther along the road toward turn one.

Christy and Michelle followed along with them. All
the while Will stood perfectly still, watching the car. He
would not move until the Ford had actually begun to
roll off the line.

"All right, cowboy. How we looking in there?"

It looked odd to see Will's lips moving at the headset
microphone but hear his voice crackling through the
earplugs. Rob keyed the radio switch on the steering
wheel.

"Everything's looking good, boss. Oil pressure. Fuel
pressure. Amps. The temperatures are starting to come
on up."

"Good. Keep an eye on the water temp. We have a
couple of strips of tape on the front end. Make sure you
check it every chance you get. We don't want to blow
the motor up."

"Ten-four!"

Will was talking about a few short strips of duct tape they had used to close up some of the openings in the front of the car that led to the radiator. The small pieces of tape were enough to help fine-tune the handling of the car. It affected the flow of air as it whipped over the car once it was up to speed. Adding a piece or taking a piece of tape away could loosen or tighten up the car as it sailed through the track's corners. Even that tiny change on the car could make significant differences in how it cut through the wind. So long as the car was running along by itself or was leading a group of other cars, the constricted opening had little effect on how hot the water in the Ford's radiator might get. But if Rob should run up close behind another car for a while, drafting in its wake, it could cause the marginal temperature to spiral upward into dangerous territory. In addition to all the other things he needed to be watching, the driver also had to keep a close eye on the radiator's temperature gauge to make sure the engine was not going to get into trouble. It would be easy to miss seeing the heat spiking and to not even know anything was wrong until the engine fractured in a cloud of steam and smoke and vaporized fuel.

Rob was growing even more impatient. What in the world was the holdup? His right foot twitched so badly on the throttle that Will looked at the engine sideways, thinking the motor must have suddenly developed a quirk, but he quickly realized Rob was revving it erratically. Still, the pace car merely sat there, lights flashing, as if it had no intention of ever leading them out to run a stock car race.

Then, finally, the brightly decal-laden automobile pulled away. Rob imagined he could hear the collective relieved sigh of three dozen race car drivers.

"Let her roll, cowboy."

The cars eased out, slowly accelerating, dutifully following the pace car. That was when it suddenly occurred to Rob once again that he was the lead car, that the others would be following him and his buddy who rolled along just to his outside all the way around this racetrack. And then they would all be doing everything they could to get on past him once the green flag fell. He and the driver of the car on the outside pole had gotten special attention from the track officials at the morning drivers' meeting, with a complete briefing on what their responsibilities would be.

Now he tried to recall all the instructions as they completed the first two of the three pace laps. The field of qualifiers eased slowly down the back straightaway again, on their way around to take the green flag for the start.

"How are the temps?"

The radio had been quiet for a while and Will's words actually startled Rob. He glanced over at the proper gauges.

"All right where they should be."

"Good, now be ready and be smart. Remember, you can't win this thing in the first few laps. You got to still be around at the finish to win."

"Ten-four."

Will couldn't help but crack a slight smile. All the coaching they'd done over the last few days made these final admonitions seem like overkill. Rob knew what he had to do. Will knew that he knew it. But somehow he felt the need to say them one more time. And God bless the kid, he only said "Ten-four" and went on about his business. Now, if only he remembered the oft-repeated instructions once he got into the heat of the battle.

"Good luck. I'll call the green flag for you," Will said, then let the radio net go silent so the kid could focus all his attention on getting a good jump on the start.

Rob rolled the car through turn three and it felt as if he were moving only twenty or thirty miles per hour, as if he were holding up freeway traffic behind him that strained to pass him. He knew, though, that they were actually going nearly a hundred as they strung out behind the pace car. It only felt slow compared to how he had been touring this place in practices the last few days.

Now he twisted the wheel back and forth, zigzagging along, scrubbing the tires of all the little bits of rubber and other debris they might have picked up on the pace laps. He certainly didn't want to stomp it, go charging off into turn one for the first time at close to 190 miles an hour, and have the car lose its grip and go spinning as if they were racing on patchy ice.

As the platoon of cars marched together through the third and fourth turns, all of their drivers tightened up the formation until it appeared that they were all joined together like a tandem freight train. The car behind Rob moved right up onto his tail, so close Rob could not even see the nose of the car, only the reflection of his own car in the visor of the driver's helmet.

Rob's chest swelled with pride for a moment as he paced the field down to the line. His first start at this famed track! His first start and he would make it from the pole. It had been a heady week for this young team from the hills of Tennessee and an especially exciting few days for the talented young driver.

Rob strained to look ahead and see the flag stand sitting at the center of the tri-oval. Up there on its hip the flagman waited, ready to throw the green if they were properly aligned behind Rob. As the field of cars snarled through turn four, the lights on the top of the pace car went out and its driver accelerated away, trying to put some distance between it and the lurching cars behind that were waiting to be unleashed onto the open track ahead.

Rob wanted so badly to stomp on the gas now, to go hurtling along, set free, instead of waiting for the pace car to drop out of the way.

Suddenly the pace car darted to the inside and steered down the pit lane, out of Rob's sight. He now was charged with setting the pace for the rest of the field as they came down to the line. Rob glanced to his right, to the car that rode along to his outside, and he could see the crowd beyond, all on their feet, as ready as the racers to get it on.

The flagman peered back up the track, the green flag at his side as he observed the two lines of race cars moving his way. He stared intently at the two cars on the front row. They rode along, perfectly lined up, side by side. But he still watched, making the decision as to whether he could safely give them the go-ahead.

With a quick flip of his wrist, he raised the flag high over his head.

He was about to set loose a thundering herd of wild horses, and God help anything or anybody who got in their way.

Green! Green! Green! Go get 'em, cowboy!"

Rob had actually anticipated the quick move by the flagman and had already jammed the gas pedal to the floor. By the time Will's words rattled in his ears, the car had leapt forward and he was building speed as he rolled boldly toward the start/finish line. Rob got a slight jump on the car to his right as they all thundered across the start/finish line for the first time, in the red 06 Ford the locomotive in the long train that trailed along behind him.

Rob was able to jump out ahead of the car on his outside. As he eased ahead of the second-place car, he felt the pull of Joe Banker's engine as it powered him to a point out front. Before he knew it, he had pulled out in front by two car lengths. As he glanced in his mirror, he realized that the car directly behind him had followed closely, tucked up within inches of the red Ford's rear deck. That left no room for the car on the outside to slide down the track and tuck in behind Rob. The two rows of race cars remained a pair of writhing, parallel snakes as they slithered off toward turn one, with no one able to do more than ride along in tandem until they could get all the way up to maximum speed.

Rob concentrated hard on keeping his foot to the floor, watching the towering first turn that shimmered invitingly up ahead in the sunlight. One advantage of having the pole was the unobstructed view out the windshield. That gave him a clear picture of the track as it stretched out in front of him, sweeping into the first two turns; then, coming out of the second turn, he would be able to see far down the way where the asphalt swooped around through three and four. He kept his mind on the portion of the track he could see, though, setting the car down low going into turn one. He nodded appreciatively as he felt her stick tightly to the track.

Every fan in the place was standing, cheering wildly, as the field crossed the line two by two to take the green flag. This was what they had all traveled down to this place to see, hear, and feel. What they had paid hard-earned money to see. The amalgamated thunder of dozens of finely tuned engines. The way it vibrated against their chests and stunned their ears. The gust of dusty wind the cars kicked up as they passed by. Each person in the grandstands strained to pick out his or her favorite driver, to see what kind of leap he might have gotten on the rest of them.

Will Hughes sat comfortably on top of the team's "war wagon," seemingly as nonchalant as if he had bought a ticket and didn't really care how this contest came out. But he was busy already, directing the action, sizing up the competition, his eyes sweeping from the very last car in the pack all the way up front where his own car pulled the rest of them along like a mule in its traces.

Billy Winton sat in one of three director's chairs that had been unfolded at the back of the pit. Christy and Michelle Fagan rested in the other two. The group had only settled down after the field had roared by to finish the first lap. Billy was already listening to the traffic on the radio as he scanned the television monitor on the side of the pit box. That gave him the best view of Rob as he pulled out in front of the others through turns one and two.

The two young women leaned forward to watch the screen, too. Christy couldn't believe the noise, the way the cars had jumped ahead when the flag had dropped, the roar of the fans as they urged the bunch of howling machines along. She could only grin at Michelle and adjust her earplugs and spin around to watch Rob disappear into the second turn in real life before she turned back to the television.

Michelle grinned back, knowing full well how her sister felt. It was still new enough to her that she had goose bumps on her arms and a lump in her throat. Somehow, too, she felt for some reason as if she might cry. The spectacle of it all was an emotional experience, one that had quickly grabbed hold of her. If anything, this start was even more exciting than the few others that she had witnessed so far.

She had no idea that the much older man in the Ensoft Racing jacket next to her, the one occupying the director's chair and looking down his nose through his reading glasses at the television set, the man who had lived through hundreds of these starts over the last thirty years, felt exactly the same way.

This race today had been a turning point for Billy. Up until this defining moment, this whole return to racing had been something of a lark for him. Even the long hours spent in the garage, helping Will get the body and setup on the car perfect, had only seemed like a temporary diversion from his regular adopted routine. Oh, he had spent a great deal of time at racetracks since he had retired from Jodell Lee's team. But today, here at Daytona, with his car out there leading the first lap, it was totally different somehow.

He was back in racing with a vengeance. And he couldn't have been any happier about it.

As the cars had droned around for the final pace lap, closing in on the start, he had felt the old sensation coming on. The feeling was deep down in his belly. And it had been a while since he had felt it. It was not the usual prerace nerves or the casual excitement every lover of this sport felt at one time or another. No, it was the burning fire of competition. And it blazed as hot and bright inside Billy Winton as it ever had before.

And he knew the time had come again. The time to compete, to win here at Daytona.

Meanwhile, his driver led the field out of turn two and on to the long back straightaway for the first time. By the time the field cleared the new grandstands coming off the corner, the outside line of cars had pulled even with the inside queue. Two by two, the field raced down toward the third turn. Rob was getting an early look at the powerful force of the draft and the dramatic effects it could have on groups of cars running close together as they approached two hundred miles per hour. He realized once again that the aerodynamics of this massive speedway equalized faster and slower cars. It was going to take much more than a powerful engine to win today!

The two lead cars raced into turn three side by side. Only now were the cars actually approaching full speed, the restrictor plates under the hood doing their jobs very efficiently. Rob wrestled with the steering wheel as the car bounced around in the rough air while the car behind him stayed on his back bumper. But rough ride or not, Rob never even considered lifting off the gas.

Zooming through the corner at a breakneck pace, the tightly packed field raced in line back down toward the start/finish stripe. The power of the Joe Banker motor allowed Rob to pull back out in front by a couple of car lengths. This time the car that had been riding along on his right outside had a better idea. Instead of running there, trying to stay side by side with the 06 Ford, he eased a bit to his left and slipped down, falling in behind Rob, ready to allow the Ensoft machine to pull him along for a bit. The third-place car closed up the gap quickly as he, too, let the vacuum created behind the other cars draw him in tight. Now the three of them, their speed enhanced by each other's presence, ran in a tight bunch. From the stands and the pits, it seemed bumpers must have absolutely been touching as they bounced along, and more than one of the assembled throng who were watching held their breath.

Since the cars from fourth on back were still running side by side, sometimes as much as three wide, Rob and his two buddies were able to break away from them. As they exploded down past the thousands of whooping, yelping fans in the grandstands, they seemed to be putting even more distance between themselves and the rest. The other drivers obviously saw what was happening up there, too, and began jockeying for position, searching for partners to draft with, and some even got four cars wide as they passed the flag stand.

From his spot up front, Rob had lost interest in the rest of the field. He had nothing but open track ahead of him, he had gotten credit for leading the very first lap

he had ever run at Daytona, and he and his drafting
partners were already setting sail for the first and second
turns. But he knew two things would likely happen. First,
some of the other strong cars would hook up and run
them down. That was inevitable. And eventually he
would catch up with lapped traffic and would have to
do more than simply kick the throttle and hold on for
the ride.

"Your pack's ahead by six car lengths," came the
word from Harry Stone, his spotter, who leaned against
a railing high on a platform above the grandstands and
had a view of the entire track.

Rob didn't answer. He kept looking from the mirror
to the windshield, watching the car on his butt and the
open track ahead.

"Wiggle a little bit, son," came the voice of Jodell Lee
on the radio. "See if you can break the flow of air on
them old boys that's draftin' on you."

Rob tried it, felt a noticeable loss of momentum, and
saw that the car directly behind fell back a few feet before he slid down to mimic the leader's move. The third
car did the same. And then they were right back where
they had been.

There was movement farther back then. As they
headed down the backstretch, the Ford sitting in fifth
place made a sudden dart down to the inside, sandwich-
ing the fourth-place car between himself and another
driver on the outside. The crowd gasped as they saw
that something had to give as they approached a narrow
part of the track. The driver of the car that had been
riding directly behind the Ford made a quick assessment
of the situation and followed him down to the inside. It
was clear he was trying to help push the Ford along and
come with him, trying to execute a classic "slingshot"
move on the cars that would now be caught in the mid-

dle and on the high side of the track. Sure enough, those two cars running next to each other began to drop back, as if their pilots had turned off the jets. But in actuality, they still had their feet to the floor, stomping the throttle as hard as they could, all to no avail. The two drafting cars moved on by and then slid up together in front of what had been the fourth-place car, now shoving him rudely back to sixth. And it all happened in less than half the back straightaway.

Now, all throughout the track full of cars, the drivers began to pick their partners, trying to link up with similarly powered and set up cars. Again some of the bunches spread out, three and four across in spots, as everyone tried to jockey to join in with the fastest group they could find. And all the maneuvering was happening at a blistering rate of speed.

And, of course, the shifting and darting back there had allowed Rob Wilder and the two drafting cars to slip even farther ahead as they stayed in line. In the television truck, the director kept switching from all the wild scurrying going on in the bulk of the field up to where the three lead cars pulled away, threatening to leave the others to race, wreck, or run wild, as they wished.

In the press box, the commentators for the telecast were obviously enjoying all the tight racing as much as their audience around the country likely was.

"Sure looks like Rocket Rob Wilder is backing up his pole-winning speed here in the early going. There's no doubt he has plenty of horsepower under the hood of the Ensoft Ford today."

"The youngster does look like he's gonna be able to back up what he was telling us about that car. He was quick as a hiccup off the green flag and he hasn't looked back yet."

"We'll have to see if the young driver has the maturity and discipline to keep the car up at the front as the race wears on. Sometimes it's hard for a young, inexperienced driver to pace himself."

"I'll tell you this. The front of the field is the place you wanna be today. See how these guys are racing behind them. Look at 'em, going three wide through the corner there. Whoa! There is no way they need to be running this hard this early in the race."

There was obvious concern in the old driver's voice as they watched a couple of the cars touch, wiggle, almost go spinning, then get gathered back up before they drove on, both of them still trying to get the advantage over the other despite their close call.

"You're absolutely right. And besides the risk of a big get-together out there, if these gentlemen don't settle down and get back in line pretty soon, those front three are going to drive right off toward the checkered flag and leave the rest of them back there duking it out for fourth place on."

"You see our clock there in the corner of your screen. Their lead has grown to fifteen car lengths. It's gonna be tough for one or two of the chasing cars to run them down. Their best bet is to gang up and go after them. Or stay close till the first pit stop, at least."

The image on the television screen switched to a shot from a track-level camera, the bulk of the field heading directly toward the position. Cars dashed left and right, looking for a better drafting partner, trying to anticipate which group would be the best to join. It looked like total confusion, fruit-basket turnover.

"They keep this up and we're going to see the mother of all wrecks out there. Look at them, running three and four wide down the backstretch."

Sure enough, in the camera's-eye view from the blimp

circling over the track, viewers could see how close the cars were to each other, how little track was left when they ran in tandem.

Christy and Michelle didn't have nearly as good a view, but they certainly had more of a sense of the speed. The field kept zooming past them, their engines painfully loud. Christy could feel the metal beneath her feet move in sympathy with the on-track roar. The packs of cars zooming past reminded her of squadrons of jet fighters streaking across the sky at an air show she had once attended with her folks. Only somehow, these crazy men seemed to be going faster and making even more noise than those planes had.

"Come on, Rob! Come on, Rob!" they both screamed in unison as the front three cars flew past them. They knew there was no way he could hear them, but they didn't care. They felt the urge to scream and they did.

Once he had passed by, they whirled around to watch the flickering television picture on the back of the war wagon. With crossed fingers, Christy watched as the camera followed Rob through the corner and on to the back straight once again. She knew enough to be glad Rob was up there with only two other cars to get in his way. Even she knew that what was happening farther back on the track was fraught with danger. She couldn't imagine how they had gone this long without somebody bouncing off somebody else. It reminded her of an L.A. freeway, but with everyone on this superhighway zooming along at warp speed.

"Is he going to win?" Christy finally asked Michelle. The field had passed them and the roar was at least tolerable.

"They've only run ten laps," Michelle said, checking, like a veteran, the scoring pylon behind her. "There are still over a hundred laps to go. Lots of stuff can happen in a hundred laps!"

"It seems like he's been leading forever."

"They'll swap up the lead here soon. Those guys behind him are just checking him out to see what he has," Michelle responded, proudly showing off the knowledge she had culled from Will and the boys during her time with them at the tracks at the end of the previous season.

Still, Rob showed no sign of being willing to surrender the point. Jodell Lee had suggested it already.

"You may want to let one of them lead for a while, kid," he had said. "Give you a chance to see how your car feels in the middle of the draft. Maybe feel out if you got what it takes to pass him back."

But Rob had only bumped the microphone switch to signal he had heard. He didn't want to ever let go the lead. Never! He didn't care if it was the prudent thing to do or not. It was the most wonderful feeling he had ever experienced. There he was, driving a wonderfully prepared racer, leading the biggest race of his young life at the very speedway he had always dreamed of running. All those nights he had lain awake as a kid, wondering what would become of him. Wondering how in the world he would ever live out the dream he had harbored since he was old enough to know what a race car and a speedway were.

Now here he was. And he was in no hurry to let the moment go. To quit living the dream. Not even for a lap!

Back behind them, the cars were beginning to stack up even worse than before as patience was already a sparse commodity. Some had certainly realized that their cars weren't strong enough and were desperately seeking someone, anyone, who could help by dragging them along until they could pit. Others were clearly frustrated as slower traffic or the lack of a decent drafting partner had kept them much farther back in the pack than their machine deserved to be.

Suddenly one of the cars on the inside seemed to make an abrupt turn directly for the outside wall, as if its driver had finally decided to go race some other track somewhere else. All it had taken was for the wind from some adjacent car to suddenly shift enough that the car lost the downdraft on its own rear spoiler. When that happened, it was as if some giant hand had swatted the rear of the car hard and had sent it plunging off perpendicular to the rest of them. There was nothing its unfortunate jockey could do but hold on and hope he bounced off the wall easy and not back down into the thick of oncoming traffic.

But even before he could get to the wall, another car drove hard into his side and bulldozered him toward the cement blockade where the word DAYTONA had been so carefully painted. They hit together hard, with a *whoomp!* that brought the few spectators who had actually sat down right back to their feet to see what was happening. As the first car whacked the wall hard, it boomeranged right back into the thick of the following racers. Everyone was scrambling, looking for an opening, more likely being blinded by white tire smoke that was instantly thicker than any fog. They had to steer more on faith than instinct, relying on luck, hoping they could get through unscathed until they could stand on the binders long enough to slow down. Of course, some plowed right into the rear of others who were quicker on the brakes than they were, and cars were headed off in all directions, sheet metal flying, dust and grass divots being kicked up below the track where some had ended up.

"Caution's out!" Harry Stone called to Rob over the radio. "Looks like it's in the short chute."

Rob checked his mirror and made sure the other two cars saw the flashing yellow lights above the track wall. He could see other cars farther back, ones that had been ahead of whatever had happened. But he didn't slow down one bit until he had crossed the start/finish line and taken the yellow flag.

"Whoa! Watch it now." It was Will Hughes on the radio now. "Back her down. There's debris all over the short chute. It's a junkyard up there, cowboy."

Rob waved his right hand to let the cars immediately behind him know he was off the throttle. He could see they were doing the same, having obviously gotten the same word from their crew chiefs or spotters.

Rob steered carefully through the carnage, weaving his car back and forth through the scattered debris that was strewn all across the accident site, hoping he didn't pick up anything that could damage a tire. There were chunks of plastic fiber and pieces of metal scattered all over the track as if the racing gods had had a tantrum and shredded a few machines.

Meanwhile, with the first hint of the caution flag, the Ensoft crew had jumped up and begun getting ready for a pit stop. Will directed traffic, but there was little need. These boys had practiced the maneuvers for hours and hours already. Now they would get the chance to show how well they had learned their roles as soon as the race officials opened pit road so the cars who wanted to could come in for a stop.

"Four tires and gas," Will ordered over the radio.

Donnie Kline watched carefully as the tires were readied, the correct ones for left and right, front and back, and as the gas cans were lifted up and propped on the pit wall, ready. He held the jack close to his chest, like a football lineman waiting for the quarterback to call the right "hut" so he could spring into action. Kline looked off to his right, toward the entrance to pit road, waiting for his first glimpse of the bright red Ford as Rob led the pack off the banking of the track, ready to turn onto the flat of the pit lane. Finally the flagman who stood at the entrance to the pit lane waved his flag, signaling that the pit lane was now open.

And there was Rob, the car shimmering in the distance in what had already become a hot February afternoon. Donnie quickly surveyed his crew and nodded at each one in turn.

The front and rear tire changers had joined him on the top of the wall as they all waited for the long line of cars to make their way down onto the pit lane. Compared to the rapidity with which they had been touring the track less than a minute before, they now seemed to be easing along at school-zone speed. And sure enough, there were officials timing the cars for speed on pit road.

As he rode toward his pit, Rob watched his tachometer, making sure its needle didn't rise above the RPM level he had set during the warm-up laps. The pace car had led the field down pit road during those laps for that very purpose, so they would know how fast they were allowed to go.

Now, sure he was legal, he looked ahead, trying to pick the Day-Glo Ensoft signboard out of all the others that were waving in the various pit stalls. Then, almost at the end of the long line, there it was. The blue-with-yellow-trim signboard was being held high over the front of Rob's pit stall. It actually came up faster than he had been expecting it to. Rob jumped on the brakes as he cut the wheel sharply, steering into the pit box. The car actually slid a bit past the markings the crew had taped onto the concrete of the pit space as a guide for him. It stopped only a foot short of the yellow line marking the front edge of the team's pit. Another foot or so farther and the crew would have been forced to push the car back inside the box that was marked by the yellow lines. That would have been costly.

When the car was still two stalls away and coming, the crewmen, led by Donnie Kline, leaped over the wall, timing their jump in front of the Ensoft Ford as it slid to a stop. Donnie was ready, shoving the jack beneath the car the instant it shuddered to a halt. He had placed it under the passenger-side door where the precise spot had been clearly marked. Then he gave the jack handle two mighty heaves and the right-side wheels were up and off the ground.

At the same time, the tire changers settled down on their well-padded knees, jamming their identical air-driven lug wrenches onto the nuts on their respective wheels. With the sharp shriek of compressed air whirling in the air guns, the lug nuts were broken loose from their studs, the tires were quickly freed from their wheels, the lug nuts themselves flying everywhere. Then the changers yanked off the hot, worn tires and hoisted the new fresh ones that were being handed in by the tire carriers, placing them onto their studs, all in one smooth, continuous motion. With a quick bang from the air guns, the lug nuts that had already been glued to the tire rims ahead of time were tightened down. Then the tire changers were gone, headed around to the other side of the car to replay the exact same routine again on the left side.

While that activity was going on, the gasman had raised the first can of fuel high in the air, its nozzle inside the filler spout of the race car. Another man stood behind him, holding a smaller can at the tank overflow. He was called the "catch can man," there to catch any spillage in his own container. He had another job, too. When most of the gas had drained from the first can, he grabbed it and held it in place while the gasman turned around to fetch a second full can from the crewman passing it over the wall. The catch can man tossed the empty container back over the wall as the gasman took the second one, pushing it into the filler spout.

From behind the pit wall, Will Hughes handed Rob a drink on the end of a long pole. If chassis adjustments had been warranted, the rear tire carrier would have stuck a ratchet into a hole on the car's right back roof area and rotated it by however many turns Will called for. Or he would have had the front tire carrier remove or add strips of tape on the front end that controlled the airflow over the snout. But not on this stop. The car seemed to be set up perfectly. Another crewman used a brush strapped to another pole to scrape off debris from the front grill of the car while yet another crewman used a third pole to wash and squeegee the car's windshield.

Donnie Kline watched the whole operation, his fingers itching as he clung to the shaft of the jack. He waited impatiently for the gasman to pull the can off the spout, signaling the car was finally full of gas. Fuel mileage often played a vital role in races at Daytona, and it was crucial that they allow every drop of gasoline possible to gurgle into the Ford's tank.

Then Donnie saw the catch can man nod as the fuel began to overflow into the catch can. The front and rear tire changers were just finishing tightening the lugs on the left-side tires. He dropped the jack and jerked it free. Will was chanting, "Go, go, go!" into his radio, but Rob was ahead of them. He jumped on the gas, popping the clutch the instant he felt the car fall from the jack. With a billow of smoke, he was out and away.

And, at sixteen seconds total, it was a great stop.

Rob pulled away, beating the other cars he had been running with out of the pit. In his wake he left the crew, throwing jubilant high-fives to each other. Then, the celebrating quickly over, they got busy, moving the discarded tires to the back of the pits so Will could study the wear pattern on them. A couple of the crew swept up the old lug nuts and other debris from the stop and made sure there were no fluids spilled that might cause a problem when the next stop happened. And that could be in fifty laps or it could come before the green flag waved again. They had to be ready for either.

Rob rolled by the official who was standing at the line that marked the end of pit road. He was holding the green signboard with the word GO painted on one side of it and a bright red STOP on the other. He was showing GO, so Rob Wilder did just that thing. Luckily, their pit stall was close enough to the end line that he did not have to worry about watching his speed. He simply gave it all he could as he accelerated back onto the track, running up through the gears as quickly but as surely as he could. He caught up to the pace car going down the backstretch and settled in behind it, proud of the fast stop which left him still sitting in the front spot.

The television crew was duly impressed, too.

"Can you believe the time on the oh-six car's pit stop? A sixteen-second stop is amazing, even on the Cup side. This kid and the Billy Winton Racing crew have led the pack in under the caution and had a stop quick enough to come right back out, still holding the lead. And that's with all these Winston Cup drivers out there, too. That is unbelievable."

"Well, I can tell you from experience, when you have Will Hughes calling the shots, you know it's going to be a first-class operation all the way around. Will's daddy was a noted short-track racer, so this young man grew up in the sport. And young Hughes himself is known around the garage as the kind of crew chief that takes nothing for granted. Will Hughes is one of the smart young lions in a garage that is filled with smart people. Look at the stop they just turned if you want a prime example."

Rob led the field single file behind the pace car as he rolled along, impatiently waiting to go back to green-flag racing. The slow speed gave him a chance to catch his breath and take stock of his first laps at Daytona.

So far, so good, he thought. Only then did it suddenly dawn on him that he had led every single lap so far. It had seemed almost too easy to him.

The rest of them wouldn't be that easy, would they? Not a chance!

The lights blinked off on top of the pace car as the flagman signaled one more lap to go in the caution period. The sound of the harnessed engines bounced off the grandstands as the long line of cars snaked along in front of the expectant crowd, already pulling for a good start and more daring racing. Everyone was back on his feet now, ready, hungry for more.

As he and the pace car led the parade into turn three, Rob readied himself for the restart. He tightened his grip on the wheel after wriggling his wrists about, getting the circulation going in his forearms once again. He glanced in the mirror and marveled at the long line of powerful racing machines that were poised right on his rear bumper, every one of them deadly determined to seize what he had, the lead in this race. Even now they were easing up closer to each other, taking up what little slack there was between them, ready to surge forward and come after him as they exited turn four for the start.

Funny, Rob thought. I ought to be intimidated, I guess. Maybe afraid one of those yahoos is going to run right over me trying to get to the front.

But he wasn't. Not at all. Instead, he felt a powerful

rush of adrenaline and a broad grin split his face.

No sir, he was exactly where he belonged.

"Get ready to take 'em, cowboy. Green flag is coming this time by. Watch the car directly behind you especially. He's been looking awfully anxious there."

"Ten-four," Rob radioed back. He was trying to focus in on the start, to not do something dumb, but his foot tingled, ready to stomp down hard on the gas pedal and get this thing to flying again.

For his part, Will kept his eyes on the flagman as the man atop the stand studied the long line of cars coming toward him out of the fourth turn. He perused the field carefully, looking for anything amiss, making sure everything in the tight line was queued up perfectly.

Rob concentrated on maintaining an even speed as he strained to see the flagstand and any indication of when the banner might whirl. The pace car dropped off onto the pit lane, leaving Rob Wilder to pace the field.

Then Rob could see the flag ready to wave again. The man's arm was starting an upward motion, and without hesitation, Rob danced hard on the gas pedal. The deep rumble of the motor instantly turned furious, becoming the snarl of an angry bear that had been too long caged but was now freed. Rob could only imagine the rush of fuel and air as the mixture poured in through the intakes, ready to explode with awesome force inside the engine block.

Will's cry of "Go! Go!" over the radio was actually a second late. Rob was already gone.

Good jump, kid, the crew chief thought as he watched the field of brightly colored racers leap away toward the start/finish line.

But he noted, too, that the car behind Rob had a good jump as well. A real good jump. Maybe even better than his young driver. The Chevy pressed that slight advantage and pulled out just as it crossed the line, diving down to the inside of the Ensoft Ford. Then the car that had been lined up behind the Chevy jumped down to the inside as well. That meant the second-place car had himself a drafting partner. Rob didn't. The result was inevitable and Will winced at the rapidity with which it all happened.

Since he was now hung out on his own, the two cars drafted right on by Rob as if he had pulled over to buy a hot dog and soda. Rob was startled with the ease with which the two vehicles flashed by on his inside, putting him into third place before they had finished with the first turn.

Now what had been a clear view out the windshield was filled with the ugly rear ends of the two cars that had whipped him off the start. They had clearly not heard all the praise the television crew had been heaping on the young, blonde driver with the lovely girlfriend. Nor had they conceded this race to the brash upstart who jockeyed the mount out of Billy Winton's stable.

To make matters even worse, a third car was now locked door handle to door handle with Rob as the pack swept into the first turn. He knew his best move would be to slide down into line behind the first two cars and hold on until he could pass them back. But he could see the other car out of the corner of his eye and it was blocking his way. To further confirm his fix, Rob could hear Harry Stone's voice on the radio from the spotter's stand and he was chanting over and over, "Inside. Inside. Inside." That meant that someone was below him on the track and there was no way he could slip into line, no matter how desperately he wanted to.

By the time they had finished the run down the back straight, the cars were still cruising right on by Rob, leaving him fighting to hang on to sixth place. Finally someone moved up behind him, likely assuming if Rob had had the muscle to lead most of the race so far, he would be a decent drafting partner. Sure enough, the car's presence off his back bumper gave him a push of air, and that at least stopped his drop backward. In the space of less than a lap, the nature of the draft at Daytona had taken him from the top of the heap to the middle of the pack that was fighting for third through fifteenth place.

Rob gritted his teeth and tightened his grip on the steering wheel. He knew he had to shake off the disappointment he felt. At these speeds he didn't have the luxury of stewing over his miscues. He still had to be patient, to work his way back up the same way the other two drivers had. The ones who had dusted him off the start.

The first dozen or so cars began to break away from the rest of the competitors, opening up a distance between them equal to twenty or so car lengths. Will was standing on the pit wall watching the four cars in front of Rob. Now they were threatening to open up a gap on the bunch of eight where Rob was now running. And especially if they kept trying to pass each other and ended up dueling side by side.

"He needs to pull down in line and quit racing the thirty-two car or that front group is gonna get away from them," Billy radioed Will from his spot in the back of the pits. He had been sitting, clocking the laps and watching the television.

Will wanted Rob to learn some of the nuances of drafting out there, but he also didn't want the kid to fall too far behind in the process. Before long he would be stuck back there, mired deeply in the pack, racing with some of the slower cars while the contenders drove off and left him. And besides that, back there was where trouble usually happened at tracks like this. Accidents like those were usually violent and massive, too, and didn't care one bit if they caught up in their vortex a new media favorite like Rocket Rob Wilder. He would be just as crunched and just as out of the race as any of the also-rans.

"Try to get back in line if you can. We can race for position later on," Will advised his driver.

Racing through turns one and two, Rob drifted high in the banking, trying to get momentum built up to take a run on the car he was racing with. The extra speed he gained from the high line allowed him to shove the car out in front enough so he could slip down in front of the car on his inside.

"Clear!" the spotter called.

"Good job, good job. Now let's work on those cats in front of you," Will said, waiting for the front pack to come roaring back around past his position.

"Ten-four. I learned a lesson there, Will," Rob said, then sucked in a lungful of air. With the car safely back in line now, he actually had a chance to take stock of where he was in relation to the leaders, who was in front of him, who trailed him. And he could also breathe normally again for a moment.

"Nothing wrong with that move, young 'un," came the drawl of Jodell Lee. "You ain't hurt."

Rob appreciated the kind words, but he wasn't so sure. He only knew he wasn't leading anymore.

Billy and Will were already on the radio, discussing strategy for the next pit stop when it came. Despite the restart, they were both pleased with how their driver was handling the terrific speeds they were turning out there as well as the intricacies of the draft.

The laps began to wind off quickly as they stayed under the green flag. This was a field full of Winston Cup regulars and a bunch of experienced Grand National veterans. Most of them obviously knew their way around this long strip of pavement. Rob and a few of the other young guns were the only ones still going to school out there, and they appeared, to a man, to have done their homework well.

Still, Rob continued to learn on every lap. The long run of green-flag racing, with his and the other cars running so close to each other, had already shown him plenty he didn't know but had suspected about the drafting process. He was surprised that so much of it seemed to come naturally to him, as if he'd almost been born with the ability to figure out what the result would be of each move he might try. Or as if there were someone sitting in the car with him, silently giving him the nod when it came time to do a particular maneuver. He had gotten that feeling before, and it would have been eerie if it had not felt so natural to him. Even when the wheel seemed to move of its own accord, as if it were some ghost giving it a nudge instead of his own gloved hands.

Now he was studying the line of the Winston Cup driver who ran along in front of him for a bunch of circuits. He watched closely how the veteran dealt with the car as it bounced around in the rough air that spilled off the other cars in the draft and those slower ones they were working their way around. Finally the Cup driver pushed down to the inside, trying to make a pass on the car that had been scooting along in front of him for the last five laps or so.

Rob almost sensed the move coming before the driver pulled out of line. And he didn't hesitate at all. He put the tires of his own car directly in the other driver's tire tracks and followed him up the track the width of one car.

The two of them, now even more tightly joined by

their aerodynamics, raced the fourth-place car, a blue Pontiac, for position. Rob held his line as they pushed past on the outside. The car that had been trailing behind Rob followed the two of them also. That left the fourth-place racer all by himself with no one to give him a push or pull.

But as soon as he was clear, the Cup driver sidled right back down, in front of the passed car. That left Rob still only a half car length ahead of the driver they had been trying to make the pass on. There was not enough room to slide down and complete the move, and he no longer had the Cup driver's race car to pull him past. He tried to push even harder on the gas pedal, struggling to find some smidgen of ooomph.

There must have been something there, waiting for his call. Suddenly he shot beyond the blue Pontiac.

"Clear! Clear inside!" Harry cried.

Rob nudged the wheel and moved over, tucking in once again behind the Cup driver.

So that's how it's done, he thought. Another lesson learned. But that had certainly been a lot of work for a single position. There had been another factor, though. And something Will had radioed to him a few laps before now suddenly made more sense to him.

"If you get out of line, try to get back in as soon as you can," he had counseled. "Even if you have to drop a few spots. Either make the pass or cut your losses or you'll be marking the end of the field before you can say 'Jack Robinson.'"

Rob hunkered down, content to maintain his place in line, still near the front, within sight of the leaders. He had to admit to himself that the level of concentration was beginning to tell on him. At these speeds and in such close quarters, things could happen before a fellow could blink. Sometimes he was afraid to blink, fearful he might miss something. There was no chance to relax at all so long as they ran under green, not even an opportunity to take a deep breath. Even if the stifling air inside the cockpit of his racer had been breathable.

Christy Fagan watched in amazement as the laps played out. Time and again the cars zoomed by where she sat, the drivers keeping them in such close formation that they seemed to be touching each other. She winced as she watched the car that was running behind Rob move up close and appear to give him a slight tap in the rear. It was puzzling to her, though, why they stayed in such long, trainlike lines. Why didn't they just pass each other and try to take the lead? She finally leaned over and yelled the question to Michelle, who actually seemed to know something about what was going on out there.

Michelle tried to explain it to her as best she could over the racket, but it didn't seem to make sense. Christy found the premise that two cars racing together are faster than one car by itself a difficult concept to fathom. But as she watched the cars on the track, she could see one example after another of how it actually worked.

The laps clicked off, taking them closer to the three-hundred-mile distance they would cover this day. Christy really enjoyed watching the wild pit stops, the way the crew scurried in such beautiful synchronicity, like a crew of robots. And they must have been doing a good job, because they always pounded each other on the back and high-fived each other once Rob had screeched away and was back on the track.

Will was pleased, too. The stops under the green flag went as well as the one during the caution period had. They were still running with the lead pack, the car was handling well, and though clearly tired, their driver was holding up well and having fun out there. He was grinning broadly behind the visor of his driver's helmet during the last stop.

Now most of the cars were on their last set of tires, ready for the final run to the "checkers." The field was strung out all around the giant track, with each pack racing for position if not for the win itself. There was still a seven-car draft up front leading the race, followed a couple of seconds back by a larger bunch of fifteen or so cars. It was clear that the winner would likely come from the lead draft, but it was still possible for some of the next fifteen to make a run, join the leaders, and still move to the front if the front-runners began to waltz side by side with one another.

That was what made the race so exciting for fans, crew, and drivers alike. As many as twenty-two cars still had a legitimate shot at the victory, and the race was almost finished.

Rob still sat in the sixth position, glad to be among those in the lead mob, and for the moment, was still content to ride around and learn and build his own confidence. Confidence in himself as well as his car. There was very little shuffling about going on among the lead cars now. The drivers knew they needed to stay in line, racing single file, putting as much distance as possible on the larger group that was trailing them.

As the miles spun out, Rob had begun to realize that the five cars that ran in front of him were actually holding him back. He was as convinced as ever that he had a better engine than they did. But he kept hearing the same word inside his head, repeated in the voices of Will Hughes, Billy Winton, and Jodell Lee: "Patience."

He had to wait for his opportunity to pull out and attempt to pass on his own, to drive to the front, to make sure he was the first to the flag. Somehow he was confident he would recognize it when it came.

"Twenty to go," came the voice of the spotter in the earpiece.

"Ten-four," he answered then, as he drove down the back straightaway once again. He dared to hold the mike button down long enough to say more. "When can I give this thing its head and make a run for the finish? She's perfect. These guys in front of me are holding me back."

It was Will who answered his question. "Keep her on the leash a few more laps," he said patiently. He liked the fact that his driver wanted to take the point, that he was tired of breathing the exhaust of the cars in front of him. He knew the kid had a fire burning inside his belly. He needed to keep it quelled for the moment, though.

"I'm ready now," Rob shot back as he set the car up for the run through the next high-banked turn.

"In a few more laps. Be planning your moves. I'll let you know when."

If the car was as good as Will suspected, it was still a bit early to show their hand. The Cup drivers in the front group had experience on their side. They could more than negate any speed advantage the Ensoft Ford might have by taking advantage of the inexperience of the young driver. He would probably only have one shot at getting to the front and that would be it. Odds were none of the veterans were going to pull out and follow young Rob either. More than likely, any move Rob made would have to be accomplished on his own, relying on the power of the car instead of the cooperation of the others. After all, they had no reason to respect the kid's abilities or the car's capabilities. They would naturally tend to hook up with one another, with the guys they had raced with for years.

The spotter called fifteen laps to go.

Rob kept his eyes on the bumper of the car in front

of him. When was Will going to let him go? He knew
with dead certainty that he could push his way to the
front and stay there. He knew there was still enough
reserve power left in the motor to propel him to the
point.

"Come on, Will, let me go!"

He whispered the words, but he could still hear Will's
patience speech before the race. He knew the crew chief
was looking at the big picture. Even if they didn't win
the race outright, they would still get a good finish. A
good finish for the team. For the sponsor. For the confidence of their teenaged driver. But if Rob stuck his
nose out too soon and got passed by every yahoo in a
jalopy, their first run at Daytona would be a disaster.

Intellectually, Rob understood. Emotionally, he wanted
to hop to the outside and leave the rest of them to decide
second place.

Billy Winton still sat leaned back comfortably in the
director's chair, watching with Christy and Michelle as
the race played out on the television monitor. He had
even seen their own images thrown up on the screen as
the camera crew looked for reaction shots from the team
owner, from the beautiful girlfriend of the rookie driver.
And one of the shots had captured a mile-wide grin on
Billy's face. They had no way of knowing that it was in
reaction to his driver's comments on the radio. The kid's
eagerness to dispense with this patience stuff and move
on to the front was heartening. But so also was the
youngster's willingness, reluctant as it might be, to heed
the advice of his crew chief and bide his time.

As Billy watched the screen, he could see the kid begin
to move the car around a bit as he followed the racer
directly in front of him, getting a feel for the air the car
was kicking back. No one had told Rob how to do what
he was doing. He had figured it out on his own. First

he'd pull out a half-car width to the high side. Then, in the next corner, he would do the same to the inside. Each time he was testing how his car reacted as he tried the different lines around the track.

Billy grinned again. He had hired drivers with plenty of experience before to pilot his cars, drivers with actual wins under their belts, but he had seen none of them do the job any better than this raw rookie was doing right now.

Billy could feel his own confidence building as well, despite his best efforts to keep it tamed. He wasn't certain if the kid had the drafting experience to actually outrace the veteran drivers he would have to beat to the checkered flag.

But it was clear the desire to mix it up with them was there.

The car should have enough left in it to get the job done.

Only the experience was lacking. And Billy Winton was nowhere near ready to discount the kid's chances yet.

Jodell Lee punched his microphone button. "That's it, kid, check 'em out. You got to know where you can make your move on them cats," he said.

The young driver didn't acknowledge except by doing exactly what Lee had suggested.

"Y'all don't go anywhere. It looks like we're going to have us one wild shoot-out for a finish," the television commentator was saying. But even he knew he didn't need to hype the next few minutes of this particular race. The audience could see for themselves that it was going to be entertaining.

" 'Wild finish' may be an understatement," the announcer said. "The drivers in this seven-car breakaway have shown remarkable patience, staying in line so they can pull away from the second bunch back there. Now that they have done that, you have to begin to wonder how much longer that patience can last. The wild card is our rookie, our pole sitter, Rocket Rob Wilder. He's never been in the middle of anything like this before on those small tracks back in Alabama. Nobody knows how he'll react when they begin to dice it up in the next few laps. Things could get very interesting in a hurry."

"You're right about Wilder. For those of you who have just joined us, this young driver dominated the early going, leading all the way till just after the first caution. You can't do that at a place like this, running against all these veteran drivers, unless you truly have a strong car."

"Well, he proved that in qualifying and in the early going here and he's been near the front all day. I don't know about you, but I'm gonna be on the edge of my seat until this thing plays out," the commentator said with obvious sincerity.

The announcer laughed. "I think the fans here at Daytona agree with you. I don't think anyone is sitting down right now in those seats they paid for!"

An opportune camera shot confirmed it. The crowd was on its feet, cheering the lead pack past the flag stand one more time, waving caps, banners, and recently shed T-shirts as they passed.

Rob was still moving around on the track as much as he could while keeping the car in front of him just a few feet off the end of his hood. He looked high, then low, and then settled back in line. But he had noticed one thing in all his darting around. The rear of the car in front of him seemed to wiggle a bit every time Rob shoved the nose of his own Ford up close to its rear bumper and then swung to either side.

The next time Rob zipped by the start/finish line,

there were only ten laps to go. He had not improved his position at all, still sitting in sixth place in the seven-car conga line.

Sixth would be a phenomenal finish for this team. And it would be a huge disappointment to Rob Wilder.

What was Will waiting on?

Rob was certain that he could take these guys. He actually considered going ahead and making the move on his own. If it worked, no one would care. If it didn't, he'd just say he saw an opening and tried to take it.

But every time he was on the verge of stepping out, he would hear Will's words. See the look in Billy's eyes. Remember the caution expressed by one of the great hard chargers of all time, Jodell Lee. Even hear that little voice that often accompanied him in the racer's cockpit, telling him the best moves to make. And he would also agree in his heart of hearts that indeed, it was not the right time just yet.

The red Ford rocketed over the dips in the pavement in turns one and two. The seven race cars ran hard, still in single file, as if in tow. As they hit the backstretch, the lead car swayed back and forth across the breadth of the track, trying to break the draft that was pulling the train of cars behind him. With the restrictor plates, such an effort was a near futile gesture, but it had worked in the days before the carburetors had been doctored. Many of the veterans didn't like to give up any of the old tricks, whether they still worked or not.

Rob held his ground, growing ever more restless. Laps were running out. Was Will going to wait until the whole thing was over? Maybe he'd let him break loose on the cool-down lap!

"It's time! Let's go," he said to the dash of the car, the windshield, the shimmying steering wheel.

Meanwhile, down on pit road, Will Hughes watched

the laps count off on the big scoring pylon in the infield. Billy had stepped over and joined him and now stood beside him on the pit wall as the cars circled with only ten laps to go. Both men seemed supremely confident, in contrast to the worried looks on the faces of many of the crew chiefs up and down the pit lane. Young or not, experienced or neophyte, whatever the shortcomings of their driver, it didn't matter. They knew Rob Wilder had what it took to get the job done.

They both knew Rob had their car right where they had hoped it would be. Everything they had done since the green flag fell to start the contest had been designed to have them in this precise position at this point. They also knew they likely had one of the strongest cars on the track and were at least in a position to race for the win.

"Reckon we ought to show these cats what we got?" Will asked, a conspiratorial grin on his face.

Billy Winton grinned right back and nodded. Will asked the same question to the headset microphone at his lips.

"Done!" came the relieved reply from their driver.

Rob almost jumped out of his harness. Then he swallowed hard and tried to slow down his heartbeat again.

You got the call, big boy, he thought. Now what are you going to do?

The line of cars stormed off turn four and down onto the short chute leading to the start/finish line. Rob held the car high through the turn, pushing into the outside line as he tailed the racer in front of him. As they approached the wide-mouthed entrance to the pit lane, Rob sucked in a deep draft of air and jerked the car to the inside. His foot stayed hammered to the firewall and he felt the car surge ahead underneath him, as if the Ford, too, were excited about the chance to finally soar.

The drivers called it a "slingshot move," and Rob understood perfectly where the name came from as his racer shot ahead of the car he had been tailing so patiently for so long.

The kid could only imagine the look on the other driver's face as he jumped ahead of him and actually put a fender up next to the yellow Chevrolet that had been running in fourth place. Quickly, carefully, he took a look in his mirror to see if the car behind him had followed his move.

Nope. That driver had decided to take Rob's position, to hold his line and try to draft up on the car he had just passed.

The leaders cut across the tri-oval and drilled on toward turn one. The crowd cheered wildly, clearly pleased that someone had finally broken loose from the lead pack and was willing to force the issue. The more knowledgeable among them knew it was inevitable. They were glad it had finally happened. Now things would get real interesting! They had not paid their money to see freight-train racing. And they were doubly excited when they noticed that the one who was stepping out was the hot young rookie in the brilliant red Ford.

What was the kid's name again? Some scrambled for their programs.

Rob Wilder!

What had the TV guys called him? Rocket Rob? Now they knew why!

Rob stayed to the inside, hoping he could steer right on by and take fourth place, but he was also debating whether he should try to ease back in behind the Chevrolet and settle for fifth for the time being.

He quickly made his decision when he heard Harry's voice on the radio yelling, "Clear!"

Rob immediately moved back up into line behind the

fourth-place Chevy, accepting fifth until he could do better.

In the television booth, the announcers obviously approved of the move.

". . . an awfully gutsy move for the young kid."

"And a smart one, too. An inexperienced driver may have tried to get more and gotten shuffled back to who knows where. I don't know. I think maybe they have been holding this kid back some. Did you see the power the Ensoft car showed on that pass? An easy move and without any help from a drafting partner?"

"That was one of the first clean single-car passes we've seen at the front today."

Jodell Lee agreed with the television voices. "Smart move, kid. Smart move," he praised.

Rob took several deep breaths as he calculated his next move. His first option would be to make another dive to the inside, re-creating the move he had just made as he tried to pick off the yellow Chevy.

The cars behind him jumped his claim first, though.

Suddenly the two of them whipped down to the inside of Rob, trying to draft on past as the cars were about to enter the third turn. Rob decided he would navigate another course for the front. He rode the car deeply into the corner in an attempt to go to the outside of the fourth-place Chevy. Meanwhile, the lead car of the two that were drafting on the inside got a fender up on the yellow race car's lower side.

Rob took the outside line then, pushing the car deep into the corner. Now there were three cars, side by side, rolling into the turn. Rob powered up the banking, miraculously gaining ground on the Chevy as he rode along outside of him.

"Look at 'em! They're running three wide going into the fourth turn. Looks like these boys have decided to mix things up a bit here all of a sudden. Nobody wants to get left behind!"

"Look at my man, Rocket Rob Wilder, trying to get it done on the outside. That car is flying! I think any of these front seven cars has a real shot at winning."

"Hang with it, son!" Jodell Lee barked.

Rob was using the banking to his advantage, even though, until this very day, he had never raced on such towering turns. Something told him he was where he needed to be.

Somehow he managed to pull in front of the fourth-place car. The Chevy was caught, racing in tandem with the other two cars that were trying to work their way past on the inside.

Rob steered back into line, but this time in front of the yellow Chevrolet, then immediately set his sights on the front three cars. Over the next lap, he tested how the different lines affected him and the third-place car running directly ahead of him. He learned nothing new. He now had a good feel for every inch of this grand old track.

Now he also had to assume that he would have no drafting help when he attempted the next pass, but he thought he knew a way to get it done. He drove in tight on the back bumper of the green and white Ford running in front of him. He watched for the telltale wiggle of the car's rear end when he suddenly shoved a wall of air up against him.

He saw exactly the effect he expected.

"Easy . . . easy now," Jodell advised, watching Rob push the car around in front of him.

"Five laps," Harry said.

"Five to go, cowboy," Will repeated.

Rob didn't answer. He tightened his grip and gritted his teeth before giving the steering wheel enough of a twitch to swing down to the inside of the third-place car just as they came off turn two. As expected, the other Ford swerved down sharply, blocking the inside line as effectively as if the car had been thirty feet wide.

Rob countered, swinging up and to the outside. The driver ahead moved right along with him as Rob anticipated, blocking his move in that direction as well. Even though he completely expected it, the move was so abrupt that Rob almost crashed into the back end of the white and green car.

"Son of a gun!" Rob spat, using about the strongest language in his vocabulary as he yanked the wheel to keep his car from drop-kicking the other Ford all the way up into the cheering throng who were showing their approval for what they were seeing out there on the track.

"Watch him! Easy!" Jodell said. "You got him where you want him."

Rob held his ground as he followed the Ford through turn three and four, then pulled down to the inside as the cars hit the short chute, ready to try to squeeze by once again. But then the fifth-place car was now back on Rob's radar as it, too, slid down the track, moving right up on Rob's bumper. That let the two of them draft right on by the green and white Ford before its driver even had time to try the block again. They easily laid claim to the third and fourth positions.

Now who was next?

There was no mistaking who was navigating the cars that ran in first and second spots. They were Winston Cup veterans, interloping for the day in the Grand National race. They were both household names among race fans, even the most casual ones. And with better than a dozen Winston Cup and Grand National victories between them, Rob knew it would not be easy to take their spots away.

But he was certainly game to try.

The cars racing along behind Rob had not given up either. They were already pressuring him from behind, as determined to claim this win as he was. Rob was forced to watch his mirror, keeping his eye on the group of cars that dashed and darted about back there. He did not need to get caught up racing with them, though. He needed to be pushing the two cars in front of him for the lead. But he knew, too, that with one tiny slipup, he could be fighting to hold on to seventh place instead of dueling with the Cup hotshots for the lead.

Or he could get sideways and ruin the day for a whole bunch of folks, just like a rookie was expected to do.

"Three laps to go," Will called.

Rob tested the high side going into turn one. His car seemed to like the outside line just fine. The two drivers in front, however, drifted down close to the white line at the bottom of the track. That line indicated where the steeply banked track surface ended and the flat apron running round the track began. Getting too low could be disastrous, but they were likely going low in hopes of shucking Rob, dropping him from their draft. But the Ford seemed to have plenty enough power in its motor so that Rob was able to hold the position and stay high. And before the other two noticed, he was threatening to pull even with them as the cars raced off the second corner. As they swung out of the turn, the front two cars moved up higher on the track, taking a line right out against the wall, doing their best to block him off.

Rob smiled as he watched their move. It was exactly what he would have done if he had been leading. He continued to push them to the outside while taking a quick glance at the mirror to check on the cars behind them. They had fallen a few car lengths off his back bumper now. He and the other two cars were running flat out, racing for all they were worth, and the others had, at least so far, been unable to keep up.

Billy Winton was so intent on watching the sparring out there on the track that he didn't notice someone standing next to him until he felt a tap on his shoulder. It was Jodell Lee. Billy lifted the radio headset off his ear to hear what Jodell was trying to say.

"Did you just see that move the kid tried to put on them coming off turn two? He's gonna smoke those two guys in front of him," Jodell yelled as a couple of stragglers in the field sputtered past.

"Yeah, I saw it. Just like I've seen it a hundred times before."

"He does drive like a veteran, don't he?" Jodell agreed as he watched the three cars going through turn three on the television.

"No, not a veteran. He drives just like you did thirty years ago."

"The kid is good . . ." Lee said with a grin, slipping the headphones back over his ears.

Will stood on the top of the pit box and craned his neck trying to catch a glimpse of the cars as they came off the fourth turn.

"Two to go this time by," he radioed Rob as soon as he caught sight of his bright red car coming his way.

There was no answer back on the radio. Rob focused in on the task at hand. He took another quick peek to the outside of the lead cars and noted with satisfaction that the second-place car moved over to block him. Rob figured that the strategy of the number-two car would be to pull out to make his move when Rob did, letting Rob push him past the leader and into first place. The driver would further assume that Rob was only an impatient young driver, unfamiliar with the intricacies of drafting, and would either happily settle for second or try for more and get drop-kicked.

Rob Wilder might be a rookie, all right, but he had just spent the last few hours learning all he could about the maneuvers that would work on this big old track. And he had practiced most of them already a dozen times each.

Christy and Michelle huddled together watching the monitor, cheering each time he passed another car. Now there he was, running in third place, the car shining beautifully on the screen as the camera followed it around the track. Neither of them noticed the cameraman as he slipped up beside and got a close-up of Christy, holding her crossed fingers to her chest as she watched Rob attempt his next move.

"Are we going to win?" Christy asked as the line of cars passed in front of their position, racing off through the tri-oval.

"I don't know. He's only got a couple of laps to get by them. It'll be close. Real close."

The television crew in the booth was having trouble tempering their excitement as well. They knew it could not have been a better race for their audience if they had scripted the finish beforehand.

"Looks like young Rob Wilder's pretty girlfriend has those fingers crossed for luck."

"Well, it seems to be working so far. The young driver has put on an impressive show here today. To be fair, though, so has this entire lead pack."

"I think it's amazing that with two laps to go, you could throw a blanket over the front seven cars."

"And any one of those lead-pack cars still has an opportunity to win this thing."

"In a lap and a half, we'll know."

Rob charged hard down into turn one, all the time looking down to the inside once more. He had a good run on the leaders and he debated going on and pushing for the lead right then and there. But the car behind him showed no sign that he would be willing to follow him if he tried to make the move now.

Rob drifted back up to within three feet of the back bumper of the car in front of him, trying to loosen up the air coming over the Chevrolet's spoiler. The car wiggled, but the driver held on as the trio hurtled through the corner.

The second-place car took another look to the low side of the leader as they came out of turn two.

No dice. He was promptly blocked.

Then the driver shifted high, to the outside, trying to pass that way, but the leader anticipated that move, too, and he effectively cut him off. That leader was going to be tough to get around.

Rob checked the car behind him in his mirror one more time and watched the shuffling by the leaders in front of him. He studied all their moves as he carefully plotted his own. He ran through his head all the strategies Jodell Lee had taught him.

Would he have what it took? Next time by, he would find out.

Going into turn three, the cars behind Rob finally lost their own patience and decided they needed to get on closer to the front if they had any chance. That meant they were soon racing side by side for position while the cars farther on back, the sixth- and seventh-place racers, were trying to make moves of their own toward the leaders. As usual, the front three were able to put a few extra car lengths on them as they lost the blessing of their own draft.

That took some of the pressure off Rob. Now he could

concentrate on what was ahead of him for a bit without having to worry about someone coming up from behind and making it a four- or five-car bid for the lead.

Now the three leaders were lined up nose to tail, a sled-dog team yoked together at nearly two hundred miles per hour. Ten car lengths back, the other four cars still raced among themselves, still side by side. The fans in the stands were all on their feet, trying to make as much noise as the cars themselves, as the leaders roared down toward the white flag that was already waving above the start/finish line. Their racket was no match, though. The awesome thunder of the racing engines drowned out the crowd's cheers.

The whole crew had now joined Will and Billy on the pit wall. Their race work was done now. They had completed their part of the team effort. Now they wanted to see if they had helped a car that would finish first or fifteenth.

Will's face was expressionless. He knew they had the car, the driver, everything they needed to get the job done. Now they needed only one thing else. Luck. Pure racing luck.

"Pick your spot, young 'un," Jodell whispered to himself.

Michelle and Christy stayed near the monitor, watching the much better view the television coverage offered them. Christy still had her fingers crossed so tightly they were turning blue, but she didn't dare uncross them until the race was over. She was convinced that would spoil any luck they might have conjured up over the last hundred laps or so.

The three cars moved as one as they went into turn one for the last time.

The leader dove as low on the track as he could, keeping the car down there as he tried to protect the inside line. The other two stayed right behind him as they raced through the center of the corner.

Rob allowed his car to drift up in turn two as he waited for his chance, for his spot.

The second-place car suddenly darted out of line, seeing the slightest crack in the leader's defense, pulling down to the inside as the cars exited the corner. The leader saw him coming, though, and cut down sharply, trying to block him off. Rob followed the car ahead of him, the challenger, giving the Chevy a push with his draft.

Just then, the two cars in front of him bumped slightly, making contact between their front and rear fenders. But though they wobbled ominously, neither driver gave any quarter at all. They held their line and maintained their speed, neither driver willing to surrender an inch of track to the other.

The leader then dropped his Ford all the way down to where the infield grass grew up against the concrete, all in a blocking maneuver, trying to keep his challengers behind him as the three cars raced down the long back straightaway.

The three of them likely all thought of nothing but being first to the flag. And of making sure they made the right moves for that to happen. Rob stayed honed in on the bumpers of the cars he was chasing into the third corner.

Time for one last shot at the win.

Which line would they take?

Who would go where?

He would have only one guess and it had to be right. They were already into turn four, a three-stage rocket ship taking full-bore aim on the prize that awaited them at the end of the tri-oval.

The second-place Chevy darted down to the inside as

the cars came up and off the corner. The leader held
his own Ford down one more time, figuring a successful
block here would likely win the race. Rob faked a move
that seemed to say he was satisfied with maintaining the
draft, settling for third place as he drafted along behind
the Chevy and allowing the Cup hoss to cross the line
first.

"Come on, baby!" he said out loud to Joe Banker's
motor out there in front of him, hoping it would have
the power left to accomplish what he wanted to do here.
"Come on!"

"You got the motor, son. Use it," Jodell whispered
softly to himself.

And then Rob pulled out high, as if he had actually
heard the old driver's words. No way was he willing to
settle for anything less if he had any chance at all to take
the race.

The Ford and Chevy seemed to have forgotten about
Rob and the red Ensoft Ford as they struggled between
themselves for position. The Chevrolet got a fender up
alongside the leader, stacking the two cars up. Rob used
their air to slingshot boldly to the outside.

Lord, what a view! Nothing between his windshield
and the flag stand but a stretch of beautiful, clear track.

And what was that? The checkered flag?

Yes! Already out and ready to wave!

The two cars on the inside touched ever so slightly
once again, the contact signaled by a puff of tire smoke.
Rob ignored them and held his foot flat to the floor,
trying to goose out the very last particle of speed that
he could tickle from the mighty engine that had run so
smoothly all afternoon.

On to the short chute, he pulled even, making the trio
three wide as they approached the line. It was so close
now Rob thought he could see the flag held tightly by

the flagman, ready to checker them home where only one of them would be the winner.

Then Rob felt as if his heart were about to burst, as if his own pulse were pounding as wildly as the pistons in the motor. He could tell that he had actually managed to put a fender ahead of the other two cars.

He was leading! Leading by only a couple of inches, maybe, but he was leading!

"Don't back down! Don't back down!" Jodell yelled, if only for his own benefit, keeping his finger off the radio trigger.

Rob could feel the flush of victory already as they closed in on the finish line in a rumbling jumble.

The checkerboard flag was waving already.

Waving for him!

The Chevy was almost off the track below them, riding on the flat surface at the apron.

The other Ford was in the middle, the meat in the sandwich, and its tail squirmed sickeningly in the wild turbulence kicked up by the other two cars.

Rob could feel his own car losing its grip too as the convoluted air spilling over the spoiler wasn't enough to hold the rear end solidly to the track's surface. He prayed he could hang on another second. Another second until he got to the line a bumper's thickness ahead of the other two.

That was all he needed. An inch was as good as a mile.

"Don't lose her, kid!"

Jodell Lee could see the car's tail wagging all the way to where he stood in the pits. He held his breath.

The basic rules of geometry, the time-tested laws of physics, both took control then. The Chevy, running on the inside of the other two cars, had a slightly shorter distance to cover to the line.

The car in the center was contemptuously shoved backward by the tornado off the two other surging cars that raced along on either side of it.

Rob held on, his foot rammed to the firewall, his hands gripping the wheels so hard they had gone numb a lap ago, his heart threatening to stop as he approached the line in a red blur.

Then they were crossing the stripe painted across the track, and the waving flag was no longer out there ahead of them.

It was in his mirror.

The race was done.

FIRST LOSER

Rob Wilder had no idea if he had won the race. Neither did the Chevy's driver. The other Ford had certainly not won. He dropped back while Rob and the other driver drove on. The two of them still ran side by side and shrugged at each other when they looked across the few feet between them. But neither raised a victorious arm outside the window yet. Neither of them acknowledged the standing ovation of appreciation the thousands of out-of-breath fans were giving them.

They simply didn't know who the victor had been.

Rob waited for word from Will or Harry on the radio. It finally came from Will.

"Great job, cowboy. We just started breathing again down here." But had they won? That was the question. Will held down the button still, the transmission not ended so Rob could ask him. "That's the way to get an introduction to this place." Then there was an ominous pause, the circuit still open. Will cleared his throat before he spoke again. "Bring her on around to the gas pump."

Rob's heart sank.

A trip to the gas pump was not a trip to victory lane.

The Chevy that had beaten him by inches slowed down along the backstretch, allowing Rob to pull over closer. He waved at the kid and gave him a thumbs-up, an acknowledgement that the youngster had run a good, clean race. Rob waved back and drove on.

Clean or not, good race or not, the Chevy was headed for victory lane and a celebration reserved for the one who won the race. Rob, though, was driving back to the garage.

Second! What was it Jodell called second place? The first loser?

". . . one of the best races I've seen in years," the announcer was saying. "You know, if this had been Talladega, with its finish line past the tri-oval down toward turn one, I think the kid would have had enough momentum to take the win. Young Wilder has got to be pleased with the run he made today, though."

The old driver doing the commentary suspected that might not exactly be the case. "I'm sure he's feeling mixed emotions at the moment. To make such a daring move, to actually grab the lead by a few feet, and then to get nipped at the line has got to be tough to swallow for a true competitor like this. But they did most of what they came down here to do. They got a good finish. They showed the racing world they are a force to be reckoned with on the Grand National circuit this year. And look out, Winston Cup, in a year or so! Wilder and Billy Winton and Will Hughes and the rest of the Ensoft crew has to be happy about that much anyway." The old driver paused for a beat, then went on. "But I'll bet you a dollar to a doughnut that kid's hurtin' right now."

Sure enough, down in the Winton pits, it appeared from all the jubilation that they might actually have won the race. Donnie Kline was high-fiving every human he could reach and even gave a few to the light pole behind the pit wall. Billy Winton had a smile on his face as wide as the track as it came out of turn two.

Jodell Lee carried a smug look of satisfaction himself, but he, too, suspected the kid would not be quite so happy as the rest of them were. He knew how it felt to have come so close and still not be able to close the deal.

Michelle and Christy jumped up and down hugging most everyone. Crew members from other teams were standing in line to get their hugs, too, but the girls didn't seem to mind.

And talk about a way to make the sponsor happy! Michelle could only begin to imagine the amount of coverage that wild finish would garner on sports shows that night and the Sunday morning papers the next day.

Rob pulled the car down onto the entrance to pit road and got into line behind the others who were being checked by the officials as they came in off the track. They measured the angle of his rear spoiler, but one of the officials held him up and walked around to the driver's-side window.

Uh-oh, Rob thought. Don't let us be out of tolerance back there. Don't let them take the second place away from us, too.

But the young official was smiling. "I just wanted to tell you what a great race you ran, Rob," he said. "That was something else to see!"

Then he waved him on.

He steered the car over next to the gas pumps and killed the engine, yanking off his driving gloves and helmet and tossing them into the floorboard. He was still rerunning that last lap over and over in his mind, won-

dering what he should have done differently. He un-
hooked the steering wheel and jammed it up onto the
dash. He was not happy with himself and he showed it
as he struggled with all the wires and hoses he was
hooked to, jerking them loose and tossing them aside.

"Good run today, Robbie." It was Will Hughes, un-
fastening the window net and leaning in to hand him a
soda and help him get free of all his tethers. The young
driver drank the whole thing in one big gulp. "We
showed 'em we came to race, didn't we?"

Rob caught his breath from the pop and tossed the
empty plastic bottle out the other window.

"Yeah, but we lost, Will."

"Hey!" Will shot back sharply. "Don't be so hard on
yourself. We can't win them all. Nobody ever did. Not
Fireball or Richard Petty or any of them. We did what
we needed to do and we have made our sponsors feel
very good about the big bucks they're spending on us."

"It hurts to be so close, though. Man! Another few
feet and I would have taken him!"

"We'll win our share of close ones. Now, get over it
and get a smile on your face for when the network people come around looking for an interview. Heck, we finished second at Daytona our first time out. We owe
ourselves a little celebratin'!"

Rob started to say more, but he noticed someone
standing behind Will.

A smile broke over his face as he reached up to grab
the roof railing to pull his tired body out of the steaming
cockpit of his racer. He unzipped the thick fireproof
driving suit to let in some cooling air, then he eased
down beside his racer, a sudden wave of fatigue washing
over him.

"Hi!"

It was the sweetest sound he had ever heard. When

he looked up, those beautiful blue eyes met his, her dazzling smile seemed to brighten up the whole place, and he suddenly didn't feel so bad about his first adventure at Daytona. He hoped she hadn't heard his childish carryings-on in the car just now.

"So what did you think of your first stock car race?" he asked her when he finally found his voice.

"It was wonderful! Wild but wonderful. Oh, and noisy and so fast I couldn't keep up with it all and I was scared for you every time . . ." She paused and covered her mouth with her hand. "Aw, listen to me. It was great, Rob. You did so well and I'm so proud of you."

She realized then she still held the bottle of Gatorade they had bought that morning at the store. She handed it to him with an apology.

"Thanks!" Rob said, thankful for something else cold to drink. He turned it up and took a deep pull. He wiped his mouth on his sleeve. "Whew, I wish I had had that about fifty laps ago."

Michelle came up, placed a cold, wet towel around his neck, and handed him a dry one to wipe the sweat off his face. Rob patted the pavement next to him as an invitation for Christy to sit down. The three of them were still talking quietly when the network crew showed up to interview him. The producer in the truck reminded the cameraman to be sure that the girl was in the shot.

And in moments Rob was expressing his pride, his disappointment, and his determination to get them next time to the national television audience.

South of the San Francisco Bay, in a beautiful hillside estate, Toby Warren was presiding over a party that had been under way for the last few hours in his huge living room. The room itself was devoid of all furniture except for a scattering of beanbag chairs and the giant-screen

TV that took up a good portion of one wall. The assembled throng from Ensoft sat on the floor and in the low chairs, cheering lustily as Rob's image filled the screen during the interview. The company name and logo was clearly embroidered on the cap that Michelle had just managed to prop on his head before the camera came to life. The logo was also visible on Christy Fagan's shirt collar as she sat there beside him, smiling, her hand resting on the young driver's shoulder.

They clapped, too, every time Rob mentioned "the Ensoft Ford" or "the Ensoft team" or the "Ensoft pit crew and the wonderful job they did today getting us out early on every stop."

As everybody tipped their drinks of soda or cranberry juice, Toby led them all in a rousing hip-hip-hooray for their driver, their car, their team.

And the boss was grinning happily the entire time.

CLIFFORD AND RANDY

Rob bounced his way along the winding driveway that snaked through the pasture between the main highway and Billy Winton's farmhouse and the race shop that had grown up behind it. The rusty old pickup truck slid to a stop in the gravel outside the main shop building, the truck's door creaking badly as Rob opened it, using the outside handle by necessity, and climbed out. He reached into the metal toolbox bolted into the bed and pulled out a worn baseball cap and tugged it over his long hair. He had simply not had time to get it cut lately and it fell into his eyes. Billy was insisting that he drive all the way up to Johnson City and get it styled properly, that the hack-'em-up little barbershop in Chandler Cove didn't do a good enough job on the kid's mop for television spots and newspaper photos.

He was about to open the door to the shop when he heard Billy calling to him. Rob turned to see him standing there in the doorway of the small log cabin he used for an office. Rob threw up his hand in a wave and headed back across the gravel toward the cabin. Billy stepped out onto the porch, his cowboy boots clicking on the wide planks. It was barely six-thirty, yet it appeared Mr. Winton had already been at it for a while.

"Morning, Billy!"

"Mornin'. Come on in here for a minute. I got something for you."

"What?"

Rob's first thought was that maybe he had left something in Billy's car the other night after the ride back from the airport. He had slept the whole way and was still groggy when he slung his grip into the back of the truck and headed on to his new apartment for a proper night's rest, something that had been in short supply lately. They had been returning from the race at Darlington, a grueling affair in which Rob had finished ninth. They had also run well the week before at Atlanta where he had led a bunch of laps and finished sixth.

Two races. Two top-ten finishes. Rob craved firsts, but everyone else seemed more than satisfied.

"I figured you might want your paycheck, that's all," Billy answered, leading the way into the office.

"Oh, you can give it to me whenever you get a chance," Rob said in all sincerity. "I got some things I promised Will I'd help with on the car. I likely won't get a chance to get to the bank anytime soon anyway, so it won't matter."

"You're the first danged driver I ever saw who didn't care if he got paid or not. Most of the ones I've been around are camped out on my doorstep just in case I got a check for them."

"Aw, Billy, I've got more money now than I ever dreamed of. Shoot, I made more money with that second place at Daytona than I ever made in a year at Brandon's Cabinets."

"Well, much as you dislike getting money, I still have to pay you. That was a nice payday the other Saturday from Atlanta. I don't have all the numbers from Darlington yet, but I still owe you for it, too."

"Billy, I'm making plenty of money. As long as I can race, I don't much care if I get paid or not. I got more than enough in the bank drawing interest."

"You sure? Look at those jeans with the holes in the knees. And at that old junk truck you're driving around. Folks'll be talking about me stealing from you just based on appearances."

"I worked hauling hay and cutting tobacco for three summers to buy that truck when I was sixteen. She may be a little rough, but she still runs good. I can get several more years out of her at the very least."

"Rob, with what you've made in the last couple of races, you could pay cash money for a new one."

"But I don't need a new truck. Old Bessie here's still got a lot of miles in her. My daddy used to say if you didn't get two hundred thousand miles out of a vehicle, you didn't take proper care of her."

Billy could only shake his head as he pulled the envelope out of his desk drawer. Sometimes he was certain the kid was putting him on, that he would suddenly break out and display the same egotistical attitude so many of the race car drivers wore as surely as they did their driver's suit or team jacket. The youngster sometimes seemed too good to be true.

He did notice Rob had mentioned his father, though. Wilder rarely talked about his family life, and Billy made it a point not to pry so long as it didn't affect the chemistry of his team. All Billy knew for sure was that his parents had not gotten along, that his father had left home when Rob was only a kid. That the boy's mother took great exception to her husband's attempts at stock car racing. From what he had heard, the kid had a scrapbook filled with clippings of his old man's aborted racing career.

Billy figured all that was none of his business, but he couldn't turn his head to Rob's financial situation, to his naïveté when it came to money. That would be irresponsible on his part. He decided to try once again to give him some fatherly advice.

"You need to get you an accountant and a lawyer to help you with your money. If you don't, Uncle Sam is going to get most of it and the shysters and shill artists out there will surely get the rest."

"Billy, I appreciate it, but I just put it in the bank and then I don't worry about it. It's drawing interest, making money every day without me having to hit a lick at a snake."

"You're getting . . . what? Three percent? Inflation's at close to four. You're actually losing money with it in a savings account."

Rob stared at him blankly. His parents had never had money enough for groceries, much less to sock away in some bank account. He felt like the richest man on earth when he handed over his checks and passbook to the teller at the Bank of Chandler Cove and saw how it added up.

"Well, what about your lawyer and accountant? Reckon they'd be interested in helping me out, too?"

Billy hesitated. "They likely would. But don't you want to find somebody of your own? I could get you some names and you could pick somebody you feel comfortable with."

"Nope. If these folks are good enough for you, then they're good enough for me. Can you set up a meeting with them for me? I wouldn't even know what to ask them."

Rob was still unsure of the need for financial advice. But if Billy Winton had suggested he needed a swami with a turban, then he would most likely say to send one right over.

"Tell you what. My two guys are supposed to fly up to the race with me. They haven't been to the track in a while and want to watch us and Jodell's team run. Why don't you fly up with us? You can meet them and get to know them over the weekend. Then, if you feel comfortable with them, you're on your own."

"All right, but I promised Will I would ride to the track in the van with them—"

"No, you fly up there with us. Look, these guys are old friends of Bubba's and Jodell's. They're not what you might expect at all. I think you'll . . . uh . . . find them interesting," Billy said, a sly grin spreading across his face.

Rob missed the smirk altogether. The telephone jangled loudly then and Rob used that as an excuse to head on over to the shop. He folded up the envelope with his checks inside and stuck them in his jeans pocket.

He could hear the loud pounding, hammer on metal, before he even opened the shop door. Several men were underneath and working on the front end of the car Rob had crumpled a few weeks before when someone spun directly in front of him. The damaged racer was up on a set of jack stands and there were several sets of feet sticking out from beneath the car. He recognized the pair of boots that belonged to Will and gave him a kick. The hammering stopped and the rest of the body slowly slid out and into view.

"Hey, there, cowboy! Where you been? Sleeping late again? I thought you were gonna be here sometime before the middle of the day to help us on this wreck, but I guess I must have heard you wrong. You always said if you wrecked 'em, you'd help us fix 'em."

"I've been here for a while. I was over in the office talking with Billy. He's still harping on how bad I need a lawyer and an accountant. I told him to let me talk with his so he'd get off my back."

Will gave Rob the most serious look he could manage while lying on his back on a creeper, his face peppered with dirt and oil and his hair laced with bits of metal filings.

"Look, Robbie. You need to listen to him on this one. And besides, you'll get a kick out of old Randy and Clifford. They've been with Jodell since him, Joe, and Bubba first went to Daytona back in 'fifty-nine. They are an unusual pair. They're good at what they do now, though."

"Well, Billy wants me to fly with them down to Fort Worth this week. He said they are going to the race with him and it'd be a chance to see how I like them."

It had suddenly gotten quiet in the shop as all the boys seemed to be eavesdropping on the conversation. Will started to grin, then fought to keep a straight face.

"You going to fly all the way to Texas in the same plane with Randy and Clifford?" he asked.

"Yeah, Billy said we'd meet them early in the morning and then we'd fly together over to the track."

"Billy tell you anything else about Randy and Clifford?"

"Just that they were the best at what they did. If Billy thinks that highly of them, it's good enough for me."

"Nothing else?"

"No, why?"

"Oh, nothing," Will said, having to struggle even harder to keep from breaking up. There was also the sound of snickering from the two guys still under the damaged car. Across the shop, someone else suddenly broke into an odd-sounding coughing fit. Will sat upright on the creeper. "You're right enough about lawyers and accountants. But right now we got us a damaged car we need to fix. Let's quit jawing and get to it and we'll see what you think of Mr. Weems and Mr. Stanley after y'all get to spend some quality time together."

Rob headed to the locker room to change into his coveralls. As soon as the door swung closed behind him, the old hands on the crew burst into laughter. Randy Weems and Clifford Stanley were well known to most of them. Not only did they handle most of Billy Winton's financial and legal matters, but the two eccentric characters were also fixtures around the Jodell Lee Racing shop, often present for the late night bull sessions in which Billy and members of his crew sometimes joined.

Will shook his head. The two advisers would be a good thing for Rob. That is, if the kid could see past their rough exterior. At the very least, it should be quite an interesting little plane trip over to Texas the next day for one Mr. Rob Wilder!

Will almost wished he could go with him so he could see it for himself.

It was surprisingly warm for so early a morning in a mountain springtime. Rob Wilder felt a surge of new-found energy as he steered the old pickup along the winding, narrow blacktop roads that led him from his new home down to the airport near Blountville. He was now renting a small apartment from a friend of Jodell Lee's. It was a small place, a cramped, two-room affair over a garage. Though it was tiny, mostly unfurnished, and with little to actually make it a home, Rob felt as if he had moved into a luxurious penthouse suite. He had lived the last few years back in Alabama at various relatives' homes, grateful for their kindness but relegated to whatever leftover room they might have after their own broods had been bedded down. He had reluctantly taken a bedroom in Will's house since he first ventured to East Tennessee the year before. But finally he had a place of his own, even if the windows wouldn't open and the toilet leaked and the refrigerator that came with the place was hardly big enough to hold a six-pack of sodas.

Simply knowing he had a place to which he could return made it far more pleasant to leave. And he was going racing again. Going to a track he had only seen on television, a relatively new facility located in a broad, flat state he had only viewed from high above it as they flew over it several times on the way to and from California.

Rob was in a particularly good mood as he fiddled with the truck's old push-button radio. He was disappointed he would miss the fun and camaraderie riding all the way to the race in the van with the rest of the crew. But on the bright side, he did look forward to sleeping on the plane on the ride up, to having an extra night in a king-sized hotel bed before the rest of them arrived and they got serious about winning the race in Texas.

Rob sang along with the Ricky Martin song that blared from the radio, actually dancing in his seat as he made the turnoff to the airport. He shifted the truck down into second gear as he turned the corner and pulled up outside the building that housed the airport's general aviation flight service. Just then the disc jockey kicked off a familiar song, the same one that had been playing on the radio the evening he, Michelle, and Christy had been making their way down Sunset Boulevard in the convertible.

Christy had insisted Michelle turn the song up and the two girls had sung along. Rob had avoided joining in, suspecting that his own off-key howling would have spoiled what had already been a promising evening. But he could still hear Christy's lovely voice, see the way her hair blew in the wind as she threw back her head and sang along.

They had spoken on the telephone only a couple of nights before, but it seemed like weeks ago. Rob had not seen her since the morning after the 500 in Daytona when they all said their good-byes at the airport. He felt awkward calling her, assuming he would be interrupting her studies, keeping her from some important social function she doubtless would be attending. Still, they had managed to hook up on the telephone at least once a week. She always seemed glad to hear from him, reluctant to hang up when he tried to let her go, and urged him to call again or let her know where she could reach him so she could call him. He knew for certain how he felt about the opportunity to talk with her. And he knew how badly he wanted to see her again. There seemed such an awful, impenetrable distance between them, the two thousand miles or so that might just as well have been a million. The hollow echo on the telephone line only emphasized the discouragingly wide span.

I'll call her tonight as soon as I get settled in, he vowed to himself as he shut off the ignition. At least he would be hundreds of miles closer to her, even if he could still only touch her by telephone line. That simple realization made him feel even better.

The truck door's tired hinges creaked as he opened it and hopped out, grabbing his small travel bag out of the bed of the pickup. He didn't see Billy's Town Car in the parking lot. He had actually beaten the boss, and that didn't happen often.

The attendant behind the desk and a couple of pilots waiting for their passengers all gave him a friendly greeting.

"Hey, Rob," the attendant, George McKinley, called. "Nice morning, isn't it?"

"Nice morning for sleeping in, but it seems like I've got a plane to catch."

"Well, she's parked out there on the tarmac waiting for you boys. Door's open. You can go on and get on board if you want to and take a little nap."

"Who's the pilot today?"

"Jim Washburn."

"Good. Thanks, George," Rob replied.

He liked Jim. He was a good pilot and made the uneasy flier in Rob feel a little more comfortable during their trips together. Rob started for the door but then turned and asked, "Have you heard from Billy? He should have been here already."

"Yeah, he called about a half hour ago to make sure Jim had the plane rolled out. He said he was running a little late. Something about having to stop and pick up a few things for the trip."

Rob nodded and headed on out the door. Jim would be checking the plane over and going back to the flight service to check weather and whatever it was that pilots kept up with. Rob figured he could get a head start on his nap.

He was halfway across the tarmac toward the plane when he remembered he had been so preoccupied, thinking about Christy, that he had left his new CD player on the seat in the truck. It and the tiny-screened television set for the apartment had been his only extravagant purchases so far. The disc player helped him blot out the monotonous rumble of the airplane engines on these long trips, or the garage noises at the track when he tried to catch a few winks here and there.

As he made his way back toward the parking lot, he noticed a couple of odd-looking characters, outfitted in worn overalls and farm work shoes, over across the way. A pair of hog farmers, maybe lost? Or possibly part of a ditch-digging crew just showing up to go to work?

He paid the odd duo little attention as he hurried out and retrieved the disc player and the small nylon case filled with CDs. But as he headed back toward the plane, he noticed that the two men in the overalls were now standing around at the bottom of the steps that led up and inside the King Air, the plane Billy and Rob were going to take to Fort Worth. They seemed to be hanging around there, waiting or looking for what?

No doubt about it. These two "Farmer Browns" definitely belonged somewhere else.

He started to shoo them off, in a nice way, of course. To send them toward the commercial terminal across the way or in the direction of the construction job at the far end of the runway. But as he approached, the taller of the two stepped to meet him, offering a big, meaty paw in a friendly enough gesture.

Maybe they were just race fans, waiting to say hello to an up-and-coming racer.

"Howdy, partner!" the stranger said while the other man merely grinned and nodded.

What was that aroma? It had been a while since he had smelled it, but it sure resembled the perfume of fresh cow manure. But there was another scent drifting his way, too. Something tangy and strong. Rob couldn't quite place it. But both scents seemed to be emanating from these two trespassers. Rob took the man's hand and shook it anyway. Somehow, appearance and fragrance aside, they didn't seem to be threatening.

"Hi. Pleased to meet you," Rob said in his friendliest

fan-greeting voice, though no one had introduced himself yet.

But just then the shorter one made a move to reach for something in the pocket of his overalls.

Hijackers! Rob suddenly thought. These two big, beefy, red-faced characters were about to hijack their plane at gunpoint!

But the man fished out a quart Mason jar better than three-quarters full of a clear liquid. Rob took a step back as the man unscrewed the cap. Immediately the soft early morning breeze brought him an even stronger whiff of the sour fumes he had smelled already.

It didn't seem to bother the man, though. He turned it up, took a healthy swig, and smacked his lips as if he had been drinking pure nectar, then shoved the jar toward the taller farmer.

"Ungmmm," the man said, clearing his throat pointedly. "My Lord! Where *are* your manners?"

"Sorry. I forgot."

The man sheepishly withdrew the jar from his friend's direction and then offered it to Rob with the flourish of a wine steward proffering his finest vintage. Rob couldn't help it. The smell of the stuff was so strong and disgusting, he screwed up his face and took another involuntary step backward.

"No," Rob said, then remembered his own manners. "I appreciate it, but I'm . . . I'm . . . not thirsty."

But all the time he was casting about, looking for some help should he need it to escape these two loony hillbillies.

But the two didn't seem to be offended at all by his rejecting their wake-up toddy. They began giggling, slapping each other on the shoulder, their blows getting more and more pronounced. Rob began to back away, a step at a time, sure he needed to put some distance between himself and these two before they stopped their cackling and started to exchange serious punches. If they were drinking that brew this early in the morning, who knew what mayhem they might be capable of!

But just then, Rob's not so subtle retreat came to an abrupt halt. He backed squarely into Billy Winton.

"Whoa there, kid! I see you've met Randy and Clifford."

"Who?"

"The tall one there is Clifford Stanley, and that's Randy Weems there about to take another slug from that Mason jar."

Clifford gave him a wave of his big freckled hand, but Randy was already taking another draft of whatever that noxious liquid was in the jar, spilling a bit around his lips and down the bib of his overalls as he swigged thirstily.

"This is another one of y'all's jokes, right?" the kid asked, wide-eyed.

Rob was always on the lookout, ever vigilant for the next in a continuing line of practical jokes. He had been the butt of far too many of the crew's pranks already to take for granted anything so bizarre as these two. He had been sent off to Kingsport to buy left-handed lug wrenches. He'd been offered lemonade spiked with Tabasco and a peanut butter and Vaseline sandwich. Once he had been handed fan mail from a famous movie star that ended with a proposal of marriage. With practice and a heightened sense of awareness, he had gotten much better at seeing them coming.

But if they had now recruited Billy Winton to participate in their silliness, then he would have to do a much better job of being on guard.

"Of course not. But I can't blame you for thinking it. I had the same reaction the first time I met these two rednecks, too." Billy laughed. Randy and Clifford appeared to take no umbrage from his insult. "Now, what on earth are you two lug-heads doing gettin' started on the hooch so early?"

"Aw shucks, Billy. We like to think of it as being real, real late instead of early. Me and Randy was just having us a little nip 'fore we got on that flying machine there. 'Sides, we're on vacation," Clifford said.

"Okay, but there's one rule on this trip. No corrupting my driver! Understand?"

"We understand." They spoke in unison, like a couple of overgrown schoolboys being reprimanded by the headmaster. The Mason jar quickly disappeared into one of the deep pockets of Randy's faded-out overalls.

"Okay. Let's get going. We have a race to get ready to run," Billy said, shooing the two big men up the steps and into the plane.

Rob eyed the two warily, still not sure he wasn't being taken for a ride in more ways than one. A lawyer? An accountant? These two rubes? Billy Winton, a man normally so practical and intelligent, actually trusted his finances and legal matters to the two "Jethro brothers"?

Clifford was halfway up the steps, Randy following close behind, when Billy suddenly yelped.

"Whoa! Stop right there. You forget something, Cliff?"

Both men stopped and gave Billy a puzzled look.

"What?" they said, again in something closely akin to harmony.

Billy nodded toward the tall man's scuffed and scarred work boots.

"Oh. Sorry. I forgot. I was out in the barn feedin' the cows before we come over here."

"I know. They can likely smell you to Knoxville."

Clifford ambled over to a small patch of grass and

cleaned off his boots, then he climbed the narrow stairs, followed closely by Jim Washburn, who had finished the preflight inspection. The pilot was grinning, clearly familiar with Randy and Clifford from previous trips.

As they taxied out for takeoff, more formal introductions were conducted. Clifford Stanley was the attorney, and despite the fact that he looked more like a struggling dirt farmer, he oversaw a thriving practice in Chandler Cove. Randy Weems was a CPA and owned his own firm along with three partners, and he had clients from the Tri-Cities to Knoxville. Still, Rob had decided to remain wary until he was sure these two were to be trusted. Soon the conversation turned to people Rob didn't know and he took that as his cue to take a nap.

He brought out his compact disc player and headphones, hooked them up, and turned the player on. He was about to pull the headphones over his ears when Clifford leaned toward him and spoke.

"What you listening to, young feller?"

"Just a singer they've been playing on the pop stations a lot lately," Rob answered, sure none of them would have a clue who the artist was even if he actually named him.

"You ever listen to any country music?"

"Sure I do. Back home that was about all I listened to," Rob said.

"He has a girlfriend from California, so he's trying to expand his musical tastes," Billy interrupted. "Seems he's drifting away from his roots a little bit."

"Shoot, Billy, I like it all——" Rob started.

Clifford Stanley interrupted him. "Well, I think he needs to get back to them roots. Heck, we're heading down to Texas, after all, the home of some of the greatest music there ever was. He needs to be listening to good old no-nonsense country music, like it was before they gussied it all up and ruined it. Where's all them records you keep on this tub, Billy?"

"Right there in that pocket behind you," Billy answered, pointing. He knew what was coming, but he tried to keep a straight face.

Clifford leaned down and rummaged through the assorted compact discs Billy kept on board for the plane's sound system. He dug around for a bit before he finally found what he was looking for, then he held it up and surveyed it lovingly. Meanwhile Randy had produced the Mason jar once again, but this time he passed it to Billy.

Winton held it up to the light, studied the contents, then unscrewed the lid and took a whiff. "Smells good," Billy said, surprisingly. "What I want to know is, where do you two come up with this stuff in this day and time?"

The odor had already hit Rob and he was making gagging noises.

"This is about as fine as it comes, old friend," Randy said, a look of sublime bliss on his flushed face. "It's a literal piece of Americana, Bill. Same formula as Jodell's grandpa used to use when he made all them fine batches once upon a time. It's been passed down through the years like a guarded family recipe."

Billy raised an eyebrow. He suspected the stuff was still being distilled and bottled somewhere near Jodell Lee's farm. He had often wondered over the years if maybe Jodell had ever really completely let go of his moonshining heritage. But he knew, too, that some questions were better left unasked.

Billy tilted the jar up to his lips and took a cautious sip. The fire burned all the way down his gullet and into his belly, but it was not a totally unpleasant feeling. It brought back a raft of memories. He winked at Rob, who watched him with eyes squinted and mouth screwed up in disbelief.

"I wouldn't normally take a nip of anything this early in the morning, and especially some strange brew like this. But that is some mighty fine stuff."

Billy passed the jar back to Clifford, who grinned broadly at Billy's pronouncement.

"Dang straight! The elixir of the angels. That's what that brew is!"

Rob had taken the CD from Clifford without looking and now had it loaded in the player. He tried to ignore the smell of the whiskey. Maybe this would turn out to be some good music after all. Maybe Vince Gill or Randy Travis or Kathy Mattea or one of his other favorites. He didn't even check the writing on the plastic disc as he inserted it into the machine, but just pulled on the earphones and cranked up the volume.

Suddenly the singing blared in Rob's ears, the words of the song moaned in a deep, raw, twanging male voice, the tune toted just the other side of off-key. Rob sat up in his seat like he had been jolted with electricity. "What in the Sam Hill . . . ?" he blurted out, ripping the earphones off and tossing them to the floor of the plane as if they had offended him mightily.

The men in the back of the plane cackled. Rob glared at the three of them.

"What is that mess?" he cried. His face was as contorted as it might have been if he had actually tried a gulp of the white liquor in the quart jar.

"Mess?" Randy retorted, his face suddenly mock serious. "That, my young friend, is the greatest country song ever sung by the greatest country singer to ever live. Ever!"

"It sounds more like a sour motor about to throw a rod to me," Rob said, pulling the offending disc from his player before it further contaminated it.

"Now, don't you be talking about the great Ernest Tubb like that. No sir! E. T. was the best there ever was. Billy, I don't know if you ought to take this young hotshot to Nashville next week after all. Not if the word gets around that he was blaspheming a true legend like he done. They're liable to run him right out of Music City," Randy groaned.

"Now, boys, I told y'all to leave my driver be," Billy said, but he was still laughing.

"Well, he needs to quit saying bad things about a legend. Bill, you remember back to that night when we took you to your first Grand Ole Opry show?" Clifford asked, ready to launch into the story of that particular evening's events.

"Yeah, but the main thing I remember is you two acting like you parked the mule and wagon right there at the front door to the Ryman Auditorium. Robbie, you think these two boys are rough and unsophisticated now . . ."

The bantering went on for the better part of the next hour while the length of Tennessee and a part of Arkansas unreeled below them. It was clear that there were some mighty deep roots to these men's friendship.

Still, Rob was missing valuable sleep. He tried to ignore them and drift off. But he couldn't help himself. He found himself captivated by these two characters, with their stories and with the odd juxtaposition of their appearance and manner and the obvious intelligence they had to possess to do what they did so well. Before he realized it, Rob had switched off the music and merely pretended to be sleeping, listening all the time to the back-and-forth conversation in the plane's cramped quarters. He couldn't help but laugh out loud at them.

And to their credit, they pretended to believe that he was actually asleep.

Rob finally opened one eye.

"I see Sleeping Beauty has decided to join us," Clifford crowed. "I been meaning to tell you. That was a good run you had at Daytona back in February."

"Thank you. I wish we could have won."

"Should have. And you will. Don't worry. It reminded me of when we went down there with Jodell Lee and them to pit the car the year it opened, back in 'fiftynine. Man, I can still remember it like it was yesterday."

"You were there for the first race at Daytona?" Rob asked, suddenly sitting up straighter in the seat, interested.

"Son, I was there for the first three. If I hadn't had to take a little detour in Uncle Sam's Army back in 'sixty-two and 'sixty-three, I'd have been to the first thirty in a row. But then the Army's how I got the money to go to college and on to law school, so I can't complain about missing a couple of races, I don't guess."

"The two of you crewed the car with Jodell?" Rob asked. He was more than a little confused. He had assumed their relationship with Jodell and Billy had been based on their professions, not from crewing the car at races.

"I've changed more tires on pit road than Carter's got pills. We didn't go to every race, but we hit all the big speedways for years with Jodell and Joe and Bubba and them. Charlotte, Atlanta, Daytona, Darlington . . . you name it, we were there."

"I can't believe you were at Daytona that first time!"

"Son, let me tell you. All kidding aside, I can still remember the first time I laid eyes on that big old speedway. It took my breath away. You could see those towering banks as you approached from the beach, and once you got inside it looked to me like the straightaways went on for miles. You got to remember, up till then, Darlington was all we'd ever seen in the way of a real speedway. Everything else was a half mile or less and the track was usually dirt to boot. We hadn't ever seen that much asphalt in one place in our lives."

"That is so cool!" Rob marveled.

"You should have seen old Jodell when he first hit that track in that Ford of his. We'd worked for weeks on that car. Then, to see it out there on the track running wide open . . . now, that was a sight to see. Almost as pretty as any plow mule we'd ever seen. Almost."

"So what was that first race like?"

Rob was clearly eager to hear more.

"Kid, like I told you, I can still remember it like it was yesterday. We rode down on the bus with Catherine, Jodell's wife, though they wasn't married yet at the time. First time me and Randy had been anywhere any farther away from home than over to Greenville, Tennessee, once to the hog auction. Neither one of us knew there was anything else in the world except those old hills and hollers of home. The sight of all those race cars in the garage just made your heart start to pumping. Nobody . . . not Jodell or Richard Petty or Ned Jarrett or any of them . . . knew exactly what to expect. Hadn't never been a track anything like it before. Some of them were nervous. Maybe even downright scared. But not old Jodell Bob Lee. He was used to driving fast, hauling that moonshine whiskey, and when he saw that place, you'd have thought he'd died and gone to heaven."

Clifford's eyes had grown misty with the memories.

Even Billy was enjoying the story, though he had likely heard it dozens of times before. Still, it seemed he picked up new details with each telling. And it would fill in another piece of the puzzle as he learned more about how all these men had come to accomplish so much from such humble beginnings.

By the time they landed, Rob had a much different opinion of the two rough-hewn men who had hitchhiked with them to Texas. He told them as much, and how their stories had him itching even worse to get back behind the wheel of his race car and take to this new track. He could only imagine what it must have been like to race in those days, to drive in a simpler time and against all the legends when they were in their prime. He vowed to persuade Clifford and Randy and even Billy and Jodell to tell him more about those days. He felt a strong kinship with those old drivers for some reason and he wanted to hear more about them.

Michelle Fagan was waiting for them at the airport. She'd flown in the night before and had already picked up a rental car. Rob rode with her as Billy took care of the plane and got his own car.

It was good to see Michelle again. He gave her a brief hug and she offered him a quick kiss on the cheek. It had only been a few days since he'd seen her at the last race, but he was excited anyway.

Michelle, a knowing smile on her face, couldn't wait to ask him his impressions of Randy and Clifford. She had met them when they completed the contracts for the Ensoft sponsorship. She thought her worst stereotype fears were being confirmed when she first laid eyes on them. Both men had shown up for that meeting in freshly starched white dress shirts with ties, wearing fedora hats, but in overalls and work boots. She didn't have to tell Rob how stunned Toby and the rest of the Ensoft crew had been when the cast of *Hee Haw* walked into their office suite.

But by dinner, they were all like old buddies. The Ensoft management team had its own streak of eccentricity and they had all ultimately blended well, even when Randy pulled out his own bucket of sorghum syrup to go on their breakfast pancakes in the restaurant at the Grand Hyatt in San Francisco.

They were so full of Randy-and-Clifford stories that they were almost to the hotel before Rob finally got around to asking about Christy.

A Track as Untamed as Texas

There was something almost unnaturally exhilarating for him about pulling onto an unfamiliar racetrack for the first time. But each time he had done so, he had instantly felt at home, as if he had been driving the track since he was born. After a few laps, he was as comfortable as he had ever been at the little bullrings around northern Alabama and southern Tennessee that he had run dozens of times each. As he steered the car onto the Texas track, though, he imagined how it must have been for those drivers Clifford had talked about, the ones who dared to pull out onto the untested Daytona speedway back in 1959. How wild it must have been to come down to Florida from those tiny dirt tracks and to suddenly find themselves running two or three times the speed they were accustomed to doing over four times the distance they usually ran.

He enjoyed those thoughts for the better part of one lap, then stomped the gas and headed back into turn one at full speed, now concentrating on the here and the now. The Ford felt good as he hit the backstretch, zooming down toward the banking leading to turns three and four. She held firmly in the corners, rolled smoothly on the straights, and felt steady and powerful, responsive to his every nudge or kick. He dreaded coming to a track and rolling the car off the hauler only to discover it wasn't close. That the setup was so far off. When that happened it made for long weekends at the track.

To the casual observer, the Texas track appeared similar to Charlotte. But that was not the case at all. The track itself appeared to be wide and racy, but that was dangerously deceiving. The truth was that the racing groove could be tight and treacherous and had been the subject of much controversy since the speedway was first opened. The racing surface itself had also been the source of quite a bit of fretting. Even with all the repairs and reconfigurations that had been done since the inaugural races, the drivers continued to have reservations.

Rob didn't care how a track was configured. He didn't care if it was square or had loop-the-loops in the straightaways, if it was dirt, gravel, asphalt, or Astroturf. He showed up to race, to try to finish first, and that was all that mattered to him. Everybody had to drive on the same stretch of track. The crew that set the car up best for the course they were running and the driver who managed to learn the best way around, and who then had the nerve to actually run it that way, usually won the race.

Rob knew he had a good car after those first few laps around the track. It wouldn't take many more circuits around for him to figure out the fastest way to make the trip. By then, this wild and woolly speedway would only be the latest "favorite" track for Rob Wilder.

Rob had quickly found that he enjoyed going to new

tracks. It gave him the opportunity to build on his experience level, and besides, it was similar to solving a difficult puzzle or finding an answer to a particularly obtuse geometry problem. There was a great deal of satisfaction in coming up with the correct solution or answer.

And this trip was quickly turning out to be very productive in other ways, too. It had not progressed quite so quickly as his learning the track, but after most of the first afternoon at the Fort Worth raceway, Rob finally realized that he had warmed considerably to Randy and Clifford. And once he had, he was amazed at what he found.

Most of their country-bumpkin facade was nothing more than just that. They liked the attention their rube act attracted, and it was an excellent way to take some of the stuffing out of the stuffed shirts they met. Clifford even admitted that the routine often gave them an advantage in most any situation. More than one opponent in court or negotiator in a stiff bargaining session had taken a look at one or the other of them and let their guard down. And it didn't take them long to see that either of these hicks was much more formidable an adversary than they could ever have imagined based on their looks and conduct.

They seemed to know their stuff, too, when it came to his finances and legal affairs. They spoke a language he couldn't begin to understand, but they were patient in explaining what they were suggesting.

Rob found the same to be true of their racing knowledge. Once past the manure-and-hayseed exterior, it became apparent that both men possessed a wealth of wisdom about the sport. Rob soon found himself trailing along behind them, listening, picking their brains. He especially enjoyed their colorful stories about racing's greatest stars, men like Curtis Turner, Joe Weatherley, Fireball Roberts, Junior Johnson, the Allisons, the Earnhardts, and Ned Jarrett.

Clifford turned out to be a master storyteller, embossing his tales with wonderful descriptions and first-hand reminiscences. Michelle was as transfixed as Rob was. She had bought some books on racing to learn more about the early days, but so far had not had time to read much of them. She likely didn't need to now. Clifford, with the occasional color commentary from Randy, was far better than a dry history anyway. Between practices over the next couple of days, Rob and Michelle were mostly in the lounge of the transporter that had been parked in the garage area, listening, urging Clifford on.

Will was pleased about the distraction. Weems and Stanley were doing a wonderful job of keeping his driver preoccupied, out of the garage, away from other temptations. The crew was busy making sure the car was set up for the difficult track surface. Will and Donnie worked diligently, tweaking the setup, trying to get the car just right. They didn't necessarily need Rob hovering over them, pestering them to let him help work on the car.

Finally, with the start of the "happy hour" practice the day before the race was about to start, Rob sat on pit road, waiting as impatiently as ever for the official to wave the line of cars out onto the track for their final drill. Donnie and Will still fiddled at something under the hood while the remainder of the crew cleaned up the garage area. Rob did exactly what he always did in the final moments before driving out onto a racetrack, the same thing he had done at the tiny tracks back home and now did before tackling Daytona or Darlington or Texas. He ran an imaginary lap, visualizing his braking points, the precise line where he wanted to set the car going into the corners, and when he would jump on and get off the gas.

Randy and Clifford joined Billy and Michelle atop the truck, and the two men shot their fists into the air and let out a shrill rebel yell when they heard the engine fire beneath the hood of the 06 Ford. The reason for the grins on their faces was unmistakable. They loved racing and everything connected with it.

The line of cars roared off into the first turn as the crews began a feverish final hour of practice, most of them trying to nail down all the changes they wanted to make to their machines before the next day's race. Rob took it easy on his first lap, riding along down low on the track, out of the way of those who were pressing already and so he could check the gauges to confirm that the temperatures and pressures were rising to normal ranges.

Coming out of turn four, he hammered the gas to set sail on his first hard lap of the session. He saw clear track ahead of him as the car swept full bore down toward the tight first turn. He felt the groove seem to narrow markedly as he set his line through the sweeping corner. The car bounced across the surface of the track and sat down hard on her springs as she did her best to hang on to traction.

Rob sawed at the steering wheel as he worked to keep the car down, hugging the bottom edge of the banking. He got back in the gas aggressively as he came off turn two, pushing the car right out against the wall as he raced down the back straightaway. Then, as he approached turn three, he pinched the car back down low, trying to get in position to hit the narrow line just right as he exited turn four. He even nicked the edge of the grass going through the quad-oval as he raced back off toward the first turn.

Some of the drivers had said the track was as hard to tame as the big, wide state of Texas had been. Rob Wilder did not disagree with that colorful assessment.

On pit road, Will clicked his stopwatch as Rob streaked by, then checked the time. He breathed a huge sigh of relief, then jotted the time down on the clipboard. The changes they had made after the last practice had not hurt the car and thankfully had seemed to take them in the right direction. It would take a couple more laps to see how much the changes would impact their speeds and also give them a clue as to what others they might need to consider.

Billy studied the car with a practiced eye as it made its way round the track. Randy and Clifford stood at the rail beside him, watching just as intently.

"He's a tad loose coming off turn four and he's a little loose getting into one. Both the exit and entrance to those corners are so tight that he's losing a tenth or so there," Clifford said matter-of-factly.

"What would you do?" Billy asked. He agreed with Clifford's evaluation completely and he was truly interested in what the big man thought might help them.

"Hard to say these days, the way they make these radial tires. In our day, I'd say we'd work on the stagger some till we got it right. But now I guess you play with the air pressure or maybe the jack wedges."

"Now you know why I have Will around. It keeps an old man like me in my place. These new radials still give me fits trying to figure out what to do. I always think all we need to do is pump in some more air and expand the circumference of the tires. Of course, that wouldn't be worth a flip with these darn radials."

"I know, old buddy. That's the very reason me and old Randy are here on 'vacation' while you and Will and them have to worry about that fancy race car out yonder."

Billy looked wistfully out toward where his young driver was bringing his car back out of the fourth turn.

"Sometimes, Clifford, I wish I could 'vacation' like you and your sidekick. But then, when we go down to a place like Daytona and run like we did, I wonder why I ever gave it up in the first place. Or how Jodell was finally able to get out of the race car for good."

"I know what you mean," Clifford said, suddenly turning serious. "I get back to a track and smell a little gasoline and burning oil or get the grit of tire rubber tween my teeth and I see the look on that kid's face when he pulls in after a good run and it takes me right back to Darlington in 'fifty-eight or Daytona in 'fifty-nine and I wish I could do it all over again."

"Same here," Randy chimed in as he followed Rob on into the next turn. "Course, we did it as much for the fun as we did the money. Best we could hope for was to win enough to buy gas to the next race and to feed old Bubba Baxter."

"Randy, you're right, but you know, if it wasn't still fun, I wouldn't be doing this at all. I can't tell you how great it was watching that kid drive these last few races. I thought I was seeing what Jodell probably looked like when he was Robbie's age."

"Bubba Baxter and Joe Banker both say that all the time. They talk as much about old Rocket Rob as they do their own car sometimes."

"Let's face it," Billy said as he watched Rob pull down pit road so Will and the boys could make some adjustments. "If it wasn't still fun, we'd be on the porch rockin' away and watching the grass grow!"

Clifford and Randy both nodded seriously.

Michelle smiled as she eavesdropped. She couldn't get over how devoted these men were to their sport. It was actually a touching thing to see.

Everyone, from Billy Winton on down, was smiling when the practice ended. At the end of happy hour, they were among the top five or six fastest cars on the track.

Clifford and Randy went to dinner with Rob and Michelle, and when it was all over, the two young people felt as if they had had a floor show with their meal. Never mind the strange looks they had gotten from the other diners around them. Everyone within earshot was soon being entertained also as the two hillbillies kept up a continual comedy performance, interspersed with heartfelt stories about racing in the fifties and sixties, about growing up in rural East Tennessee, and more.

When they all met back at the hotel afterward, Rob's sides were aching from all the laughter. He was thankful these two didn't come to the track for every race. He wasn't sure his constitution could take it. But he admitted to Billy as they rode the elevator up to their rooms that the evening had left him as relaxed as he had ever been on the night before a big race.

"Shoot, Billy, I've been so wrapped up listening to all their carrying on that I haven't even had time to worry a bit about tomorrow."

"So there was some method in my madness after all, asking those two bumpkins to come along with us," Billy said with a grin and a wink.

Rob smiled back as Billy stopped at the door to his room. But there was one other thing Rob wanted to say before he told his boss good night.

"Billy, have I ever thanked you for bringing me along on all this? I'm having the time of my life. And I really appreciate all you've done for me, for letting me be a part of all this. But mostly for all the trust you've put in me. I don't think I'll ever be able to repay you."

Billy blushed brightly. "You think for a second I'd keep your butt around here if you weren't the best young driver I've ever seen?"

Rob hesitated, embarrassed by the praise "I reckon not."

"All right. Now, go on and get a good night's sleep. You'll need all you got to tame this Texas twister tomorrow."

Then Billy closed the door.

Rob Wilder turned on his heels and whistled all the way down the hall to his own room.

GUITAR TOWN

Racing luck finally caught up with them the next day. The Billy Winton team had another truly outstanding run going at the Texas speedway. Then, late in the race, Rob ran over something on the track and cut a tire. What looked like a sure top-five finish deteriorated to a frustrating eighteenth place after the late pit stop, and Rob had to drive his heart out to salvage even that much.

Still, with the notable exception of Rob Wilder, the team left Forth Worth with their heads held high, happy with a mostly good showing at an especially difficult track, one that even had many of the veteran Winston Cup drivers befuddled.

"Sometimes the racing luck just runs against you," Will said, trying to cheer up his disappointed driver.

"I know. I know. I can't help feeling like it was my fault somehow, though."

"Yeah, you're right. At a hundred and seventy miles

an hour you should have seen that little old bitty piece of metal out there in the groove and dodged it. Or stayed in the lead pack for the rest of the race while you were running around on the tire rim. Yeah, that was a pretty sorry display of race car driving, all right!"

Clifford Stanley overheard the crew chief's sarcastic words. "He's right, Rob-roy." Clifford had taken to calling Rob "Rob-roy" for some unknown reason. "If you had swallowed a few sips of me and Randy's Smoky Mountain mouthwash before the race like we tried to get you to, you would have been wobbling so much you likely wouldn't have never run over whatever it was. And even if you had, you'd have been so happy and spiritual you'd never even have noticed you had a flat tire."

Rob couldn't help smiling.

"That's better," Will said.

"Lord have mercy! He's so pretty! I'd give anything if I had me a girl-baby so I could marry her off to old Rob-roy here and they could raise me up a whole litter of race car drivers."

With the Texas race behind them, their thoughts quickly turned to Nashville, the next stop on the Grand National circuit. Despite the bad luck in Texas, they all had a good feeling as they headed back closer to East Tennessee. It would also take them closer to a track that Billy Winton had always considered to be one of their "home" tracks when he had crewed Jodell Lee's cars.

Rob had more than one good reason to be looking forward to the Nashville race. First, he was excited to be back so close to home so his friends could drive up and watch him run. He had stayed in touch with the guys who had helped him run his old red Pontiac, but Rob and the 06 crew had not yet raced close enough to Hazel Green for them to actually come see him.

Nashville was also a track on which he knew he would

be comfortable driving. That had been the raceway where Billy and Will had given him his successful driving audition the year before. He had instantly felt as if he had been driving it since he was piloting a tricycle. He had also watched quite a few races there with his buddies and had always dreamed of running in competition there.

And there was one more thing about the weekend that he was looking forward to. Christy Fagan was planning on hitching a ride back east with Michelle and Toby Warren aboard the Ensoft jet on the Wednesday before the race. Warren was headed for New York and a session with stock analysts, but he wanted to stop in Chandler Cove on the way so he could see the racing operation and visit with Billy, Will, and Rob. Toby would circle back through Nashville to take in the race, but Michelle and Christy would ride over with Rob, just the three of them all the way to Nashville.

Rob had planned on picking them up at the airport and bringing them to the shop in his old truck. But when they heard, Donnie and the rest of the crew gave him grief for even thinking of such a thing. At their behest, he finally asked Billy if he could borrow his Lincoln, and Billy immediately agreed. No way would he allow Rob to ferry such important folks in what Donnie called the kid's "hog hauler."

Rob still didn't see what was wrong with fetching the three of them in his old pickup, though. It might be a little tight in the cab and there was no air conditioner and the windshield had a good-sized crack in it on the passenger side, but it was a fairly short ride from the airport to the shop. As Billy handed him the keys, he jawboned some more about Rob getting himself a new car, a vehicle more in keeping with his young-racing-hero image.

Rob simply waved him off and drove away.

Soon he was standing outside the flight service building watching the Ensoft corporate jet come in low, settling down on the runway with a puff of smoke when the gears hit the pavement. It was hard to believe it had been two months already since he had seen Christy. As he waited for the plane to taxi over and for the door to open, he caught himself wondering if she still held the same feelings for him that they had shared that night on the beach at Daytona. Had they both simply been caught up in the moment, spellbound by the ocean, the beach, the excitement of the upcoming race?

He hoped not. He prayed not.

The engines powered down as the plane rolled to a stop, and finally the door to the jet opened slightly, seemed to pause for a second, then swung wide open. One of the pilots dropped the stairs, then hopped down them, waiting at the bottom for the passengers to disembark. Rob headed that way at close to a trot, watching for familiar faces to appear at the door.

Michelle was the first out, stepping into the sunshine, shielding her eyes against the brightness, then seeing Rob and waving excitedly to him. She quickly headed his way, running to meet him and give him a hug.

Toby Warren followed closely behind her. He was hardly to the bottom of the stairs before he jumped the last few steps, put an arm around Rob, and started peppering him with questions about the Texas race. Rob tried to answer as best he could while still keeping an eye on the plane's doorway.

But he was engrossed in his conversation with Toby and didn't even see Christy until she was standing there right in front of him. Lord, she was gorgeous! Even more beautiful than he remembered, even more stunning than she had been in his dreams ever since February.

He tried to say something cool to her, something clever, but his tongue got all tangled up when he opened his mouth and nothing came out.

"Hi there," was the witty quip he finally stammered.

"Hi," she replied. She wore dark jeans, a white, ruffled shirt, and had a silk Ensoft racing jacket thrown over her shoulders. The soft breeze played with her hair. All Rob could do was stand there and drink her in for several awkward moments until she finally spoke again. "Well, I was kinda hoping for a hug."

"Oh."

He didn't hesitate then. Rob swept her up into his arms, squeezing her tightly. She hugged him right back. He inhaled the fresh fragrance of her perfume, basked in the warmth of her, finally so close to him. Neither of them noticed for a while that Toby and Michelle were standing there, staring at them with silly grins on their faces.

Rob didn't care. He gave her a quick kiss on the lips, held her a few seconds longer, then finally let her go. Except for her hand. He held on to that as they walked back toward the car.

They piled into Billy's Lincoln and Rob gave them the grand tour as they made their way through the hills and past farms on the way back to the shop. He pointed out the turnoff that led to Jodell Lee's place and the mountainside behind where Jodell's granddad had once distilled what was purported to be the best moonshine whiskey in the area. He reminded them that Jodell had learned to drive a race car right there, on those very same roadways they were crossing, while delivering that brew. Toby mentioned that he would like to see Jodell's shop as well, and Rob promised to take him over there on the way back to the airport.

Christy quietly watched the rolling tree-covered hills

as they stretched off toward the much higher Smokies. The landscape was nothing like what she expected.

"So what do you think?" Rob asked her as they swung off the two-lane blacktop and into the wide drive leading up to Billy's house and the race shop.

"It's so green here!"

Christy was accustomed to mountains, and the steep hillsides here were so similar to those back home in Southern California, but she couldn't believe all the trees, the grassy pastures, and the distant lush mountains. It was all a marked contrast to the dry, grassy scrub hills around Los Angeles.

"Well, here we are," Rob announced as he made the last curve in the drive. The compound of buildings on Billy's farm spread out before them, cupped in a bowl formed by the hills that swept up from all sides. "The cabin behind the house is Billy's office, and that new building over behind it is the race shop. That old barn over there is where they used to work on the first cars they ran when Billy first decided to get back into racing."

"This is so cool!" Toby marveled. He was clearly impressed with all the empty, fenced farmland that surrounded the few buildings. Such wide-open spaces were unheard of back in the Bay Area.

Work in the shop stopped abruptly as Rob brought the group through the front door. Billy was hunched over in the front fender well of the car they were planning on taking to Nashville. Will was standing nearby, helping Billy with the geometry of the front-end setup they were trying to put under the car before they loaded her up and headed west. Greetings were passed while Billy crawled over the fender to shake hands with everyone. Then Rob, Michelle, Toby, and Billy retired across the drive to Billy's office to talk business and take a look at some new ideas the marketing department was proposing.

Meanwhile, Will offered to take a break from working on the car and show Christy around the shop. She realized again how much bigger a business this all was than she could ever have imagined, how downright scientific it all was with machines and equipment that seemed to belong more in a laboratory than a race shop. It was fascinating to see how the cars that Rob drove were put together and then prepared specifically for the track they would run on that week. Will was a good tour guide, too, explaining in layman's terms what she was seeing and how it applied to trying to win a race.

She was, however, quite a distraction to the crew. They tried not to get caught as they stared at the lovely blonde. Donnie Kline whacked a couple of them on the backs of their heads and put them back beneath the car they were supposed to be working on.

When the meeting ultimately reverted to spreadsheets and stacks of papers and binders and financial statements filled with rows and columns of tiny numbers, Rob excused himself and eased out. He told himself he needed to check on the car and make sure everything was getting done, to see if maybe Will needed him to grab a wrench and give him a hand. But he knew it was really only that he wanted to check on Christy and see how she was doing. All through the meeting he kept seeing her as he had that morning, standing there at the base of the airplane steps, the bright sunshine in her golden hair, that wonderful smile and her mesmerizing eyes all lit up because she was with him again.

It was late afternoon when Rob dropped Toby off at the airport and wished him luck in his meetings in New York. He couldn't exactly figure out what "analysts" were or what they had to do with computers and software and such, but he didn't ask. Afterwards he headed over to his apartment to pick up the bags he had spent the night before packing and then back to the shop where everyone was waiting for him.

The trip over to Nashville in Billy's car was uneventful. Billy had stayed behind for some business he had to take care of, so Will Hughes drove the Town Car. Michelle sat up front with him and they talked about business, the stock market, the economy, and other stuff that sounded interesting, but not interesting enough for Rob to actually join in the conversation. Instead, he sat in the back, talking quietly with Christy and watching the mountains roll by, as the small towns marked by exits on I-40 came and went, as the bright blue Tennessee sky tried to outsparkle Christy Fagan's eyes.

It failed miserably.

They were all tired when they finally rolled through the limestone cut where the freeway dropped them down and allowed their first view of downtown Nashville. Christy and Michelle had been up since before sunrise that morning, had flown all the way across the country, and both were yawning as they checked into their hotel. The day was almost done anyway, and after a quiet dinner at an Italian restaurant over near Vanderbilt University, they called it a night.

But as soon as he got to his room, Rob picked up the phone and dialed the hotel operator, asking for Christy's room. Thankfully she answered instead of Michelle.

"I hope you don't mind that we didn't go out tonight," he said.

"No, not at all. I'm bushed and I know you need an early start. You have a busy day tomorrow, Mr. Stock Car."

Billy had explained to all of them before they left how compacted the schedule would be for this race, how everyone would have to concentrate on the job at hand. Both Christy and Rob had assumed the lecture was primarily for their benefit.

"Yeah, we all do. I've got a good feeling about this race, Christy. I'm glad you're here to see it."

"Me, too."

And something in her voice when she said those two words made them eminently believable.

There was no scrapbook this night either. As usual, he had stuck the thing into his overnight bag, but as soon as he lay down, he began reviewing the day in his head, looking for things he might have done better or differently. Before he could get to the part where he typically looked ahead to the day coming up, he was gone, lost in a dreamless sleep.

The next morning Rob was awake even before the telephone on the nightstand jangled with his wake-up call. Normally it was a struggle for him to climb out any earlier than he absolutely had to, but he eagerly awaited the start of this particular new day. Apparently some other folks were ready to get going, too. Christy and Michelle were already in the hotel restaurant on the mezzanine when he came down. Michelle seemed genuinely surprised to see him so early.

"It's alive! It's alive!" Michelle growled, using her best Dr. Frankenstein voice. She knew he now tended to sleep in when he was on the road. Billy had all but dictated it. He wanted his driver well rested.

Rob frowned and nodded toward one of the chairs, silently seeking permission to join them. Christy was already shoving it back for him to sit down.

"And a warm and wonderful good morning to you, too," he said. "I just didn't want you ladies to eat up all the breakfast before I had a shot at it." He looked pointedly at the eggs, grits, sausage patties, milk gravy, and southern biscuits piled up on both women's plates. "What happened to the granola and yogurt this morning?"

"We decided we needed to pack some carbs for the long day," Michelle said sheepishly.

"Actually, we just wanted to see what it tasted like." Christy grinned. "When in Rome, you know. And it's not half-bad."

"I'll have what they're having," Rob called as the waitress passed by.

They spent the rest of breakfast talking, laughing, carrying on about anything and everything but racing. It was when they were walking through the lobby toward the parking lot that Rob realized his usual racetrack butterflies were gone, long since wiped away by grits and eggs and the wonderful company.

The three of them took Billy's car over to the track. Will and the crew had gone ahead to begin getting the car unloaded and ready. But pleasant as the breakfast with Christy and Michelle had been, when Rob parked the car in the lot just behind turn two, his mind was back on the job at hand. He was ready to go racing.

Still, when Christy offered him her hand, he took it and held it as he steered her around a big pothole next to the gate to the parking area. When he looked back for Michelle, he couldn't help but notice an odd expression on her face, though. Could that have been jealousy?

Rob let the thought drop. That was a far too complicated question for him to consider on such a beautiful morning.

Some of the crowd that had gathered already at the entrance to watch the drivers come in called to him and waved slips of paper for him to autograph. Some of them seemed to recognize Christy, too, from all the television

shots she had shared with Rob in Daytona. A couple of
them even asked her for her autograph, too. She looked
startled, suspecting they were putting her on, but the
sincere looks on their faces confirmed they really wanted
her signature. They weren't sure who she was, but she
was with Rocket Rob Wilder, so they wanted an autograph.

Donnie Kline was directing the lowering of the race
car from the top of the hauler when they walked up.
The bright red plumage of the Ensoft Ford glinted in
the warm early morning sunlight as the lift slowly eased
the car to the ground. Rob stopped abruptly, still holding Christy's hand, and watched as the boys unchained
the car, literally setting her free. Then they slowly
pushed her off the lift and stopped her.

Rob stepped over, took his free hand, and caressed
the smooth surface of the car's fender all the way back
to the rear deck.

"You've got to agree she's beautiful, one fine race
car," he said softly to Christy. It was almost as if he were
talking about a racehorse. Or a woman he loved. "Here,
feel her. This is what a winner should feel like. Sleek
and smooth and powerful."

She did as he said and reached out and touched the
freshly waxed and polished skin of the race car. She was
surprised. Sure enough, it felt warm, almost as if the car
were alive, a breathing animal. Somehow she was able
to appreciate the same sensuous feeling Rob had for the
car. And to realize it was far more than a mere machine
to him.

Her eyes widened and she smiled when she spoke. "I
see what you mean! It's almost as if I can feel a pulse,
like some kind of raw power coursing through it before
the motor is even turned on."

Rob ignored Michelle, who was rolling her eyes. And

Donnie Kline, who was on the verge of saying something embarrassing. Rob gently pulled Christy aside so the crew could go to work.

"I can't wait to take her out there. This place is almost like home to me. You know, the first time I drove a race car for Billy was right here," Rob said, and remembered back to that hot summer day the year before when he had tested here all day without more than a few minutes' rest. He had been testing the car and testing himself at the same time.

"I didn't realize this was where you got started with Billy." She had never really thought about the fact that, as a race car driver, he had had to start somewhere. Nor that Nashville had been that place. She suddenly realized why Rob was so sentimental about this short asphalt track, its covered stands along the front stretch, and its cramped infield. It was nothing compared to the vastness of Daytona. But it clearly held a special place in Rob Wilder's heart. "I guess this place does mean a lot to you."

"It does. If I had failed to impress Billy and Will that day, I'd likely still be back in Hazel Green, Alabama, working for Mr. Brandon at the cabinet shop and racing late models whenever I could save up enough to buy the gas and a set of tires."

"This is a special place, then. And you'll drive well here," she said with a confident nod of her head and a tight squeeze of his hand.

"Yeah," Rob agreed with a flashing, self-assured smile. "We'll run good here. Real good."

And he returned the squeeze.

An hour or so later, the car was finished with the initial inspection and was sitting up on jack stands behind the truck. Rob emerged from the small shower/

dressing area in the hauler, already wearing his driving suit.

Michelle was sitting in the shade of the hauler, talking on her ever-present cell phone, conducting some kind of important business back in California. It was still before seven out there, but apparently things were popping already.

Christy sat in one of the director's chairs outside the back of the truck, sipping a bottled water, soaking up the warm sunshine, and watching the crew working on the car. She wasn't sure what all the tweaking and nudging they were doing meant, but she knew it was important and her best move would be to stay out of everyone's way. She did enjoy all the hustle and commotion, the irreverent shouts and carrying on of the crew. They all seemed so dedicated to what they were doing, so fixated on doing every little thing just right, but they also seemed intent on having a good time at it.

Will was busy making notations on his clipboard while he ruffled through the sheets of paper that were attached. They were doing a final review of what they wanted to accomplish in this first practice session. Rob would listen to whichever notation Will would read out loud, then he would nod his head in agreement or point at one of the sheets for clarification. It was a ritual they did before every practice session, and Christy noted that it varied very little from the same routine she had seen them complete during preparations for the Daytona practices.

Finally Rob settled into the cockpit, more than ready to go. Will leaned on the windowsill, checking the safety belts.

"You ready to see what we got, cowboy?"

"Yeah. Yeah, I am. I just wish they'd hurry things along. I'm gettin' an itchy throttle foot."

"She's going to be fast. We got her set up pretty close to what you used when we tested here last year. This place will eat up your tires, but then it'll eat up everybody else's, too. Let the tire pressures warm up before you start pushing the car. It'll take four or five laps for the pressures to ease on up. Then we'll get to see what she'll do."

"No problem."

Rob twisted on the steering wheel, making sure it was set a comfortable distance away from his body so his arms wouldn't tire so quickly during the race.

It was a great relief when he finally was able to fire the engine. He allowed it to warm up for a few seconds before the line of cars was waved out onto the track. Rob pushed the shifter up into gear, then eased out on the clutch. The car bounced across the pit road exit and merged out onto the track. It felt wonderful to be in motion, to be taking to the track, even if it was only for a practice session and not true competition.

But Rob knew, too, that the competition actually began hundreds of miles to the east, back in the shop in Chandler Cove as they prepared the car. Then it continued here as they worked feverishly to set the car up for qualifying and racing. The race itself was only the culmination of all that had gone on before. A race could as easily be lost in the shop several days before they even arrived at the track, before the crowd cheered them on at the race. Lost as surely as it could be out there on the track itself.

Rob took the first lap at three-quarter speed, allowing the engine and tires to fully warm up before getting on the gas.

As he kicked the throttle and charged off into the first turn, Rob finally felt as if he had returned to a wonderfully familiar place. This was his first trip back to this track where he had felt so much at home during his only other tour the year before. The exhilaration was a powerful stimulant and he wanted to push the car to its limit, to see what they had. But as badly as he wanted to let it all out immediately, Will's instructions for those first few laps rang in his ears like a distant echo. He forced himself to be patient, to wait for the tires to warm, bringing the pressures up.

Even then, without pushing hard at all, the car still felt plenty fast beneath him. He couldn't wait for Will to unleash him.

As he waited to finally push the car hard, Rob concentrated on driving smoothly into and out of the corners. It only took a couple of laps for his feel for this track to come back as surely as an old but pleasant memory. It seemed like only last week that he had run here.

Rob tucked the car down low in the center of turns three and four, right down on the white line, then he got back into the gas hard, precisely when he hit his mark. He felt the powerful motor jump beneath his feet, seemingly as eager as its driver was to be set free.

"Let 'er rip, cowboy," came the welcome voice crackling in his radio earpiece.

Rob didn't take the time to reply. He lit the car's fuse and held on for the blastoff, coming off the corner at full speed, wide open. He never saw the empty grandstands as he flashed by, nor did he see any of the activity in the crowded infield. Every bit of concentration he possessed was focused on driving the car where he knew it needed to go, on getting her down into the first turn as fast as possible.

He set his line, taking him low down on the track, hugging the apron. The car rocketed into the corner with the right side digging into the banking. There was faint complaint from the tires, but the car stuck, hanging in, grabbing traction as if it were on a set of rails. He got back in the gas going through turn two and hurtled down the backstretch, looking for all the world as if he were unaware or had somehow forgotten that the track took a hard left turn just up ahead.

At exactly the correct spot, he cracked the throttle, set the car into the curve, then accelerated as he came up off the turn-four banking. Across the start/finish line he flashed, ready to make another lap and, if it was at all possible, make it all the faster.

Christy and Michelle climbed up to the viewing platform on top of the truck to watch the practice. Michelle offered Christy the scanner she was carrying to see if she wanted to listen in on the conversations between the crew, the spotter, and the driver. She declined, though, doubting she would know much of what they were talking about anyway. And she suspected it would only make her more nervous to hear Rob talking while he was trying to hang on to that bucking bronco out there.

Besides, she wanted to stand up there against the railing and take in everything, the noise, the smells, the wildness of this brash, swaggering sport she had suddenly learned to love. She had noticed how Rob had lounged nonchalantly around the car before climbing in, as if he were about to take the minivan down to the market for a gallon of milk. The more she watched, the more she was around these people, the more she admired the courage it took for them, and especially Rob Wilder, to go out there and hurtle around the speedway in those steel boxes. And almost as much as she admired their bravery, she had developed an equal appreciation for their determination to win. Everything they did was for first place. Not to merely finish strong, but to finish first to the flag in every race they entered. It was such a determined mission, from Billy and Will right on down to the men who gassed the car and wiped the windshield. It was a single-mindedness that was impressive to watch but hard to fathom.

Will scrambled up the ladder to join them as the practice session started. He left Donnie in charge down in the pit area, ready to make any necessary changes. Not only did Will want to watch his car from somewhere where he could follow it all the way around the course, but he also wanted to see who else among the practicing cars would be running strongly. With a crowded field on hand, and with the likelihood that some decent cars might be forced to go home before the race ever started, he needed to know who was a threat and who was not. He was already plotting race strategy, and they weren't even ready for qualifying yet.

He explained to Christy and Michelle what he was looking for as he watched with a practiced eye every move that Rob made during those first few laps. He studied intently how the car got into and off the corners. He looked to see if it tended to push up in the center of the turns. Even before he finally gave Rob the okay to finally push the car, he had a relatively good idea of where they stood and what changes he needed to convey to Donnie down in the pits. What he saw when Rob set sail only confirmed those ideas.

He jotted down a few notes on the clipboard, then he hit the microphone button on the headset to tell Rob a timed lap was coming up, to drive it the way his instincts told him it should be driven. Will clicked the stopwatch then, ready to time the first hard lap.

Rob raced hard off into the corner as Will watched every bounce and push. Will accidentally revealed a slight grin on his normally stern countenance as the car stuck perfectly to the low side of the track. Centrifugal force dictated that the car give way and slide up the track, and especially at speeds such as Rob was now turning out there. An object in motion tends to follow a straight line, not some artificially curved one, like a race-course at the Fairgrounds in Nashville, Tennessee. But everything Will and Billy and the crew had built into the car had been designed to overcome that natural compulsion. And all of Rob Wilder's driving intuitions were honed on overcoming that force of nature, too.

Will Hughes never took his eyes off the car as it roared around the track. He clicked the watch again as Rob passed the finish line. A quick glance at its face told him all he needed to know.

They were fast. Very fast.

Later that evening, Rob waited behind the pit wall for the start of the qualifying session. He was beginning to realize, even more than before, that everything now depended even more on him and his performance inside the racer. The car was plenty fast enough to win the pole position. It was his job now to go out and actually win it. The car couldn't do it alone. It would take a perfect lap for him to pull it off. They had already seen that there were four or five other cars that were just as fast or faster. That meant that it would ultimately come down to the driver. The one who made the cleanest lap would lead the rest of the field down to take the green flag when the race started.

For once, Billy Winton wasn't at the track for quali-fying, the business he had keeping him back home until he could fly in early the next day for the race. This was a first for Rob. He had always had Billy's calming influ-ence at the track, always had his unwavering counsel whenever he needed advice.

Not today. With Will busy getting the car ready, Rob was left to his own devices.

He talked quietly with Christy as he waited for the

qualifying round to start. It was still amazing to him that the two of them could find so much to talk about, even though they came from such dissimilar backgrounds. But there was so much he wanted to know about her, about her home, growing up, school, that he doubted he could ever find out everything. And she, too, seemed vitally interested in him, how he had grown up. He mostly dodged the subject, though, and usually managed to turn the conversation back to her.

One thing they didn't talk about was racing. And that kept Rob from stewing over the qualifying, worrying about whether he could give the car the run it deserved. He finally mentioned it to her.

"I appreciate you keeping me distracted. I'd be a nervous Nellie by now, and especially with Billy not here to hold my hand."

She reached over and took his hand in hers as if on cue.

"That's my job this trip," she said. "You know, Billy asked me yesterday if I would keep an eye on you during practice and qualifying. Wanted me to keep you from worrying so much about how you would do."

Rob squinted as he looked at her hard. "So you're just doing the boss's bidding, baby-sitting me?"

"Yeah! I didn't want to spend time with you at all, but he made me!" she laughed, and the smile on her face told him how silly it would be for him to be mad about the setup.

He grinned and blushed. "Well, thanks for making the sacrifice. We do need a good starting spot here. It gets real crowded back in the pack and it's easy to burn a set of tires slap up trying to catch up to the leaders."

"Slap up," she confirmed in her best imitation of a southern drawl.

They were both still laughing when one of the net-

work reporters walked up to them. Rob politely introduced him to Christy. When he described her as his
friend, she gave him a sharp nudge in the ribs with her
elbow along with a questioning look. The reporter made
a mental note to pursue this relationship a bit more the
next day if he got the opportunity.

"You know I got to ask you the standard question,"
the television man said. "How you think you'll do in
qualifying? Do you have a chance at the pole?"

"Does a one-legged duck swim in a circle?" Rob said
with a laugh. Then he got serious. "The pole would be
nice, but we've all been concentrating on getting the
setup right for tomorrow. We'd be pleased to start anywhere in the top ten."

Rob wanted to tell him that he was dead certain they
would claim the pole position and that they would be
more than disappointed with anything less. But he held
his tongue. He didn't want to appear overly cocky.

The reporter thanked him, told Christy how nice it
had been to meet her, and then moved on in search of
more stories. This little romance between the hottest and
most eligible young driver on the Grand National circuit
and the beautiful stranger from California would con-
tinue to make good fodder for the reporter's story mill.
Today's race fans were interested in far more than
merely the horsepower of their favorite drivers' engines.
They wanted the inside stuff, too.

"What do you mean, 'friend'?" Christy asked as soon
as the reporter was out of earshot. She had squared
around and faced him, her jaw out, her blue eyes flashing.

"Uh . . . well . . . I . . ." Rob stammered. He didn't
know how to react to her sudden apparent anger.

"I didn't fly all the way across the country just to see

a car race. I came to see a particular driver who would
be in that race."

"I just thought you might be embarrassed if I introduced you as anything else."

"I don't chase men. I came because I thought you
wanted me to be here. I could be home, getting ready
for finals."

"Christy, listen to me," Rob said, and moved closer,
looking into her eyes. For a moment he felt as if he were
going to lose himself in their deep blueness. But he
couldn't look away. He didn't have the strength. "I wish
you could come to every single race with me. Two
months has been way too long since the last time we
were together."

She smiled slightly, then stepped into his arms naturally. He wrapped them around her and pulled her in
close to him.

"It has been much too long," she whispered softly, so
quietly he could hardly hear her words.

He didn't hesitate. Rob bent down and kissed her
deeply, forgetting that he was standing in the middle of
the motor pits at the Nashville Speedway, surrounded
not only by his crew but by all the men he competed
against. But he didn't care. As he stood there, his lips
on hers, his heart was racing much more furiously than
it ever did when he was behind the wheel of the Ford.
And it was as thrilling a moment, too.

Finally, reluctantly, their lips parted, but he continued
to hold her tightly, as if she might run away if he let her
go. As he watched her eyes, he hardly noticed that the
first race car to attempt to qualify had already made its
way out onto the track and was coming up to speed.

"Okay, lover boy, it's time to get in the car if you still
got the strength," Donnie Kline hollered across the wall.

Rob jumped, embarrassed for a moment, but then he

leaned down and kissed Christy again before finally letting her go and hopping away, across the wall and in the direction of his waiting car.

"And you . . . you can just shut up," he called back over his shoulder to Donnie. He wished he had a snappier comeback, but that was the best he could do.

To his credit, Kline knew when to leave well enough alone. He dismissed the kid with a wave of his big paw and began pulling on his radio headset, mumbling all the time.

Will Hughes caught up with him and joined in step. "I don't need to tell you we need us a good solid run. Don't try to win the race in qualifying. We'll do that tomorrow."

"The car's right on, Will. We got a good shot at the pole. If we don't take it, it'll be my fault."

"Not necessarily. But we do need a good starting spot tomorrow. Just go out there and run us a good smooth lap."

"I'll do it," Rob stated emphatically, then he swung his long legs in through the open window, grabbed the roof strip, and shoehorned himself into the driver's seat.

Out there in front of him, other cars kept rolling off the line to take the green flag for each of their runs. As Rob meticulously fastened up his seat belts, he glanced over to where Christy Fagan stood next to the wall, looking his way. As he watched, Michelle ambled up next to her, still with the small telephone at her ear.

He finished putting the radio earplugs in, then pulled on the helmet. Once fastened in, he stared straight ahead, focusing on the track as it led up to the banking of the first turn. There were only a couple of cars left in front of him now.

He was ready to run. But he could also feel Christy's body next to his, her lips on his, her arms around his neck, squeezing tightly, as reluctant to let him go as he was to move away from her.

Once again he pulled his eyes away from her, watching the rear end of the car in front of him. He imagined the strip of narrow asphalt was mocking him now, defying him to try to conquer it if he could. He pretended that the driver in the car ahead of him was laughing, daring him to better his time if he thought he could. And he tried to picture some of the fans in the grandstands, laughing and pointing at him, assuring each other that Rob Wilder and the 06 team didn't have a chance at outrunning their own particular favorite.

Challengers. All challengers. All determined to deny him what was rightfully his.

He gritted his teeth hard and felt himself becoming more and more determined, almost to the point of anger.

Now he was ready to show them all just what Rob Wilder and the 06 Ford team were made of.

FIRST TO THE FLAG

First in line now, finally, Rob hit the starter switch and fired the engine. He reveled in the powerful vibrations that reverberated throughout the steel frame that surrounded him.

"Remember, we need a good smooth lap here," Will's voice crackled through the earpiece.

"Roger," Rob radioed back.

He didn't mind Will's repetition of the theme. It didn't hurt to hear it again. Rob flexed his arms and clenched and unclenched his fists as he waited for the official to wave him out on the track.

He felt good about the car. Winning the pole was well within his grasp if he only went out and ran a perfect lap. The pole win at Daytona had only whetted his appetite for more. Now he no longer approached qualifying as only an opportunity to make the field, to claim a decent starting spot. Instead, he focused with all his might on actually winning the top spot. To Rob's way of thinking, there were two races to be run and won this weekend: the run for the top starting spot as well as the race itself.

Then he got the signal, the wave to drive out onto the track. Rob eased out on the clutch, then hit the gas. He charged off into turn one, trying to build up as much momentum as possible on the warm-up lap. The roar of the accelerating motor echoed off the concrete and the steel-roofed grandstands where the spectators who had gathered to watch the qualifying and final practices stood and cheered each car past.

Will stepped back to where Christy and Michelle stood with the rest of the crew next to the wall. He held his stopwatch in his gloved hand as they watched Rob take the car into turn three, now at almost full song. Then he cocked his head to listen at the precise moment when the pitch of the motor changed noticeably as the car charged out of turn four.

Christy tucked her arms across her chest and crossed the fingers of both hands. She knew, even from her limited experience, how important the next minute would be to their hopes for the weekend.

"Nervous?" her sister asked.

"A little. I don't see how they do this every week. It's so nerve-racking."

"That's all part of the game to them. They want to win so badly. It just trickles down to every little thing they do."

Michelle followed the car through the last turn as it came roaring down the front stretch to take the green flag.

Christy stood on the tips of her toes as she strained to see over everyone's head. Rob flashed by in front of her and she tightened her crossed fingers.

"Come on. Come on, Rob," she whispered.

For a moment she considered not even watching, but she reconsidered and stayed locked on the bright red car at it shrieked off toward the first turn.

Will watched, but with an odd twinge of apprehension. He knew they had a good, fast car that was capable of not only winning the race but also possibly dominating it. He could sense the quiet confidence in his driver. Rob knew he had a good car and he was certain he would dust the field in the qualifying run. But Will knew there were other good cars entered.

And he also knew all too well that lots of things could happen in one flat-out lap.

He was sure that having the girl here had helped keep their driver from peaking his intensity level too early. Billy had been right about that. For them to take the next step and begin to win races, they needed to make sure they kept Rob pulled back from the edge just enough so he would listen to their coaching and drive smart. They were more convinced than ever that the kid had the natural instincts and the innate ability to do amazing things with the car. But he also had an almost unnatural drive to win.

Now it was time to pull the car, the team, the driver, and his amazing skills all together. The result would be many trips to victory lane. There wasn't a better place to take that next step than right there in Nashville, the track where legends like Darrell Waltrip, Sterling Marlin, and Bobby Hamilton, along with up-and-comers like Jeremy Mayfield and Casey Atwood, had all cut their teeth.

Rob took the green flag in total flight, his foot jammed hard to the floorboard. The car was inches from the wall as it zipped by the flagstand. He raced down toward turn one, angling the car for the low, fast line around the track. The car went hard into the corner as he manhandled the steering wheel, twisting the car around the turn using almost brute force. Out of the gas, with a slight tap on the brake, he paused only a moment, then was back into the throttle as the car rolled through the second corner.

Will glanced quickly at the stopwatch as the car exited turn two. The speed was right where he knew it should be. Right where he would have hoped it would be at this point.

The lap was very fast so far. But it was less than half over.

"Come on now! Come on!" Will yelled, balling his right hand up into a fist as he watched the car start down the back straightaway, the first two turns now behind it.

The Ford seemed to jump off the second corner as it bounced over the bump in the pavement where the tunnel into the infield passed beneath the track. Rob never even noticed it. He was only watching the track ahead, getting set already for the line he would take into turn three. His hands and feet worked in unison, in one fluid motion, as he dived deep into the curve. Rob did know one thing. He was certain he had a good lap going. Still he didn't let up, pushing the car hard as he hit the line perfectly, staying in the gas as long as he dared.

Then, once again, Rob pegged the speeding car right down to the white line at the bottom of the track. The car bounced a bit as it crossed a little bump in the center of the corner. Rob sensed the rear end break loose ever so slightly then and he grabbed the wheel even harder, giving it the tiniest nudge to try to make certain it didn't get worse.

Suddenly the back end seemed to jump out from under him. He wrestled with the wheel, trying his dead level best to hang on.

Will watched him drive hard into the third turn. Rob

seemed to actually be a bit too hot going in. Maybe the kid knew what he was doing. He prayed the car would stick.

But then he could see the rear end begin to wiggle and he felt his heart sink.

"Hang on, cowboy, hang on!" he shouted to nobody in particular.

The last thing they needed was for their car to take a sudden hard turn toward the fence. He held his breath until he saw that the kid had somehow managed to save it, to get control and come on around to take the checkered flag. But he knew without looking at the stopwatch that making the pole was no longer a possibility, that they would depend on what the other cars did to see if they even made the field without relying on a provisional starting spot.

Rob hammered the throttle hard and brought the car on around to take the checkered flag. He felt sick to his stomach as he crossed the line and reached over and hit the kill switch to shut off the motor. Disgusted, he pounded the steering wheel with his fist and coasted the car onto the apron, drifting slowly down the backstretch as the next car accelerated out to start its own qualifying run. Maybe to bump the 06 from the field.

Rob eased down the pit road, jerking down the window net. As he pulled the car behind the wall, he ripped off his driving gloves and launched them into the floorboard.

"Dadgummit!" he fumed as he struggled with the clip that held the steering wheel on its shaft. He finally managed to get it unsnapped and he angrily slung the wheel up on the dashboard. Now able to get out, he grabbed the roof railing and pulled himself up to sit in the window opening. He was still sitting there fuming when Will came scurrying over.

"You okay?" Will asked.

"Yeah, I'm okay. I guess that's what I get for thinking I was God's gift to stock car racing. I just pushed the darn thing too hard into three and she broke loose on me. Everything was perfect. The motor. The setup. Everything but the dumb driver."

"It cost us a couple of tenths. We'll have to wait and see how bad it hurt us, but we should still make the field on speed. If not, we got a provisional we can use."

"I can't believe I didn't listen to you, Will. As many times as you've told me. All I had to do was be smooth and I had it in the bag. Instead, I tried to push it just a tad too hard and it's gonna cost us big. I could kick myself. Or bend over and let everybody line up and do it for me."

"Don't be so hard on yourself. The car before you might've dropped a little bit of oil over there in three and you just got into that. Might have been a different story if we had made the run a few cars earlier."

"I don't know. It did come loose awful easy, it seemed like. Either way, though, I blew it. That run was gonna be good enough to take the pole."

"Don't matter now. We just have to suck it up and concentrate on winning the real race," Will said, giving the kid a tap on the shoulder.

"I guess you're right. Will, if I don't listen to everything you and Billy tell me from now on, you have my permission to take a switch to me."

Will gave his driver a slap on the back, showed him a sincere grin, and helped him climb on out of the car. He needed the kid to get over his disappointment so they could get on with all the things they needed to get done to prepare the car for far more than a single lap the next day. It was no time to panic or to give up. They would still be in the race, one way or the other, and now, more than ever, they needed the car to be set up perfectly.

Will signaled for Donnie and the boys to push the car back to the truck while he watched the rest of the qualifying session. Will knew they would be back in the pack somewhere, but he anxiously waited to find out who would be surrounding them.

Rob stood watching the beautiful red race car being pushed away and hardly noticed that Christy had walked up. She stepped closer and put her arm around his waist. The disappointment was palpable. She had known something was wrong when she saw the look on Will's face when the car bobbled in the corner. She couldn't imagine what it could be. The race car seemed to be flying, still headed straight, and roaring right along to where the checkered flag was waving. She was even more aware of there being trouble when Will failed to even check his stopwatch, but ran off to where Rob would be bringing the car in a few moments.

Now Rob Wilder's demeanor was far different from the wild celebration she had seen him put on after the qualifying run at Daytona. She was struck again with the depths and heights the participants in this game had to endure. Riding high one minute, stopped cold the next.

Somehow Christy sensed that she had a job to do now, that maybe her trip here had been for more than making small talk with this handsome young man for whom she had developed such a liking. She hoped she was up for the challenge.

Rob Wilder needed cheering up in the worst way. He needed his confidence restored, his mind freed of the guilt he was feeling for letting the team down in that split second. He hadn't suddenly forgotten how to drive a race car. And the car itself would be just as fast tomorrow. They weren't beaten yet, and she was determined to make him understand that.

She smiled at him, and his mood brightened noticeably.

"I was just thinking how bad I want some of that southern barbecue you talk about so much," she said.

"I think I know just the spot," he replied, almost smiling himself as he locked his arm in hers and led her away.

They were still sitting in the hotel lobby that night talking when the rest of their entourage came in from their own evening on the town. They had gone to a big country dance club downtown. Even Will Hughes had joined them. He usually preferred staying in the night before a race, poring over the charts and graphs to make sure he had not missed something that might break. But the car had still been perfect in the final practice laps they had run, and the weather conditions were predicted to be similar come race time, so Will had decided to abandon his clipboards and went out with the others to sample the Nashville nightlife. He figured with both Michelle and him along, the rest of the crew couldn't get too rowdy. And who knew? Maybe having a good time would make everybody a little looser for the race. Even Will admitted they had all been a little too intense all day.

Rob was up early the next morning, ready to go. He had his jaw set, a renewed look of determination on his face. They had a lot of ground to make up once the race started, but after another wonderful evening with Christy Fagan and a good night's sleep, he was confident he and the car and its crew could get the job done.

"Christy, I know you came out here to see a winner, and I'm going to show you one tomorrow," he had told her. He was still embarrassed she had seen him blow the qualifying lap.

"Look, you don't have to prove anything to me," she said with a half smile on her lips.

"Yes, I do," he replied emphatically. "You, Billy, Will, myself, my dad . . ."

He stopped abruptly, blushed, changing the subject to country music and pointing out they might see some of the stars later at the track. Christy didn't miss the reference to his dad and the quick change of subject.

They arrived at the track only a few minutes after the pits opened. Rob carried in the sack of drinks they had picked up for him to use during his pit stops. Will Hughes was already inside the hauler when they got there.

"Mornin'," Rob said, and he realized he was almost as embarrassed by his attitude the previous afternoon as he had been over his driving gaffe.

"What about it, cowboy? We ready to go out there and get 'em?"

"Yes. As a matter of fact, I am."

"That's what I like to hear."

"And I'm going to listen to you, too. You tell me to run the whole dang race in reverse, that's exactly what I'm gonna do."

"I'm not worried. You know I'd rather you mess up running too hard than lagging around out there. We came here to win, and I don't think we can do that coasting home."

"It's like I heard Jodell Lee say one time. 'Second? That word ain't even in my dictionary!' " Rob growled in a reasonably good imitation of Lee.

Will believed him. The close second at Daytona had only whetted the kid's appetite for a win. It wouldn't be easy, but today could just be the day he got it.

"Rob, I want that win today. If we knock down the fence trying to do it, then we'll just have to fix the car and try again next week. But you'll earn it if you get it. We've got all those Cup drivers here because of the off week, and you saw how strong some of the regular Busch guys qualified."

"I want to take that guitar home with me."

Rob was referring to the guitar the speedway awarded the winners of the races held there in Music City.

"You win it, I know enough chords I can teach you, you'll be able to sing Miss Christy Fagan a beautiful song," Will said with a wink.

The two men slipped into the trailer's lounge and plotted the race strategy they wanted to follow while Christy and Michelle watched the crew ready the race car. Michelle had a group of guests who would be wandering through soon to meet their driver and get their pictures taken with a real, live race car in a genuine pit stall. Rob's old friends from Hazel Green were supposed to stop by, too, and visit awhile with him.

Right now the car had fluttering checklists taped everywhere in, on, and underneath it. A different crewman slowly worked his way through each item on the list and dutifully checked it off when he was absolutely sure it had been taken care of. Bolts were tightened, fittings checked, and clearances noted in every nook and cranny of the Ford. It was nothing new, the same routine they followed every race. But the final checkout was as crucial to winning as the driver, the tires, the motor, or any other cog in the machine.

After the mandatory drivers' meeting ended, the drivers and crew chiefs scattered back to their various trucks and haulers, each one as sure as the other that the day belonged to him.

Meanwhile, almost three hundred miles to the east at

the airport near Kingsport, Billy Winton was growing more and more anxious. All but one of the passengers had climbed aboard the airplane, and he was only going to give the tardy one another five minutes before they flew on without him. Besides, the waiting was only allowing some of those already aboard to get even rowdier.

Finally, tired of waiting, Billy announced, "I've got a race to get to," as he reached down to pull up the ladder. But the final passenger came sprinting out of the flight service toward the plane, and Billy had to drop the ladder back down.

"Some things never change!" Billy snapped as the others laughed.

"Sorry," the man with the windblown hair apologized as he climbed the ladder and settled into a seat, panting for breath and wiping the sweat from his face with a handkerchief. He flashed Billy a grin, showing perfect white teeth. His hair was still thick and dark without even a hint of gray despite his age.

"He ain't never been on time in all the years I've known him," one of the other men volunteered. "Don't reckon he's gonna start now just to please you, Billy."

An hour or so later, the King Air touched down softly on the runway at Nashville International Airport. The group spilled out of the plane and into a van waiting to ferry them to the racetrack. The talk on the flight over and in the van on the way to the track was subdued, mostly spent debating how the bad starting position might best be overcome and what their chances were. It was the consensus that if the kid got a few breaks, if Rob could steer clear of trouble back there, and if he didn't burn the tires up trying to get to the front, then they still had a shot at winning. But that was a lot of "ifs." The Ensoft racing team had its work cut out for it.

The group parked the van and made their way through the tunnel into the infield. But it took them a while to make the walk. They were repeatedly stopped by friends and acquaintances and fans with relatively long memories. Finally growing tired of all the talk, the two women in the group headed on over to the truck, leaving the men behind.

Michelle saw them walking up and came running out of the back of the truck to greet them.

"Catherine Lee! I didn't know you were coming."

"I didn't either. Not until Jodell woke up this morning and called Billy and invited himself and me along. You know this bunch. If there's a race, they're bound and determined to be there."

"Well, I'm sure glad you came!"

Michelle had met Jodell Lee's wife the previous year at Charlotte. She had immediately liked the older woman and appreciated her kind hospitality.

"Me, too. It was going to be such a pretty day and I haven't been to a race in a while, so we just decided to tag along and make sure our men behave themselves."

"From what I've seen of that crew, that's going to be a pretty tall order."

"Joyce and I've had plenty of practice. Have you met Joyce Baxter? Bubba's wife and keeper?"

"Nice to meet you, Michelle," Joyce Baxter said.

"This is my sister, Christy," Michelle offered.

"Nice to meet both of you," Christy said with a smile. These women seemed so friendly, so totally unfazed by all the noise and race-day activity around them. They might just as well have been at a church social somewhere as there in the pits with a stock car race about to break out around them.

Michelle asked a couple of the crew members to haul

some more chairs up to the top of the hauler when they got to a stopping point.

Rob sat nearby on the ground, leaning back against one of the big truck's tires, talking with one of the television reporters who had tracked him down. They were recording an interview to be a part of the opening of the race coverage. He fielded the usual questions about the car and what he thought his chances for the day were. But one of the reporter's questions took him by surprise.

"Is there any reason you've brought the big guns in here today?"

"Huh?"

"Rob, we know you have a fast car. You proved that in practice. But as I sit here and see all the people you've brought in to cheer you on, I get the feeling that you've left nothing to chance today."

Rob looked up to where the reporter was pointing. There was Billy and all the others, now approaching the truck. Rob saw then what the reporter was talking about. They were all there. Racing legend Jodell Bob Lee, his easy saunter making it clear that he was still an athlete. Jodell's cousin and revered engine builder, Joe Banker, still rumpled from his late night and nick-of-time arrival at the airport. Big old Bubba Baxter, a sack of hot dogs in one hand and a large cup of soda in the other. Randy Weems and Clifford Stanley, taking turns at a jar of moonshine liquor they were not-so-discreetly passing between them.

"Well, we run engines that we get from Joe Banker and Lee Racing, so I guess they all just wanted to come and see how we would do with their motor today," Rob suggested. But still, he did wonder himself what they were all doing here.

The camera panned over to the six men just approaching the race car. The reporter watched the tiny monitor screen he had left sitting on the ground nearby.

"Those men on your screen right there, folks, built and raced some of the best cars this sport has ever seen. There are those who say his protégé, Rob Wilder, looks remarkably like a young Jodell Lee when he's out there on that track. Rob, does talk like that put extra pressure on you?"

"No, I go into every race thinking I can win. Today is no different."

"Well, there you have it. We have one very confident young race driver here and a very distinguished cheering section here to help him."

Will, Billy, Jodell, and Bubba disappeared inside the team hauler, likely to discuss race strategy. Meanwhile Joe Banker had crawled beneath the hood of the race car and was busy jetting the carburetor himself. With a fistful of wrenches and screwdrivers, he had gone right to work. Finally he signaled to Donnie to fire the motor up. He cocked his head and listened to the sweet sound of the engine for a moment. A big smile on his face, he pronounced the motor ready to race.

Rob and Christy walked together up to the front straightaway to wait for the driver introductions while the crew finished setting up the pit and Donnie Kline supervised the stacking of tires. He personally checked the pressures on each set.

As they walked along, Rob turned to look at his car. The bright red Ensoft Ford sat there, forlornly lined up three rows forward from the very tail end of the field. The kid could only shake his head. It seemed wrong somehow for such a fine machine to be stuck back there with the also-rans.

Rob stood talking with Christy until the last possible minute to cross over to the stage in front of the grandstands. Since he was buried so deeply in the field, Rob was one of the first drivers to get introduced to the big crowd. He acknowledged the cheers from the fans with a wave, then crossed through the gate back across the track to where Christy stood waiting. She knew it was time to leave him so he could get to work. She gave him a quick kiss and wished him luck. As she walked away, Rob called to her.

"Have I told you how glad I am that you're here?"

"Me, too. Just win this thing, okay?"

He gave her a smile and a thumbs-up and headed off to the car. Will and Jodell Lee were standing there waiting. The old driver motioned the kid closer.

"Son, I've been looking over the time sheets from your practices. I've run a lot of races here. You got a car here that can win this thing. But this is a tricky old track. It's awful easy to burn up a set of tires trying to come from the back like you're gonna have to do."

"What would you do if you were me?" Rob asked.

"First off, I'd be danged patient, no matter how bad it hurt to run along back there. I know you get tired of hearing 'patience, patience, patience,' but that's the ticket today. You need to move on up, all right, and you got the car to do it, but you have to be easy on the tires. You are not going to be able to catch the leaders under green. All you want to do is get up to the top ten or so. Once you get there, the caution flags will let you catch up to the leaders so you can race them."

"What if there are cautions early? If there are, we're in trouble."

"That's why it's so important for you to pass as many cars as you can early while the tires are still fresh. If there's a bunch of early cautions before the leaders start lapping cars, you'll be half a lap down on the restarts 'cause of the darn single-file restarts."

"Then I'll go hard right when they drop the green flag."

"Just make sure that early caution ain't caused by you! With all those slower cars in front of you, you'll be tempted to try to put the car where you shouldn't. A busted-up race car ain't very likely to win."

"Thanks, Jodell. I appreciate it."

The call came then for the drivers to go to their cars.

"See you in victory lane, kid," Jodell called, then he was gone, striding off quickly before he was stopped by a fan for an autograph.

"Let's load her up," Will said. "We got a race to run."

"No, Will. We got us a race to win."

Will pounded his driver on the shoulder.

Rob climbed in the window and settled down into the padded driver's seat. He pulled the heat-shielding pad up on the back of his right foot, then calmly arranged the belts as he hooked them together. Will hooked the radio up and passed the earplugs over. Rob grabbed one of the small pieces of duct tape stuck on the mirror and pressed it to the back of the earpiece, then used it to secure the piece in his ear. Once he had done the other ear, he pulled on his helmet. Will yanked on the belts, made sure they were tight and secure, then backed out of the car and fastened the window net.

He stood beside the car then, waiting for the signal to start the engines. He keyed the mike for a radio check, called the spotter to make sure they could communicate, then he spoke to Rob over the circuit.

"Did you copy Harry?"

"Loud and clear."

"Gentlemen, start your engines!" The cry echoed over the public address system.

Rob flipped the starter switch, Joe's motor rumbled to life, and Rob gave the gas pedal a couple of pumps, feeling the vibration of the headers beneath his feet. He glanced at the gauges, then stared straight ahead out the windshield, waiting for the field to begin rolling away.

The crowd of people who had assembled on top of the Ensoft Racing Team truck all came to their feet at the sound of the engines. Clifford and Randy had been doing a running comedy routine. Catherine and Joyce were well acquainted with their antics. Michelle had sampled their act at the Texas race. But poor Christy didn't know whether to laugh or run for her life.

The start of the engines put an end to the show. Everyone, even the "two stooges," was suddenly serious. They were all ready to get to racing.

Will Hughes climbed up on the pit box and settled in with his computer and clipboard. Donnie and the rest of the crew stood poised, ready whenever the first pit stop occurred. Will waved Bubba Baxter up onto the pit box next to him. He radioed Donnie and asked him to fetch a radio for Baxter. Will figured he might just as well put the man's expertise to use since he was there and available.

Soon the pace laps were done and the cars came around for the last time, lining up to catch the green flag. The cars began to tighten up for the start. Only then did the challenge he faced become perfectly visible to Rob Wilder. The lead cars were exiting turn two while he was still going into turn one. It seemed like miles up there to where the leaders ran proudly and strongly. His first impulse would be to stomp it, to try to pass the whole field ahead of him from the get-go in order to get up there where the leaders were.

But the words of caution Jodell had given him still echoed loud and clear in his mind. He took a deep breath and got ready, all the while checking the cars around him, and especially those just ahead of him.

"Tighten up! Tighten up!" Rob yelled over the sound of the engine, as if those in front of him, so slow in closing the gaps between their hoods and the rear bumpers of those ahead of them, could actually hear him. But his pleas did no good and he was still entering turn three as the pole sitter, way up there ahead of him, was already preparing to take the green flag.

"Green! Green! Green!" Will screamed into the radio, walking all over the spotter, who was yelling the same words.

Rob would never see the green flag until he worked his way down the front stretch. But he certainly heard the words in his radio earpiece. He stomped on the gas and gritted his teeth in determination. He was careful, though, not to pass on the inside until he crossed the start/finish line. That would be a penalty. But as soon as he was beneath the flag stand, he jerked the wheel to the left and blew by a couple of cars as the pack charged off through the dust cloud into the first turn.

The whole bunch tightened up in front of him as the cars stacked up two by two as far ahead as he could see. Rob now found himself blocked in, apparently unable to make any attempt at a move up. But he sensed that the car wanted to run. And Lord knew, Rob Wilder certainly did. He made it three wide down the backstretch and somehow managed to pick up another couple of spots before the corner tightened up. He slid quickly back in line through the turn, tucked a foot or two off the back bumper of the Chevy in front of him.

Rob dove down low coming up out of turn four trying to get a run on the Chevy. The Ensoft Ford was clearly superior to anything close by. He was able to pass easily as long as the cars weren't stacked up in front of him.

Patience. Show patience and take what is there to be

taken. You'll know what you can claim and what you can't. Patience. Show patience.

Rob could almost hear the words echoing in his head. Sometimes they actually materialized over the radio. Sometimes he realized he was uttering the mantra himself. Other times it almost seemed as if it were a disembodied voice riding right there in the car with him.

But as more laps wound off, the field began to string out more and more. With the cars starting to get single file in front of him, Rob was able to emphatically show them all what he had under the hood.

Will and Bubba watched anxiously as the youngster tore his way up through the field. By only the twentieth lap, he had already passed half the cars in the race. But then it was also apparent that the tires were starting to wear down, so the remaining cars would not be nearly so easy to pass. Will was proud of Rob for trying to conserve the tires, but since he was coming hard through the field, he was quickly using them up. The leaders didn't have that problem, and the top four or five cars began to put some distance on those that were trailing.

"He's doing good, Will," Bubba called over the crew channel on the radio.

"Yeah, but his tires are going away faster than the leaders', and they don't have to deal with all this traffic like he has. We need a caution pretty soon so we can get some fresh rubber."

"The way those guys are racing back in the pack, I'd say you'll get it pretty soon."

"Okay, gang. Let's be ready when it happens. Get four tires ready. I'll give you the pressures for them as soon as we decide," Will instructed the crew.

Donnie Kline already stood there with his jack resting on his thigh, the sun reflecting off his shaved head. He, too, anticipated an early caution. He looked around him to make sure the others had heard Will's instructions. If they got a caution, the crew was going to have to deliver a good, fast stop to keep from losing some of that hard-won track position. And maybe they could even give their driver a little edge.

Rob was oblivious to everything but the cars in front of him and the sound of the spotter calling out information in his ear. Suddenly the car in front of him wiggled going into turn one. Reflex caused Rob to crack the throttle a tiny bit and yank the wheel to the left. Somehow, miraculously, the driver gathered the loose car back up again, but not before Rob had slid by with just inches to spare. Still, the close encounter left his heart pounding, but he quickly settled back down, setting his sights on the cars running in the top ten.

The announcers covering the race had so far concentrated most of their attention on the Winston Cup drivers day-tripping in the Busch series or on the race leaders. They had failed to notice Rob as he continued to pick his way toward the front, working hard to earn every single position. At forty laps into the race, he was threatening to break his way into the top ten.

But someone noticed. Christy Fagan watched him pass the car that was running in eleventh position and then she jumped up from her director's chair and yelled like the cheerleader she had once been. One of the hand-held cameramen happened to be focusing on her, and when the technical director saw the lovely blonde dancing about, he hurriedly chose the shot for air. The lead announcer saw the scene pop up on his monitor and paused in what he had been saying.

"Well. I wonder who . . . wait . . . that's Rob Wilder's girlfriend. And she obviously saw something out there she liked," he said.

"I'll tell you what she saw," the commentator said, even as another camera picked up the brilliant red Ford carrying the 06 number. "Rocket Rob Wilder is just about to crack the top ten. That means he has already picked up almost twenty-five spots. I think we better start keeping an eye on him. It looks like he's trying to push his way to the front. Remember, we told you he had one of the fastest cars in practice but had a little trouble on his qualifying lap and had to start way back in the field."

"I've been watching him as we've been talking," the announcer chimed in. "I think he may well have the fastest car out there right now. He's just been stuck in all this traffic while the leaders have basically had a clean track to work with."

"The key question is going to be how bad he's used up his tires coming up through the field. If they're gone, then they better be praying for a caution."

"I think there are a lot of drivers out there desperate for a caution," the announcer agreed.

"You're right there," the commentator agreed. "You certainly don't want to be the one who causes it, but as a driver, you hope desperately to get one so you can get some fresh rubber under you and a chance to catch back up to the leaders."

Rob indeed was one of those drivers who desperately needed fresh tires. His charge through the field had taken its toll on the rubber. He found it harder and harder to keep the car pegged right down on the white line at the inside of the track. The car was incessantly pushing up the track, fighting him all the way through the turns.

"Will, I think the tires are gone. When we gonna stop?" he finally called in.

"You're fine. Everybody else's are going away, too. You're still faster than the leader."

"I don't see how. I'm skatin' all over the place."

"We'll let you know," Will said.

He looked over at Bubba and raised his eyebrows beneath the visor of his Ensoft Racing cap. Bubba only nodded back. There was plenty of life left in the tires. They weren't perfect. But they would be fine. Yes, they would be fine.

And the kid knew how to drive it the way it was. He absolutely did.

Rob charged down into turn one, getting a run going on the car to the outside. He pushed up beside him, twisting the steering wheel as the car hit the banking. The driver of the race car on the outside tried to pinch him down low. Rob gritted his teeth even harder and held his line. The two cars touched, sending up a puff of smoke as Rob's right front tire left a big black doughnut where the number used to be on the other car. The wheel jerked in his hand, but Rob stayed calm, not overcorrecting, no matter how his normal senses screamed for him to do just that. Instead, he got back into the gas and cleared the car cleanly coming up off turn two.

The four women watched the action from the top of the truck parked down next to the fence in turn two. The men crowded the rail while they stood back, taking everything in. They had not been in their chairs in the last few minutes as they cheered every time Rob Wilder passed somebody on his determined charge to the front. Catherine Lee and Joyce Baxter exchanged knowing looks. They loved the enthusiasm of the two younger women. It brought back memories of when they had been their age and when it had been Jodell out there racing hard.

Christy grew more and more excited as the laps reeled off. The racing at this place was much more up close and personal, different altogether from what she had seen at Daytona. Here there was not a second she could relax or she'd miss something. How could she have been around for twenty years so far and not have known how exciting this stock car racing stuff could be?

She watched Rob start to make a pass on another car as he entered the turn directly in front of her. As she watched, the car on the outside of him suddenly seemed to steer right down against him. The two cars clearly touched. There was smoke! She closed her eyes so she would not have to watch the crash she was certain was about to happen. But there was no screeching of tires, no *wham!* of a collision. She took a peek, fully expecting to see nothing but smoke and mayhem spread out in front of her. Instead, Rob was exiting the corner, past the car that had bumped him, charging off after the next victim in line.

"Did you see that?" she said, her eyes wide as she turned to Catherine Lee.

"At least a thousand times, and I still want to cover my eyes every time too, honey," Catherine said, and put a reassuring hand on her shoulder.

Will jotted the latest lap time on the clipboard. Suddenly he felt a tap on the arm. Bubba was pointing toward turn four. A car was hard into the wall over there. The yellow flag was immediately waving from the flag stand, and the flashing lights around the track already blinking.

"Caution! Caution! The caution flag is out," sang Harry Stone from his spotter's position above the track.

Rob was entering turn one as he heard the call. He glanced in his mirror, making sure no one was close to his rear bumper before he eased out of the gas. He waved his right hand to the cars behind him, signaling he was slowing down until he could see where the trouble was.

"Four tires and gas," Will ordered. "We have to be quick now, boys. We don't want to get lapped here in the pits or have to pass all these cars again."

"Gotcha!" Donnie yelled, placing a foot up on the wall, already set to hop over it and get to work.

"Watch your pit-road speed coming in, cowboy. We're going to do four tires and half a round of wedge. That should help you on the longer runs."

Rob guided the Ford down pit lane and slid to a stop. Donnie led the charge over the wall and slid the jack under the car, raising it up with two powerful strokes. The air guns whirred, sending lug nuts flying over the shoulders of the changers. Fresh tires were hoisted up and bolted on. The crew jumped up in unison, participating in a perfectly coordinated blue-collar ballet, racing around to the other side to repeat their dance. Gasoline spilled out the overflow into the catch can, the jack dropped, and Will was shouting into the radio's microphone.

"Go! Go! Go!"

As soon as Rob felt the jack drop, he hit the gas and jerked the wheel, steering his way out of the pit. Back onto the track, he settled into line, using the moment to catch his breath. Only then could he relax, stretch his tired arms, wriggle his head from side to side and try to unknot the muscles in the back of his neck. He stuck his left hand out the window, trying to draw some fresh air into the steaming cockpit.

"Good job, boys," Will praised. "We picked up two spots in the pits. That's two we won't have to earn out there on the track."

He then twisted around to find where Rob was on the

track as he spoke to him on the radio. "We were ninth going in and we came out seventh. You got good tires, so go ahead and show those cats in front of you what you can do!"

"I'm ready!"

Then, in no time, they were down to the last hundred laps. Rob had not disappointed. It took him another thirty laps after the caution, but he had finally pushed his way into the lead, steering boldly around one of the Cup drivers who glared at him as he went by. From there the lead seesawed back and forth among a handful of cars as the teams made pit stops during several short caution periods.

There was only one set of fresh tires left behind the pit wall to go on the car. The quandary facing Will would be deciding when he should use them. Wait too long, they could lose track position and risk a crash. Use them too early and they would be at a disadvantage at the end.

Now they were running in third place with tires that had twenty more laps on them than those on the two cars ahead of them. And it was clear that Rob was slowly losing ground to them. They needed another caution period badly, and within the next thirty or forty laps, or they would have to make a green-flag stop. At a track like Nashville, that was a risky proposition. A green-flag stop would virtually concede the win. The laps were winding off quickly, so the decision would have to come soon if the racing gods didn't send them a yellow flag soon.

Will leaned over to confer with Bubba. He wasn't one bit too proud to seek the big man's advice. And he wasn't one bit surprised at what he said.

"Hang on as long as you can," he said. "Long as he's

in the top five, he can run the rest of them down with new tires."

But with his driver begging for new tires, it was hard to be patient. He knew the kid was doing a masterful job just keeping the racer between the fences on such worn tires, not to mention staying within hailing distance of the leaders.

With sixty laps to go, Rob felt for all the world as if he were driving on an ice rink. The car was skating all over the track. It was all he could do to hold on to her. Luckily, the other lead cars were beginning to have the same trouble. Diving into turn three, he twisted the wheel hard, trying to set the car in the center line through the corner. He had long since given up on trying to run down on the bottom. The car simply refused to stay there.

But this time the car didn't even stick down the middle of the track. Rob felt the back end wiggle and break loose. He feathered the throttle, trying to regain control of the Ford, but as he did, the car behind him shot by on the inside as Rob drifted upward on the track toward the outside wall.

If I get in this loose stuff, I'm dead, he thought as he struggled to keep the car off the wall. The upper part of the track was littered with spent tire rubber and other debris and would be treacherous if he got into it.

At the last instant he managed to pull it in, to regain mastery over the vehicle, but he had lost the position. He breathed again, but he slapped the wheel with his palm in frustration. Would he drive too cautiously from now on, afraid the rear end of the car would betray him again?

Will watched as the car broke loose and slid up the track. He was sure their day was done. At the last instant, though, the kid seemed to will himself back in charge, keeping the car out of the marbles on the high side of the track and off the wall. He charged on, seemingly never missing a beat.

"What do you think, Bub? We need tires bad. I thought we were a goner there."

"Everybody else is in the same boat. We'll all get our caution," Bubba said confidently, relying on his years of experience and a sizeable but usually accurate gut.

"I just hope it's not us that gives it to 'em!" Will growled as he watched Rob slide around some more.

A couple of laps later, Bubba's instincts proved accurate. Three lapped cars tangled exiting turn four right in front of the grandstands, bringing the packed crowd to its feet. The wreck was right in front of the leaders, sending them scurrying to avoid joining the melee. Rob threaded his way through the mess, feeling bad for the teams whose day had ended so abruptly but happy to finally see the caution flag waving brightly. Now he could get some fresh tires and show everyone else whose race this was supposed to be.

"Okay, everybody listen up. We need one more good, clean stop. No mistakes. We'll win or lose the race right here," Will said, and started to climb down from the pit box to oversee the crucial stop close at hand.

He was about to step off the box when he looked up to watch their car coming down the road toward their pit. He stepped down without looking where he was going and tripped over a piece of equipment. He went forehead-first into the corner of the toolbox. The lick stunned him as he sank to his knees, then he shook his head and stood up, wobbly and disoriented.

The rest of the crew, intent on getting into position for a good stop, didn't see him take the tumble. Bubba looked down, though, and saw Will standing there, blood pouring down the side of his face. He quickly took over, keying the microphone switch, calling the distance as Rob drove toward the stall.

Rob cut in sharply, bringing the car to a stop. He knew it wasn't Will on the radio and glanced up to see Bubba Baxter, all alone up on the pit box.

Where's Will? he wondered as he felt the jack go under the car and raise him up.

But he took the offered drink that appeared in the window of the car and took a deep pull. The crew was already coming around to the left side then, quickly changing the tires over there. The jack dropped and Rob hit the gas and smoked away. He hardly had a chance to wonder about Will again.

"Go, kid," came the gravelly voice of Bubba Baxter over the radio.

Donnie turned around to see Will Hughes standing there, the side of his face and the front of his team shirt already covered in blood.

"Jesus . . ." he muttered. "What happened to you?"

"I tripped coming down off the box."

"Let me take a look at you," Donnie said as Will settled into a sitting position on the pit wall and tilted his head back. The wound gaped open. Donnie grabbed a clean towel and pressed it hard against Will's head to try to stop the bleeding.

"I believe I could see your brain if you had one. You need to go get some stitches, bro."

"Soon as we win this race."

"Now!" Donnie boomed.

"After the race."

"I said now!" Donnie said emphatically, effectively ending any argument. "I ain't gonna have nobody bleedin' to death in my pits."

Will couldn't see all the blood or how wide the cut was, and he was certainly still stunned from the blow.

Donnie waved down some of the medical personnel manning the pits. They took one look before hustling Will off toward the care center for immediate attention.

"Wait!" he said, waving his hand toward the big man atop the toolbox. "Bubba, you got to bring him home. We need this!"

Bubba just nodded and turned back toward the track to pick up the Ford. Jodell and Billy had wandered several pits down to watch one of the other leaders stop and had missed all the action.

Rob had removed from his mind anything that might be going on in the pits. He'd get the story later. Right now he was focused on nothing but what he was going to have to do in order to pass the four cars that stood between him and the point.

The cars received the one-to-go sign from the flag-man.

"Okay, kid, let's show 'em who's boss," Bubba drawled over the radio.

Rob still thought it odd that Will wasn't on the radio net, but he only punched the mike button and replied, "Ten-four."

He flexed his fingers one last time before tightening his grip on the wheel once again. Four cars rolled along directly in front of him while a line of lapped cars ran queued up to his left, presenting their own set of problems.

There were enough laps left to win this thing. But he knew he had to drive smart. So many fans thought it was merely a matter of driving real fast. There was much more to it than that.

Going down the backstretch, he pulled up tight on the back of the car just ahead of him.

"Remember, kid, be easy on the tires on the restart.

Don't let these lapped cars burn them up. Save your tires for the end!" Bubba coached.

"Gotcha," Rob answered. A strange feeling came over him then as he listened to Bubba Baxter's gravelly voice. For an instant he was certain it was 1960, that he was steering a '58 Ford just like his father once had done, that the PA was playing an Elvis Presley song out there.

He shook his head to clear it, but another strong feeling washed over him then. It was a surge of pure confidence. He knew then that if he followed Bubba's suggestions, if he did what he knew how to do, what he had been born to do, he was about to win his first Grand National race. There would be no denying him and the history he was carrying with him.

"Green flag!" Bubba shouted.

Rob saw the flag go up and he stomped on the gas, chasing after the Ford that sat in front of him. He stayed glued to its bumper as they raced off into turn one. The leader broke out, opening a span of twenty or so car lengths, as Rob and the trailing cars were forced to deal with the lapped traffic. He wanted to shove some of the other cars out of his way and drive on past them, but he forced himself to be patient, to wait and pick his spots, saving his tires for the final assault.

Slowly, patiently, surely, he began to work his way up. With fifteen laps to go, Rob was soaring. He had claimed second place and now had a clear shot at the leader, who was ten car lengths in front. There was something else he could see ahead. It was a group of lapped cars half a straightaway ahead that would almost certainly come into play before the end. He found it reassuring to listen to the cadence as Bubba Baxter called the interval between him and the car he was chasing.

"Okay, kid, go get 'im. It's time to cut that old mule

loose and let the racehorse in her come out."

Rob didn't bother to confirm his understanding. He just gritted his teeth one more time and concentrated on driving as smoothly as he could. Two laps later he was right up on the back bumper of the Chevrolet that was leading the race. Leading for now, that is.

Rob pulled to the inside going down the front straightaway, getting a fender along on the inside. Most of the fans were delighted that someone was challenging the Cup driver who was leading. They were, to a man and woman, on their feet, either cheering for Rob or, if they were fans of the other driver, for him.

The Chevy drove a little deeper into the corner as Rob pulled alongside. That allowed the leader to zoom back into the front all by himself. Rob wouldn't surrender that easily, though. He kept the car within a couple of feet of the Chevy as they exited turn two. Down the backstretch they ran, with Rob diving down underneath him once more as they went into the corner. The Chevy kicked up in the center of the turn just as it had the lap before, and that once again allowed Rob to slip by on the inside, but this time he stayed there as they left the corner behind.

Flashing across the line with ten laps to go, Rob led by a full car length. Donnie Kline and the rest of the crew pumped their fists high into the air and whooped. Bubba Baxter, though, never cracked a smile. There was still plenty of work to do if they were going to win this one. Ten laps could seem like a thousand. Too many things could yet happen. One slipup and they were done. Somehow it seemed that first win was always the hardest to get. He could imagine what was going through the young driver's mind out there as he assumed the lead, then began watching his mirror.

"Leader," was all Bubba said to him once he had

completed the pass and claimed the lead. He didn't want to do anything to distract his driver's focus at this point, and that wasn't merely because he was a rookie. He would have played it the same with Jodell Lee or anybody else in this position.

It was up to the kid now. All that was left for Bubba to do was call down the last couple of laps for him.

Rob felt as if his heart were going to jump right out of his chest when he finally took the undisputed lead.

"I have to be smooth," he kept telling himself. "And concentrate!"

Then, as he roared down the back straight, he felt a sudden vibration.

"What was that?" he asked himself out loud.

The car seemed to be steering okay. It wasn't a front tire at least. He put the car perfectly through three and four without slowing any more than he had been, glancing in his mirror at the widening lead he was putting on the Chevy that was still chasing him.

He ran hard down the front stretch without feeling any more of the shaking. It was gone. Or was it? Did he get just a hint of vibration again when he set up for the next turn?

"Five to go," Bubba called calmly.

In the heat of the cockpit, Rob could definitely smell oil burning. He glanced around the cockpit to see if he could see the smoke. He wanted to look in the mirror, to see if he could see telltale smoke out the back of the car, but he stayed focused on the track ahead instead.

"Focus! Focus!" he yelled at himself. And quit imagining things, he added silently.

"Three to go."

Rob suddenly noticed how excruciatingly hot it was in the car. His arms felt like they had lost all their strength. Sweat covered his face.

"What was that?"

The vibration. Had it returned? Had it ever been there in the first place?

It felt like a pack of butterflies had taken up residence in his stomach. He glanced in the mirror. The car behind him was definitely closing, coming fast.

He sensed then that he was about to panic, to scare himself right out of a sure win.

But then something strange happened. He heard a voice, a calm, soothing voice, reminding him that he had the car and the ability to win this thing. It wasn't on the radio. There certainly wasn't anyone in the car with him. But he could hear the confident words as sure as if there had been. He focused out the windshield with a fresh, determined outlook. He could do it!

"White flag, Jodell."

No mistaking that voice. It was Bubba Baxter, speaking calmly, matter-of-factly, as if there were still a hundred laps to go instead of a single one. And Rob Wilder never noticed that the big man had actually addressed the call to Jodell Lee.

Jodell himself smiled when he heard Bubba's slipup on the radio headset he wore. In some ways he did feel as if it were he out there driving the car, with Bubba calling him to the finish exactly as they had done it countless times way back when.

Billy watched Bubba closely. He'd seen that same set in his jaw many times before. The big man wouldn't show any emotion until he brought the car home in first. And how lucky was it that Bubba had been standing there, the radio headset already on, when Will had gone down?

This win seemed destined, ordained somehow.

The crew watched anxiously, waiting for the final lap to play out. Will came trotting up, a fresh bandage wrapped around his head. He'd refused the doctor's order that he get into an ambulance and go get checked out at the hospital. And he had postponed any stitches that might be necessary for the moment. There was no way he was going anywhere until this race was finished, one way or another.

Donnie Kline stood precariously perched on a stack of tires, watching the final lap, his hands folded in prayer.

On top of the truck, an anxious crowd of folks watched, too. Christy was so excited she could hardly watch. Michelle kept squealing, waving their car on.

The girls' excitement was infectious. Catherine coaxed Christy to keep her eyes open so she could always remember the moment. Toby Warren, who had sprinted in just as the cars took the green to open the race, was like a little boy, jumping up and down in place in his excitement. Rob's friends from back home jumped and slapped hands down below behind the pits, living their own dreams through their old buddy.

For some reason, Joe Banker flashed back over forty years as he watched the 06 car circle the track. He remembered that first win at Hickory, North Carolina, when it all started for him, Jodell, and Bubba. He expected Billy, Will, Rob, and the crew would soon feel exactly as they had on that night, suspecting it was only the first of many more victories to come.

Randy Weems and Clifford Stanley were already dancing their victory jig, toasting each other with their Mason jars, even as they followed Rob for that final time around the track.

Rob dove into the first turn on his way into the last lap of the race. The car drifted up slightly in the center of the turn. The Chevy, still trailing his red Ford, was a good dozen car lengths behind. All Rob had to do was drive smoothly through turns three and four. The hard part was over.

He pushed everything else out of his brain besides putting the car exactly where he had been as he got through the two corners. Then, coming out of four to the line, he saw it up there ahead of him.

It was a beautiful sight, waving away down there, the one thing most dreamed of by the men who drove these steel chariots.

The checkered flag!

Rob flashed under the flying banner.

"Yes!" he screamed over the radio.

"Good job, Jodell! I mean . . . good job, kid," Bubba called, and he finally allowed a smile to crack across his face.

A grinning Billy Winton turned to shake hands with Jodell. Both of them knew what they had just witnessed. The only question now was where all this might someday lead. But they would save that for another time. Right now there was a celebration in which to partake.

They all followed the crew over to the car as Rob stopped it at the start/finish line. When he climbed out, the excited crewmen mobbed him. He accepted the guitar from one of the officials and waved it over his head to the cheers of all the fans in the stands.

Billy stood aside and watched as Rob mastered the delicate art of shaking up champagne and spraying everyone in range with the bubbly. Toby Warren braved the deluge, stepped up, and slapped him on the back.

"What did you think of that?" Billy asked him.

"That was great. I just have one question. When can we go Winston Cup racing?"

Billy grinned and didn't hesitate a second. "Anytime you want!"

Rob spied Christy in the crowd and he fought through

it to get to her, picking her up and spinning her around. Then he gave her a long, passionate kiss, not caring who saw or who made rude noises. Even in his elation, he knew for certain that the only thing as good as winning that first race was having her there to share it with him.

Half an hour later they were all still standing around, taking the victory-lane pictures. There were shots of Rob, Rob and the crew, Rob, Toby, and Michelle, and then the whole group. It was only after the photographer had almost exhausted his supply of film that Rob finally asked Will Hughes about the bandage on his noggin.

"What hit you?"

"The toolbox. Can you believe I managed to miss most of the last fifty laps of the first race we win?"

"I wondered what happened when I heard Bubba on the radio. It took me a while to realize who it was. He sure knows how to call races," Rob said admiringly.

"He's the best there is," Will said, turning back to the celebration.

Rob grabbed his shoulder. "I still wouldn't trade him for my regular crew chief."

The two men embraced for a moment, then, both of them blushing as bright red as the 06 Ford, they parted.

The party was finally beginning to break up when Billy demanded one last picture. Rob and Christy held the checkered flag in front of the race car. Then Billy waved for Catherine and Joyce to step in, along with Jodell, Joe, and Bubba. He had to corral Randy and Clifford, too, and ordered them to quit dancing and stand up straight. The photographer lined them up and snapped the happy picture of the entire group, most of whom had been together, doing this, winning races, for four decades.

The network color commentator, an old-timer once

on the circuit himself, made his way down to talk to Jodell and the gang after the broadcast ended. He stepped through the gate and watched as they were all being lined up for that last photo. He noted the Mason jars being passed around by Randy and Clifford, the checkered flag unfurled across the race car, the mix of old-timers and youngsters, all of them beaming happily.

What an impact this group had made on racing through the years, he thought. And what promise the next bunch coming up had already shown. This would be a photo suitable someday for the wall of a museum or a hall of fame or to illustrate a book on the history of the sport.

But as the old driver stopped in his tracks and watched the photographer snap the picture, as the dying light made the scene appear washed out and colorless like an old black-and-white snapshot, he was seized by a sudden, odd thought. The scene over there next to that winning race machine looked exactly like all those photos he had seen taken years before. Exactly like those that had survived since 1960 and before. Similar to the ones that filled scrapbooks like those the old driver had stacked up in his own closet back home in North Carolina.

A picture of a young driver, a new winner, his ecstatic crew, his happy owner, a fast, lovingly built race car, a beautiful young lady, her eyes bright with excitement for her man's victory.

And for a moment he was wafted back there, to that time, that place, as surely as if the clock had suddenly been wound backward.

He shook his head, cleared the sudden fog, and walked on over to congratulate the kid for the first of what would surely be many more victories yet to come, to tell Billy and Will and the crew how much he had enjoyed watching the youngster guide their car so far.

And with every step, the old driver felt younger himself.